THE ABBEY
IN THE WOOD

THE ABBEY IN THE WOOD

ANTONY LAMBTON

Quartet Books

London   New York

First published by Quartet Books Limited 1986
A member of the Namara Group
27/29 Goodge Street, London W1P 1FD

Copyright © 1986 by Lord Lambton

British Library Cataloguing in Publication Data
Lambton, Antony
    The abbey in the wood.
    I. Title
    823'.914[F]   PR6062.A48/

ISBN 0-7043-2588-8

Phottypeset by AKM Associates (UK) Ltd.
Ajmal House, Hayes Road, Southall, London
Printed and bound in Great Britain
by Nene Litho and Woolnough Bookbinding
both of Irthlingborough, Northants

To
Helen and Ferdl

This story was suggested by an incident in the fragment of autobiography left by Heinrich Heine and is usually considered to have been a figment of his fevered mind. My additions are entirely figments of my fevered mind.

1

At the turn of the eighteenth century, there stood on a side-road three quarters of a mile outside the old gates of Düsseldorf the ruins of an Abbey built in the perpendicular Gothic style. The main church, originally of considerable height, had been constructed with a single nave which led up to a slightly obtruding transept. In place of the usual rounded apse, three high Gothic arches had once soared on the flat wall behind the altar, but the outer two had both been filled in, and only a gap at the top of the central window remained to hint at the formerly aspiring shape of the trio. The remainder of the stone fabric had suffered from age and decay, but within the ruin, extending from the left transept to the outline of the central window, stood an old house with a high-pitched roof, which tottered upwards at its apex to a height of four irregular storeys. Its old timber and stone walls had over the centuries become dotted with small windows which looked out on to the overgrown nave, and those who lived in the house were not infrequently disturbed during windy or frosty weather by the crash of falling masonry.

The inhabitants of Düsseldorf had long forgotten which religious order built the Abbey, and none of them could understand why any man should ever have chosen to build a house in such a shady, cursed spot, reached by the sun from a few angles at rare intervals. Yet only few of the city's inhabitants had not at some time heard of the ghosts which thronged the surrounding wood, and fresh rumours were constantly circulated by travellers who, on their way into the town, claimed that, as their horses passed the Abbey grounds, they showed signs of fear and distress and could only with difficulty be prevented from bolting. Pedestrians, mainly neighbouring farm workers who often passed close by the precincts late in the evening, would also tell of hearing a shriek followed by a thud. Such tales kept alive the legend that the builder of the house, having lost his wife by a falling stone, had determined the same fate would never befall him, and had hired from some distance builders to block in the three Gothic windows. Their task was nearing completion when, a few months after the death of his wife, he was found crushed beneath a fragment of masonry from the central arch, causing the locals to believe that the ghosts of the man and his wife still haunted the Abbey. It was also said that, when the man planned the house, it had been prophesied he would never live to finish it. This forecast was proved wrong, but on the other hand it was argued that, once the house was built, the Abbey had revenged itself effectively on both husband and wife.

The subsequent history of the house was not known, although it was said that foreign soldiers had at some unknown period been quartered in it, but the next day they unanimously told their officers that they would revolt rather than sleep another night in such a doomed place. All that was known of the present occupants was that, twenty years before, the local executioner had died and been replaced by a hated man, described as 'coming from the north'. Yet before he could take up his lucrative post, a difficulty needed to be overcome: a temporary dwelling had to be found for him. This proved to be impossible, as the local people were violently prejudiced against his profession and obliged him to search outside the city walls for a residence. At last, it was said, he discovered with delight the abandoned house within the Abbey, and immediately purchased the building from the Bishop. The townsmen then declared with satisfaction he would never find a builder for miles around to aid him in the necessary reconstruction, but again were proved wrong when a dozen burly, taciturn young men arrived who the gossips soon discovered were sons of the executioner's numerous relations, as the close-knit aristocracy of death often faced such difficulties as those they were faced with in Düsseldorf and, to assist their blood brothers, the fathers of families had dispatched younger members as yet unqualified in their ghastly trade to help with the building of the house. The strangers were willing helpers, undistracted by the usual interests of the young, since even their courting had to be confined within the circle of their family. Certainly, they were considered as belonging to a damned race, and the odium attached to them was so strong it was claimed no girl from outside the family had ever been tempted, by a high price, to ally herself with a clan cursed by God and man.

The new executioner, it soon became known, had married late in life one of his first cousins. After a few years, his young wife had won the hearts of certain tradesmen by her gentleness, beauty, white skin and long red hair, but such admiration was confined to the men, as their wives would go out of their way to spit or talk loudly at her as, with head hidden by a long bonnet, she meekly walked about the town on her weekly visits to buy groceries. She was married to her husband for five years, and it was generally agreed the marriage was unhappy as she was never known to have smiled. But this was surmise.

Then, just before the turn of the century, she started to give birth to a little girl with labour pains so violent that, it was said, her husband in the middle of the night desperately ran into the town and knocked on the doors of no less than four midwives, begging them to accompany him back to the Abbey, crying out frantically, 'My wife is screaming with pain.' All resolutely refused, despite substantial offers of gold, and the young woman died after twenty-four hours of unceasing agony. However, it was later said that one of the midwives, belatedly lured by a rich reward and justifying her action by a sudden conviction that 'the sins of the fathers should not be visited on the children', had gone secretly to the Abbey, too late to save the mother, but in time to save the baby, who, it was whispered, was still tied to her dead mother. At all events, the child, a girl, lived, and the midwife's career prospered, for such was the fascination of the mysterious house and Abbey that she stole away from her rivals many patients who wished to hear her account of how, during the second day of her attendance, 'in doing what God bade me was my duty', she had been surprised to hear the sound of wheels.

Peeping out of a window, in fear of a ghostly visitation, she had seen four old men dressed in long red cloaks with their swords pushed out behind them (the working clothes of executioners), followed by another four unarmed men, carrying a pitch-black coffin. Here the midwife would declare to her breathless audiences that, not wishing to even see such men, she had locked herself in her room, but from the window could not help seeing the coffin carried slowly out of the house and along what had been the nave of the old church, followed by the widower and his four sobbing colleagues still wearing their swords. After a short interval, the nine men returned from their task and stayed an hour or two drinking while the trembling midwife bravely remained in the locked room to save the baby. At last they went away, when she too quickly slipped out of the house, never, she swore, to return 'as long as there is a breath in my body'.

The dead woman's place was soon taken by a distant cousin, Anna, an old maid with a pasty white face, spotty skin and fair hair which trailed in a long greasy pigtail behind her back. She never smiled or left the precincts, except to make her weekly visits to the tradesmen, who accepted her custom because it was possible to overcharge her with impunity. Like her predecessor she also kept her head down, even when giving orders for food. Although she was extremely unattractive, Anna looked after the child with reasonable care, the girl being, it was said, a replica of her mother, with the same dark red hair, green eyes and white skin.

The child, called Sefchen or Red Sefchen, an abbreviation of Josepha, never received any affection since it never entered Anna's head to kiss or cosset her. It was not that she was unkind, rather than she simply ignored the child as she spent her time endlessly washing floors, wiping patches of dirt off the walls, waxing furniture, or attending to her chickens and the pig which she killed herself each Christmas. Consequently she had little time for the child, whose nursery became the old nave and who only returned to the house when she was hungry. Of this period, the child had but the scantiest of memories, and only remembered that when she returned barefooted home, her cousin always gave her a large platter of bread and milk. Later she tried to remember whether it was in this period of her life that she first heard voices, or if her confused childish mind had only imagined, in her lonely games, the presence of an older man and woman. After a time she almost ceased to notice them as they never interfered with her or the footprints she liked to make in the mud outside the house after it had rained. But she was certain she was seldom alone, and was only irritated by them as she grew older and extended her playground beyond the confines of the old Abbey, when the woman began to grow worried, and although they never touched her, she could feel them willing her to stay. But she was determined to wander off among the trees, and soon grew used to the secret arguments, which she always won.

When she was five, her complete freedom ended when her father said one day to Cousin Anna: 'It's time the girl learned to read and write. I'm told you write a good hand yourself. See the child learns your tricks as well.'

From that day on, her playtime was curtailed, and every morning, after a plain breakfast, she would be sat down at an end of the freshly scrubbed kitchen table and taught, first, to recognize letters, and then form them into elegant shapes. Later on, she was given books, and made to read, and when she was six, she had to work an extra hour each afternoon. They shared the kitchen with Sefchen's father, and each afternoon, when he was not away, he would appear as the clock chimed five, sit down in front of the fireplace, stretch out his legs and begin to turn the pages of a large brown leather folio. She noticed he always brought a new book home every time he made one of his unexplained journeys.

Sefchen learned quickly. She was a clever child, and Anna enforced her teaching with a ruler, which she would bring down hard on her pupil's fingers if ever she made the same mistake twice running. One evening, the sun shining on the trees made Sefchen long to escape into the wood. She could not attend and Anna had hit her four times, the last time with such force she let out a cry of pain and looked toward her father, who was, with an expressionless face, holding up a large folio. If she had expected mercy or an intervention on her behalf, she was disappointed. He merely turned over a page, and she, conscious she would never receive help from him, tried hard to stop her tears and make no more mistakes.

Sefchen was unaware that her father was ill, and in later years she could never remember his face distinctly, so closely did he resemble his own father, the grandfather with whom she subsequently lived, and the two men, with their small noses and pointed beards, came to be merged into a single entity. It was confusing as it made it impossible to place in her own mind the dates of various events, but she learned early she had to make her own amusements as she neither received affection or excited interest. Her great consolation was the birds and animals in the few acres of wood that surrounded her home, which, she was told later, marked the limits of the Abbey grounds, and she was enchanted when she found she could tame any creature. It delighted her to wander through the woods with flocks of little birds darting from branch to branch behind her. Then, she would stop and with dry crumbs on her palms, stand completely still with arms held level with her shoulders as more and more birds fluttered down, seized a piece and flew away. Later on, they would settle on her hands and peck away until driven off by hungry newcomers.

She also succeeded at last in taming a squirrel. She noticed how they collected nuts, and carefully watched as they carried them up into a tree and dropped them down a hole into what she supposed must be a winter store. But it took her a long time to make a friend of her selected favourite and she had to stand still for hours on end before he (she was sure he was a male) would come near her. At last he would sit on his hind legs on a nearby low branch, peering at her and chattering. Then, to her great delight, he would leap down, seize a nut, climb again to safety, sit on his back legs as he held his prize between his front paws and crack it with his teeth. She collected hundreds of nuts and piled them beneath his tree so she could watch him carry them away and drop them one by one into his store. Sometimes she persuaded herself he spoke to her, and said, 'Thank you,' and although he never stayed long enough for her to caress him, she came to regard him as her own friend, who watched her sympathetically out of little eyes bright with interest at her little sorrows.

But her greatest consolation was a huge rotten old tree root that lay at the centre of the wood which she decided one day was the home of 'the little folk' who lived among the trees. She guessed that this was their habitation after her cousin had started telling her fairy stories every night before she went to bed. The tale had excited her imagination, and she looked all over the wood for the little folks' home, until she found the huge half-decayed root, full of crevices, holes and little cavities out of which fungi grew like tiny umbrellas. She was sure they ate their meals beneath them before dancing hand in hand and singing in squeaking voices. She studied the rotting wood with infinite care and pictured where the different families lived, which were their front doors, sitting rooms and larders. Close to the latter, she would place small pieces of meat or fat taken off her plate when her cousin was not looking and hidden in a piece of sacking in her pocket. She left them pieces of salt as well, as her father said food had no taste without it, but after a time she wondered if he was right, for she noticed they never ate it. Twice during the last summer she had acted bravely, choosing fine warm moonlit nights to steal out on her bare feet – she never wore shoes in the summer – and creep up to try to see and talk with the little people. But, however quietly she moved, she never caught a glimpse, although once she was sure she had heard their voices.

Whenever her cousin was particularly severe and hit her hard, or if, for some reason she did not understand, she felt forlorn and longed for playmates, she would go and kneel by the tree trunk and tell the little folk, whom she would picture hiding in their rooms inside the roots, listening to her, letting her know they lamented her cousin's unkindness.

Although, to begin with, she was entranced by the fairy stories, she noticed after a time they were told in an unnatural singsong voice and Anna sometimes read words which Sefchen did not understand. But when she asked her cousin what they meant, Anna would merely crossly repeat herself and say impatiently, 'That's how the story goes. Little girls should listen and not interrupt.'

She never remembered her father saying a kind word to her, but she knew once she dropped a plate and made him angry as he had glared at her with such cold eyes that she looked away quickly. The next day, she thought she had erred again when outside the front door she saw a white plate covered with a white cloth standing in a patch of sunshine. Surprised, she walked closer and saw laid out on it a number of dried objects four or five inches long. She picked one up and saw to her surprise it was a dried shrivelled finger with a broken dirty nail. Looking at her hands, she thought how unlike it was to any of her own slim fingers, and in amazement turned the others over to see if any resembled hers. When her father's voice broke into her examination, 'What are you doing?' Sefchen jumped with surprise.

'Why are you playing with these things? Who said you could? They're mine, I'll have you know.' And then he paused before going on in a softer tone: 'I don't usually deal with such things, but their value's gone up.' He hesitated again before adding, almost kindly: 'Now run along, and perhaps it's a good sign you like playing with such toys. Be off with you.'

Sefchen, relieved he had not been angry, immediately went to tell the little people of her good fortune and noticed a new yellow mushroom and, surely, beneath it a ring marked out by dancing footsteps. In the excitement of her discovery, she forgot the drying fingers, but at supper remembered her fright and looked at her father nervously, wondering if he would tell Cousin Anna how he caught her playing with drying fingers. To her relief he sat as usual with a sad faraway look in his eyes, speechless at the head of the table. Afterwards, in his chair by the fireplace, he sighed more than usual, blowing the candle by his side as he turned over the pages. The next day he went away in his red cloak with the sword sticking out behind, and as he walked down the nave, Sefchen saw Cousin Anna raise her right hand and lower it quickly, then draw it sideways. She wanted to ask why, but didn't, knowing she would only be told to mind her own business. When her father came back, he looked younger, his eyes shone, and as usual he brought a new folio with him. Later she wondered if this was the first time she had noticed how, whenever he was reading, he always looked at the clock before turning over a page and remembered Cousin Anna had once said crossly: 'Why he looks at those books I don't know. He can't read. But then men are always up to some silliness.'

The next time her father went away, Sefchen plucked up her courage and asked, 'Where's he gone?'

Her cousin started to say something sharp, but changed her mind and said slowly: 'Your father's a good man who rids the world of bad men.'

The answer satisfied her, and afterwards she looked at her father with increased respect.

Only on one occasion was she really frightened. It must have been in the May shortly before her father died, when she was about six and a half and had never played with any other child, since it had never entered her head they would play with her. She thought of them as beings apart, only seen when Anna took her into the town, and everyone stared at her, and she would bury her face in her cousin's skirts. But that evening, to her surprise her father said quietly: 'Girl, run to the letter box. I'm expecting a summons which hasn't come.'

When she had got over her surprise and delight that he had actually spoken to her, she seized an old doll which had been her occasional companion ever since she had found it in an attic a year before, and which, although it never quite attained the magic of the little people, the squirrel or even the birds, all of which were alive, had become a good friend. At all events, on this occasion, she picked it up and ran down the old nave, through the wood to the gate, opened the letter box and found it empty. As she shut it, she suddenly heard the sound '*Sssst*'. Scared stiff, she stood, unable to move, staring into the bushes.

'Do you live here?' said a voice, and a big boy suddenly appeared out of the undergrowth, followed by two more, one of them a great hulking lad. 'Do you live here?' he repeated, but she could only stare at him in terror. No one in the shops had ever spoken to her. 'Do you live here?' the boy asked for the third time, but, terrified, she remained tongue-tied, clutching her doll.

'Ah, she's the man's daughter all right,' said the hulking lad, 'and her aunt's the warlock. My father says she bewitched one of our cows. There was no other reason why it should have died.'

They stared at her with an increasing hostility, which, if she could have spoken, would have disappeared, but as she continued to stare at them with her deathly white face, huge green eyes and red hair, her appearance made them in turn frightened and uneasy – which they were determined to hide from such a little creature.

Suddenly the hulking boy laughed. 'I'll teach you,' he said, and with a sudden movement jumped forwards and snatched her doll.

She remained motionless looking at him, but her silence frightened the boy even more. 'I'll get my own back for our cow!' he shouted, and, pulling out a large knife, sawed at the doll's neck until the head came off and a stream of sawdust gushed out over his hand. He yelled out in fear as he threw the doll at her feet. The boys looked at each other and dashed on to the road and out of sight.

Sefchen picked up the two pieces and felt fonder of the doll than she had ever been when it had a head. It never occurred to her to blame the boys, or even to dislike them. She understood simply the world was against her and she meant nothing to anybody. On her way back to the house, she restrained her tears and, without knowing why, put the doll on the kitchen table before going to wash her hand in the trough outside, as her cousin ordered her to do before every meal. When she came back, she found to her surprise her father was carefully examining the doll. He turned to her, put the pieces down and shook his head.

'Sawn not struck off,' he said. Then he sat down and peered at his latest folio until the food was ready.

After they had eaten, to Sefchen's surprise Cousin Anna also carefully examined the doll and said she'd make glue and stick it together, but Sefchen never felt the same again about it. The sight of the sawdust running out had told her it would never again understand if she spoke to it. Later, she crept out to the tree with crumbs and ham, and placed them into the cavity and peered

7

as hard as she could into the cleft, feeling sure the little people were telling her not to worry since they were her true friends. She was grateful. The doll no longer mattered; she was no longer unhappy.

A short time after this fright her father died. Cousin Anna woke her up at five one morning to say he was dead and she was going into the town to try to find a pastor to bury him. Would Sefchen be afraid to remain by herself? She shook her head and, when her cousin had gone, went into his bedroom. He was lying on his back, his mouth, his fallen chin set in a snarl. Later her cousin returned, red spots standing out on her white face.

'I can find no pastor or graveyard to accept him. All I could get was an Irish priest in an inn. I've had to promise him gold. He's bringing two men, who will bury him here. I shall sew him up in a white sheet. Change into your best clothes. Wait for the men in the kitchen, and bring them to me when they come.'

Sefchen, tired after her early waking, fell asleep by the kitchen fire. In a dream she heard men singing loudly, and awoke when the noise stopped. A moment later, three unshaven red-faced men staggered unsteadily into the room, two of them carrying a long, thin wooden box. She wondered if they were ill, and then understood these were the men her cousin was expecting. Without speaking, she led them upstairs to her father's bedroom, where Cousin Anna greeted them with a furious look and said slowly in icy tones: 'You are late. I've finished sewing him up. Carry him down and lay him on the kitchen table. When I'm ready, carry him to the monks' old burial ground at the end of the Abbey on the right. It's the only resting place I can offer. Sefchen, go downstairs.'

Sefchen did as she was told, and, hearing movements and bumps overhead, wondered what was happening. A little later she heard knocks and creaks on the wooden stairs, followed by a tremendous noise as the two men and her father's body half out of his box shot, mixed up together, into the room. The men picked themselves up and cursed, one of them stamping up and down, shouting with pain as he wrung his right hand. The fall had broken the coffin apart and a naked leg protruded through the sheet. Then the priest reeled downstairs and spoke some singsong words in an unknown language, before sitting down and falling asleep. A little later, Cousin Anna appeared, her hair tidy, and at once began an argument with the men, who were demanding something. 'No, no, no!' she shouted, but they shouted back, 'Yes, yes, or we don't shift him!'

The priest stood up and said in a blurred voice: 'Do as you are asked, woman. It is God's will.'

This silenced her, and looking white and angry she fetched them some cups and a large square black bottle. Sefchen's last sight of the group was of a receding procession, led by the priest unsteadily waving about a broken wooden cross and intoning foreign words. He was followed by two men dragging her father along by his arms, his open mouth jerking up and down with each tug. Her cousin followed, muttering furiously. Sefchen changed into her everyday clothes. She had always been told she should only wear her best on important occasions.

The next day, two other old men appeared, wearing swords and red cloaks, as her father had done whenever he went away. Sefchen was in the wood when they came bumping along the rough track in a gig, followed by a farm cart carrying a gleaming black box. The little procession stopped. Sefchen led the two old men into the house. An argument followed, which she could not understand, but realized the men were very angry, shouting the body had been too quickly and incorrectly buried. That they had their own place and a pastor to bless him. When Cousin Anna noticed she was listening, she pushed her out of the kitchen and she heard no more.

That night, her cousin announced she would be leaving the day after tomorrow, but Sefchen was not to worry.

'Your father's rude friends have arranged you will be taken to your grandfather's house in some forest, and your aunt from Goch will be arriving to live in this house tomorrow. I have done my best for you. At the very least you can read.'

They looked at each other without affection, yet, while Sefchen did not mind her cousin going, she dreaded the thought of a new aunt and felt like bursting into tears. She stopped herself by wondering what would happen to the little people without her. Who would feed the birds, the little people, the squirrel? The next day, she took her remaining store of acorns and placed them in a crevice beneath the squirrel's favourite tree, and cut large slices of bread, cheese and ham and stuck them in the crevices in the old root. Surely they could cut up the food and store it? Anyhow, it was all she could do.

Before supper, her aunt from Goch arrived, with several large bundles. She ran in and out with her parcels, which she would not let Sefchen touch.

'So you are the dear little one, are you?' she asked, patting Sefchen's cheeks before finally running upstairs, leaving her niece bewildered. Never before had her father or cousin or anyone said such polite things to her, but Sefchen did not like her. She wondered why. Certainly it was not her aunt's appearance. She looked, at first sight, friendly enough, with her neat grey-brown hair above a little brown face, and a small nose, a thin pursed mouth and shining black eyes. Yes, surely that was what she disliked: the eyes never kept still and never looked straight at you. Yes, they gave the impression, even while she was saying nice things, that she was not to be trusted and did not mean what she said. Despite her fear of the unknown, Sefchen felt glad she would be leaving next morning. She would not have liked to stay here with the woman. Her conclusions were confirmed when, after supper, her aunt talked of her 'dear dead brother' and wiped her eyes, which was silly. She was not crying and had no tears to wipe away.

Late that night, the wind rose and the branches rasped against the chimney in their usual fashion. But Sefchen was used to such noises and paid no attention until she heard an enormous crash and knew, at once, one of the remaining arches on the south side of the church had fallen in. She was sorry, but the arch had always looked dangerous, and whenever she had picked her way through the bushes, she had always looked carefully upwards as she passed underneath it. She found it difficult to fall asleep again and found herself hearing voices. She shivered and although she shut her eyes tightly, was sure a man and a woman were kneeling at the side of her bed imploring her to stay. She felt icy cold and, despite her shut eyes, knew that the woman wore a white dress, while the man, who stood behind her, was dressed in clothes dissimilar to any she had ever seen before. What was stranger was that, although she could distinctly see the clothes, the faces remained vague. The woman wept and wrung her hands, begging her to return and help release them. Sefchen felt sorry for her and, without knowing why, said out loud she would come back. At this, the woman had jumped up from her knees, opened her arms and bent forward to fling them round her in a fit of wild joy, although Sefchen could feel nothing touching her. Then they disappeared, and in the morning she couldn't be sure whether she had been awake or dreaming.

She got up early to say goodbye to the little folk in the tree trunk, leaving them another loaf of bread and half a ham. Then she called her squirrel, who, for once, jumped calmly on to her hand. She cried as she gave him some walnuts, then walked into a clearing and held out her arms, on which three or four small birds settled. But since they flew away when they saw she had no food, she felt no sadness. After her farewells, she climbed into the cart as Cousin Anna moved as if to kiss her. Unintentionally, Sefchen moved back and received instead a venomous look. She found herself looking for the couple, but they weren't there as the cart drove away. Her cousin stood still, alone with her arm on her hips and a look on her face which made Sefchen know she was thinking: 'I'm glad to see the back of her.' Almost at once she fell into a deep sleep, and remembered only flashes of the journey until she arrived, while it was still light, at a house in a forest which looked as old as her home, although it was not surrounded by the walls of a ruin. She could remember nothing about the peasant who drove her, except that he carried her bags into a large kitchen.

She never forgot her first impression of her new home, as she stood speechless, stiff with fear, alone by the door, looking into a long room with, on the left, a huge grate with, behind it, an oven for baking bread. To one side stood a cooking range with a pot above the fire, and another in the corner, hanging from an iron hinge. The room was full of little windows, and another open fireplace stood in the middle of the right-hand wall. Before it, on high-backed chairs, sat three old women, spinning and paying not the slightest attention to her entrance. She looked at them in terror. Could these be the three witches from the North Pole, with an eye, a tooth and an ear between them? But no, they were all spinning, and you could not spin if you could not see. Later on, she found out their real names and that they were her cousins, but when she first saw them she had given them her own names: Aunt Fat, Aunt Thin and Aunt Old. And this was how, ever afterwards, she thought of them.

As she stood, frightened and ignored, the door opened and into the room came a tall woman with dark hair collected in a long pigtail hanging down her back. She had large eyes, a large nose, and a wide thin mouth. She looked at Sefchen with an unchanging expression, turned her back and began to poke the fire. Sefchen would have burst into tears if Aunt Fat had not suddenly got up and walked towards her.

'Welcome, little child, to your new home. Your grandfather's ridden away on his stallion on business. He'll be back tomorrow or the next day.'

She held out a hand and led Sefchen upstairs to a little room from where, when she was alone, she peeped out of the window, and at once felt happier at the sight of an oak standing in front of the house. It reminded her of the Abbey and its trees, while, beneath it, stood a wooden table. She thought what a nice place it would be to sit. Nicer than in the nave at home. But her bed was very different from her old one. It was not a four-poster, but a sort of box into which you climbed over the side. Nevertheless she liked the look of it. She had never liked the old wooden canopy hanging above her head threatening to fall down and squash her. That was her last memory of the day, and when she woke up early next morning, she was amazed by her unexpected surroundings. The sun was already shining across the tops of the trees, and as she quickly clambered into her dress, she thought with excitement of exploring the forest which stretched away endlessly. Creeping downstairs, she opened the door, pulling back with great difficulty the huge plank of wood encased in iron used as a bolt. She stopped dead as, in front of her, a large pile of fur quickly transformed itself into two enormous bloodhounds, who stood up, as she retreated back into the house, and started to wag their tails. Relieved, she put out her hand, and they at once started to slobber with affection. At last she managed to push them aside and walk towards the oak tree as the dogs whined sorrowfully behind her at the end of their long chains.

She felt sorry for them, but not for long. The grass was cool and exciting on her bare feet, and she did not care if she might be scolded for not putting on her clogs. Looking into the wood, she saw a carpet of unending green grass which called to her. But what if she got lost? She thought a moment, remembered what to do, and went back past the dogs into the kitchen and through an open door into the larder, filled with great jars and barrels on the floor and rows of bowls and dark-green bottles on the shelves. She searched until she found a large jar of white beans, a handful of which she put in her pocket, like the heroines of many fairy stories who would otherwise have lost themselves. As she went out, she looked up at the old house and thought again it was not unlike her old home. She noticed another similarity: no birds sang but she could hear their faint notes in the distance.

The oak trees looked magnificent, their lower boughs sweeping the ground, and she thought how nice it would be to climb up high into their branches. In places they were interrupted by clumps of beech planted close together. Thick silvery columns rose branchless so high she thought that they must be close to the sky. She looked carefully for her squirrel, having persuaded herself that the little animal would have followed her. At last she thought she saw him scampering around a tree, but although she sat for a few minutes and called quietly, nothing at all happened. She sighed and realized sadly he must have stayed at the Abbey. She felt lonely, and wandered about until she found a rutted track with grass growing between the wheeltracks. She walked along the dew-sodden centre, following the path, occasionally stooping to leave a bean on a patch of bare earth or an upright stone.

After a quarter of an hour, she came to a grass circle surrounded by low dark green trees whose falling branches hid from her the surrounding forest. At the centre of the clearing two huge poles connected by a cross-beam stuck upright in the ground, from which hung a number of chains carrying six bodies swinging gently in the wind. She was not frightened. They must be the bad men whose wickedness her cousin had explained. She looked at them with the acute, dispassionate observation of a young child, and noticed how one of them still wore what was recognizable as a long smock and his face was still covered with skin although his eyes were only holes. Another body still wore one tattered shoe, while bones protruded where the other had been. Strips of smocks flapped on the others and one still wore loosely around his neck the rim of a straw hat whose centre had disappeared. She felt neither fear nor horror, but looked with interest at a sight she had read of many times in fairy tales, and was pleased such men had been caught. Unexpectedly, a faint gust of wind brought to her nose a nasty, sweet smell. Holding her nose with her fingers, she walked homewards, thinking, as she went, of the atmosphere in the house after her father had died. But she did not forget to collect, one by one, the beans and put them in her pocket. Before long she reached the house, where Aunt Fat, who had been kind to her the night before, stood by the door.

'Where've you been?' she called in a friendly voice with no hint of the disapproval which Sefchen was used to hearing whenever her Cousin Anna had spoken to her.

'I went to where six men were hanging amid dark trees.'

Her aunt, who had been looking carelessly around, stared. 'Ah, Sefchen, you've started early, haven't you? You saw without fear, did you?'

'What was there to be afraid of?' she asked simply.

Aunt Fat looked at her with surprise. 'Well, I'm sure you're right. Still, there are many who fear what you have seen, and sometimes, on wintry nights here, we do hear scratchings at doors and windows. My sisters say the men have come down to get their fingers back, for as you know, your grandfather does a good trade in them. There's not an innkeeper for miles who won't swear that you get twice as much out of a barrel of beer with a thief's finger in it. Mind you, they've got to be bad thieves, or there's no magic, although some say an innocent man's are the best of all. Your aunt from Goch has gone into business in Düsseldorf now, and is to buy from your grandfather, as doubtless you know.'

Sefchen was puzzled. She did not like to say that she had only seen her aunt once, and in the end said nothing, but felt relieved that no comment had been made about her naked feet, for she hated their imprisonment in clogs.

Two days later, her grandfather came home. She was exploring the wood when she heard a faint plodding sound and, glancing through the trees, saw in the distance a huddled figure in a red coat riding his black stallion. The sight made her lift her hand fearfully to her heart, for the man looked the image of her father. She waited a few minutes then ran back to the stables behind the house, which had several doors with their top halves open. Out of one of them looked a black face, which, when it saw her, threw up its head and whinnied. She walked closer and tried to stroke its muzzle, but each time she tried, the animal threw up its head and showed its teeth. Determined to win his affection, she went into the forest and picked dandelions and the greenest grass she could find. He accepted her offerings and allowed her to stroke his black neck. Happy with her new friendship, she went in to eat, hoping her grandfather would welcome her. A place had been laid for him at the top end of the table, but he did not appear until they had nearly finished the vegetable soup. Instantly silence fell. Aunt Fat stopped shouting at the dark-haired housekeeper and the other old women stopped whispering. Nothing was heard but the scraping sound of knives on pewter. Sefchen felt shy, dreading he would ask her a question, but although she felt his eyes pass over her, he remained silent and, at the end of the meal, stood up and left.

Her feelings changed. She felt hurt he had ignored her and, as he walked out of the room, she raised her eyes and looked at him. Once again, she had a shock. He really was the image of her father, stood the same height with the same nose and beard. As he opened the door of his private room, he must have become aware of her examination. His heavy eyelids raised and for a second he stared back before slamming the door. But she had seen into his eyes, and they too belonged to her father. She did not know why, but she felt a deep bitter unhappiness. Getting up from the table, she ran out of the house and through the wood until she found a spreading oak tree, which she climbed and sat on a branch and clasped the main stem, before giving way to the momentary, utterly hopeless grief of childhood.

2

After a while, Sefchen grew used to her new life and imagined it was perfectly normal to live in a house with three old women sitting whispering, spinning and tippling all day long, ruled over by a morose old grandfather. Apart from the peculiar inmates of the house, there was an old groom with bow legs and leather leggings. It always amazed her how far his legs stood apart from each other, and whenever he walked towards her, she could clearly see between them. He was very old and bent, and, when he took off his cap, as he always did when he entered the house, his hair was snow white. Sefchen soon found he was unable to speak, and when he caught her playing with the dogs, ugly rumbling noises came out of his throat as his wrinkled face twisted with anger. She thought it a pity he was dumb as the only person who ever spoke to her was Aunt Fat, who sometimes, if the weather was warm, dropped her spinning and sat outside under the oak tree and told Sefchen fairy stories. She knew many more than Cousin Anna, and nearly all of them were about forests and the giants and castles which, she would say, waving her big stick towards the forest, 'are to be found all about here, but there are those who cast spells so we can't see 'em'. She often repeated the same stories over and over, so Sefchen soon came to know the best of them by heart.

The other two aunts whispered unceasingly, but never spoke out loud or stopped spinning except when they ate or drank. Their grey hair, which was fluffed out all around their heads, was never washed, and next to them stood an equally dirty large square dark bottle of spirits, from which Aunt Fat sometimes drank until she became wobbly on her feet. At such moments her voice grew blurred and she often repeated herself, but Sefchen never minded, for she felt that this woman with her pale moon face and heavy-lidded eyes did not dislike her.

Every night, before going to bed, Sefchen would drink a cup of gruel slammed down on the table by the dark-haired Margaret before taking her candle and tiptoeing up the wooden stairs, pulling herself up by the rope fastened to the wall since she hated the creaks of the old wood if she stepped on the centres of the steps. After she had washed herself in cold water and boned and cleaned her teeth, as she had been taught to do in Düsseldorf, she got into bed and would soon hear the welcome sound for which she was waiting. First came the creaking of the tightening of the rope, and then, gradually, a series of complaints as the planks groaned and creaked at the weight placed on them.

The door would open and in come her Aunt Fat, who would lean over the bed, put her arms around her, hug her, and sometimes, smelling strongly of the brown stuff, say what a good girl she was. Then she was pulled to the huge old bosom, and Sefchen felt a delight she had never known before. It was as if she was enveloped by security and made feel safe and secure.

Then the old woman would creak downstairs again and Sefchen would sink back happily on her feather mattress and fall asleep. But if the old woman was ill, or had fallen down and could not mount the stairs, or maybe had drunk too much of the nasty stuff, the child would wait in vain for the welcome noises and wake up frightened by creaks in the night. She would look at her aunt the next morning to see if she was well, and Aunt Fat knowing the child had missed her the night before would say, in a voice mixed with pleasure and guilt: 'Ah, so I didn't come to say good night, little one, did I? Well, I promise you I'll come tonight,' before she went back to her spinning.

After Sefchen had recovered from her original shock at her grandfather's disregard, she watched him closely and noticed that he had a peculiar way of walking when he was not wearing his sword. You could tell when he was not wearing it by the way his cloak hung, and the way he held his hands uneasily behind his back instead of one of them gripping the hilt while the other swung confidently at his side. He often looked down at the ground, and sometimes softly shook his head. As he had never spoken to her, she remained in awe of him, and was certain that he neither knew nor cared who she was.

One day, to her amazement, she was summoned by Margaret to his room off the great kitchen in which she had never set foot as her grandfather always locked the door every time he came out. She entered, trembling with fear, and found him sitting in silence, his eyes gazing down to the floor. She looked around, curiosity defeating fear, and saw in one corner a wooden bed like her old one in the Abbey while around the fireplace, in which turf smoked, stood large high-backed chairs. In the centre of the room stood a round table cluttered with axes, knives and clippers, while on the walls hung swords, more knives and clippers. In one corner stood a strange contraption of wood and leather and a great round stone. The room had a curious close smell which she did not like, and bookcases lined one wall, part of it stacked with metal boxes. Her furtive examination was interrupted by the old man saying in a cold, quiet voice: 'Josepha' – using the name she never used – 'they tell me that you can read.'

'Yes,' she said, on the verge of tears.

He took a large book out of a shelf and asked her to sit and read to him. She read the words with difficulty, not understanding what many of them meant. He did not seem to mind and from that day onwards would often call her to him and tell her to read aloud. It was strange to sit by the candle in winter or the little window in summer, slowly reading as he sat with his eyes closed in his high chair by the smoking fire. To begin with, she thought he had fallen asleep and would sometimes stop reading until the quiet, sad voice said: 'Read on, child, read on.' On the other hand, she wasn't sure he understood what she was reading either, for often, in the middle of a sentence, he would rise to his feet, thank her and say she could go.

It must have been about four months after her arrival that Aunt Fat told her excitedly a great execution was to take place inside the forest as a number of criminals had to be punished.

'Meals will have to be laid on for eight every day, for friends of your grandfather and other officials will be coming to discuss business. It will be your duty to carry plates, since these men eat a lot before working. Watch me carefully, because next year it will be your task to look after the silver goblets. But harken, child, and have courage, for now you will learn theirs is a profession of gloom and sorrow, for though these men eat and drink, they can never be merry. Ah, child, I'm sometimes sorry you came here, even though you interest me and I enjoy telling you stories.'

She continued to examine Sefchen with her dull eyes and said slowly and sadly: 'Sometimes I watch you walking in the forest, and, while you never laugh, I can see you are in a happy world of your own. Make the most of it, child. Be happy while you may, for our family live dolorous lives. You know, don't you, we cannot marry outside the family?'

'Yes,' said Sefchen, not thinking much of it as she was only seven and marriage seemed a long way away.

'Anyhow, child, be happy, and I'll go on telling you stories. Your grandfather's taken to you. He lets none of us into his room except you, you know. But I'm forgetting. When his friends arrive to dine, it will be your business to fill up their glasses and draw jugs from the barrels. Later, you know, you will see the wine come out of their eyes.'

She gave a little shudder and went and poured some of the dark liquid out of the black bottle into a clay cup and tossed it down and started to spin away at a great rate as the two other old crones looked balefully at Sefchen, hissing into each other's ears.

She found her Aunt Fat's warning of the invasion of visitors was accurate. Several men appeared during the next month, and all of them drank so deeply she had to fill their tankards again and again. She could not help noticing how the men resembled her grandfather, having the same pointed little beards and wearing identical clothing. All except two, one was very old, and the other younger by many years, although he tried to look aged and behave in the same sedate, sad manner as his elders. After the meals, Sefchen loved to run out into the forest, and she would often make her way to the clearing where the gallows stood and watch the corpses swinging and clanking gently in the breeze. It was a reassuring sound, and she usually fell asleep. But as the weather was getting colder, she found she had to run back to warm her bare feet. One night Aunt Fat met her and said fiercely: 'In future you must wear clogs.' Then came winter, with deep snow, and she was often forced to stay indoors and read. By the time spring came, she had read a translation of Anson's *Voyages*, and the outside world had become full of mystery and wonder. Curiously enough, her grandfather approved of the book and actually spoke a whole sentence: 'I am pleased. Goethe read it as a boy.'

At last, as the weather grew warmer, she began to explore the forest again, but always took her white beans with her in case she lost her way. More than anything she feared the Devil and his Grandmother, but her favourite story was that of Rampunzel, who she turned into a young man, while she often wondered what she would do if she found the garden of the enchantress with, inside the wall, the king's long black-haired son, leaning out of a window high up in a tower. Would she dare to sing, 'Rampunzel, Rampunzel, let down your hair to me,' and what would happen when she climbed up it and the Prince saw it was only dull little her? Sometimes, after she had walked down what she was sure was an enchanted path and found only more trees, she wondered, if she lay down instead and closed her eyes and wished with all her heart, she would be transported to fairyland and find, if not the castle in the garden, the house of Rose Red, although she knew, if a bear appeared, it would take all her courage to believe that beneath his thick hair lay a handsome prince. In the end, she decided that she only wanted to meet a safe elf or two, but certainly not those who lived in sugar houses – that would be too dangerous.

When she first arrived at her grandfather's, she found the animals in the forest were quite untameable. Not even the little birds would come and sit on her arms, as they had done in the Abbey wood. Instead, they would fly up in a panic, perch on branches and watch her with beady eyes before flying away. She never again tried to train a squirrel, for in her childish mind she thought that her earliest friend had betrayed her by not travelling to her new home. Nevertheless, she found the forest an enchanted lost land of bewitchment, and whenever she went for a long walk was sure that the trees would in the end tell her their secrets.

One day, after she had walked further than usual, she felt daring and decided to sit with her back against a tree, close her eyes and wish herself in the enchanted forest, 'which is there, but can't be seen', as Aunt Fat had told her about. But before she made her wish, she tried to prepare herself for what would happen if she woke up to find herself with a witch, or even a disguised fox or wolf, who would be planning to deceive her. Without knowing why, she found herself thinking of foxes and their deceitfulness, and how Aunt Fat said they were the 'most wicked and cunning and difficult animals to get the best of'. She tried to remember all the stories she had heard of them making fools of wolves, although she couldn't understand how wolves, being wilder and fiercer animals, three times their size and with much larger teeth, could be made to look stupid. It must surely mean foxes were braver and more cunning. At that moment, as if interrupting her dream, she heard a confusion of yapping and growling coming from over the hill. Immediately she recognized the sound of foxes. Very carefully, she crept forward, keeping her head down, for it might well be foxes playing one of their tricks on wolves, and if they saw her, they would turn and eat her up.

At last she reached the top of a sandy bank, from where, keeping her head hidden under a bursting green bush – it was May – she saw before her an unexpected sight. Halfway down the bank lay a gaping hole with, in front of it, a flat patch of earth littered with bones, rabbit skins and feathers. Further down the bank was a larger flat space, almost bare of grass, standing above a little stream which tumbled over mossy rocks along the bottom of the valley. On this space, five fox cubs rolled together in a yapping, squeaking red ball. As she watched, one leapt away, ran a few steps and turned, its nose pointed flat on the earth and its tail stuck out straight behind it as it kept its tiny eyes fixed on its playing brothers and sisters. Then, with a little dash, it joined the mingled throng again. Suddenly, one of them must have received a sharp bite, for it leapt backwards out of the wrestling match. For an instant, Sefchen saw the little front paws clawing at the top of the bank before the cub disappeared down the hill. A moment or two later, a soaking wet little animal, half its size, scrambled up again and, avoiding the others, ran whimpering with fear down the hole. The others paid no attention and went on with their endless game. Sefchen looked at the hole, wondering whether the little fox would come out again and how otherwise it could dry itself in the damp earth. After a few moments, however, the nose and eyes came peeping out, followed by the little animal who, after looking carefully from side to side, shook itself and waved its tail. Gradually it seemed to grow bigger as its fur stood up and dried. Slowly it forgot its fright and began once more to study the game. At last it began to edge towards the others, with tail and nose flat before it suddenly dashed down and rejoined the dusty fighters.

Sefchen held her breath. Perhaps these charming little creatures were really queen's children, her wish had come true and she had entered fairyland. At that moment, some way off in the forest, she clearly heard a sharp bark. As if by magic, the little foxes stopped their game and stood, listening with pricked ears, before bolting up the bank into the hole. Almost immediately she heard a rustle in the bushes and a large vixen, with a young lamb almost as big as herself thrown over her shoulder, jumped lightly on to the flat space and, without pausing, carried the heavy load up to the mouth of her hole and laid it carefully down before sitting back on her haunches and panting, her long thin red tongue moving from side to side. The litter fell furiously on to the lamb, tearing away and growling at each other as if continuing their game. Sefchen felt no sorrow for the lamb, and thought what a good mother she was to carry a heavy animal such a long way home to its cubs, and then to sit selflessly watching them eat without making any attempt to join in. After ten minutes, they had gorged themselves and some disappeared into the earth, while the others fell asleep on the sloping earth.

When they had finished eating, the vixen stood, stretched and, giving a quick look around to be sure she was alone, looked unblinking into Sefchen's eyes and examined the girl with interest. Sefchen tried to look back and make her know she was a friend who longed to play with the cubs and would do nothing to hurt them. After a moment, the vixen's body relaxed as she lay down, put her paws forward and happily started crunching the bones without paying the slightest attention to her visitor. After she had eaten enough, still ignoring Sefchen, she curled up and fell asleep.

Sefchen crept away and made her way home feeling happy and delighted. She had been seen, judged and accepted by an animal who had treated her as a friend. Her heart was full of love.

The day after she found the foxes, Sefchen asked Margaret if she could take some bread and cheese in an old leather wallet. She received a stare and nod, and later on Margaret cut slices of bread, which she soaked in hot bacon fat before laying thick slices of bacon between them. Sefchen would have liked to kiss her, but the woman looked so severe she only dared to say, 'thank you', and was going out of the kitchen when she saw a mutton bone in the slop bucket. She looked at it, but said nothing, as she knew that she must never tell anybody about the foxes, whether they were magical or not, otherwise disaster might threaten them. She also knew that, every day, Margaret took the waste food into the wood behind the house to throw into the undergrowth. So Sefchen went and hid herself in the bushes and watched. She was not disappointed, for soon Margaret appeared, head held high, expressionless, carrying the bucket in her hand. Carelessly she emptied it, turned and went away. Sefchen could hardly wait for her to disappear before she ran out and found, to her delight, that the mutton bone still had plenty of meat on it. She picked it up, but dropped it distastefully as it was covered with cold grease. She picked some grass and wrapped it round the bone and set off at a run for the foxes' home.

Arriving, she peeped over the bank and this time saw a big dark red fox with the most beautiful fluffy tail sitting outside the hole, gazing into the wood. She had never seen such a beautiful creature. As she gazed in wonder, two of the little foxes came tumbling out of the earth and ran into him. Like a flash, the pointed face turned, white teeth flashed and a cub ran whimpering back into the hole. Sefchen thought he must be cruel, but hadn't her own father been unkind? She ignored the thought – the fox was too beautiful to be bad – and continued to gaze in silent delight. Then, without warning, he jumped down the bank and, with a flick of his tail, disappeared into the bushes.

Sefchen watched, trying not to breathe or sneeze, for what seemed a long time before the mother came out yawning, the babies tumbling all over her without receiving a bite, and went and sat down and looked straight into the bushes at Sefchen, who very slowly lifted her right hand, grasping the mutton bone, and carefully edged herself out of the bush. The fox continued to watch after her cubs had vanished down the earth, keeping her eyes steadily fixed on the girl, who knew she must not make a clumsy move as she half-crawled down the slope and up the bank. She slipped once, but the fox paid no attention, and then she saw that the only parts of the vixen's body moving were her black whiskers and nostrils, which constantly quivered.

At last she was near enough. She held out the bone. The vixen moved forward, delicately took it in her teeth, moved back, sat on her haunches, dropped it and stared again at Sefchen, still wrinkling her nose. Sefchen was enchanted. Here was a friend, and she felt certain that, if she was clever and

19

careful enough, she might be allowed to stroke the pretty red head. Very gently, she put out her hand, and very gently the fox's testing nose moved forward and a narrow little tongue came out and licked her. Encouraged, she stroked the head and then, again and again, ran her hand up and down the furry back. Suddenly, the vixen made a strange squeaking noise and lay on her back, her legs gently pawing the air, inviting Sefchen to stroke her white stomach. She did as she was asked, and the fox rolled from side to side, squeaking, baring her gums and smiling. Sefchen suddenly saw a number of little red eyes looking out of the earth at her. But she had done enough for one day. She mustn't ask too much. She stood up and walked away, only looking back once as she passed over the brow of the hill, and saw her new friend now sitting up watching her.

As she walked home through the forest, full of love, completely happy, she noticed flocks of small birds darting about among the bright green spring leaves. It was surprising. No birds had come near her in this way since she had left the Abbey. Remembering their tameness, she stopped and stretched out her arms to see if they would settle, but that was too much to expect, although they went chirping and fluttering around her, and followed her to the door of the house, where she had never seen a bird before, and then settled in the great oak. From that day onwards, the atmosphere changed. No longer was the house surrounded by silence, and each morning the birds sang. That evening, she was so full of happiness that, as she sipped her gruel, she could hardly keep her feelings to herself. When Aunt Fat came up to kiss her good night, she flung her arms round the old woman's plump neck, so that the breath was knocked out of her and she gasped, 'There now, there now, child. What's come over you? I don't care for you squeezing me so hard.'

The next morning, during breakfast Aunt Old unexpectedly broke the silence in a harsh voice as she said: 'I don't know what has happened. The birds are here for the first time.'

Her grandfather looked up and said in a frightened way: 'Birds – here?'

'Yes, drat the little creatures,' said the old woman, each word cracking like a broken stick. 'They woke me up with their squeaks. Lord knows what it means,' and she raised one hand to her forehead, bringing it once down and once across her breast.

Her grandfather's face changed and looked relieved as he said, in the kindest tones Sefchen had ever heard him use: 'Cousin, you're a fool to lament their arrival. Remember who was the friend of the birds. I am glad. I never liked their absence. It shows they've forgiven me and understand how I was chosen to do God's work.'

He made the same strange crossing sign as Aunt Old and Sefchen thought he looked different as he muttered strange words in an unknown tongue. Then, even more amazingly, he placed the palms of his uplifted hands together and looked upwards so that the whites of his eyes showed. Sefchen said nothing, but wondered who God could be and thought he would be nice to talk to if it pleased him that the birds had followed her.

A week later, as she sat under the oak, she heard a scratching noise and, looking up, saw a squirrel looking down at her. She jumped up and put her hand to her throat. Was this her friend who had, after all, followed her all this way? She ran into the storeroom and boldly asked Margaret for a nut, then hurried back under the tree and there held up her hand exactly as her fading memory told her she had once done in Düsseldorf. But this squirrel took no notice and chattered a moment before leaping away to another branch. Excited she decided to wander into the forest down paths where she had never before seen animals. A hare jumped up and lolloped slowly away; and on a piece of cropped grass lay rabbit droppings. Everywhere she heard birds in the trees. Eventually her walk brought her to the gallows circle. She stood still and listened. Despite a faint breeze, which made the trees rub their branches together and the hanging figures clank on their chains, she could hear birds singing and thought, with pleasure, it must all have something to do with her making friends with the foxes.

3

One night, a few weeks later, when Aunt Fat came to say good night, the old woman remarked before leaving: 'Your grandfather has work to do tomorrow. You know, as an executioner he's proud to use his sword, but not on peasants. However, tomorrow there's a special hanging. You're still too young to witness the sight, but I and the others are going. Not that it amuses us much, but there's so little to do here, we are glad of any excitement which brings a little variety into our dull lives, and there's no doubt it's profitable work. But stay away from the circle for a day or two, child,' and she hugged Sefchen good night.

Instead of feeling comforted, Sefchen was disappointed. Why shouldn't she go to see the hanging? She'd never been frightened by the men on the gallows, as she knew they had been wicked. She made up her mind that, the next day, she would hide and watch, feeling neither fear nor sorrow, merely curiosity and the desire to see what bad men looked like when they died.

Early the next morning, her grandfather left the house without his sword. She followed him by a circuitous path and hid in the bushes on the edge of the clearing. In the centre stood a large cart constructed of long thick pine trees bound together with iron chains and supported by six thick, metalled wheels. She had often seen this cart moving through the wood, laden with huge beech and oak trees, but today it stood with empty shafts beneath the gallows' cross-posts, its four draft horses standing unharnessed and grazing contentedly on the new grass. Near by her grandfather, in cocked hat and black cloak, was standing beneath the dangling bones, directing a young man, who she recognized as the one he called his 'assistant', who was up a ladder pulling their skulls through the rope on which the skeletons hung. One by one the rib cages lunged downwards and doubled up over a chain, which also descended from the crossbar and hung loosely round the dead men's middles. Then, going up the ladder again, the youth stretched and unhooked the chain so that the skeletons fell to the ground, shattering into pieces. Six times the action was repeated, until the crossbar was untenanted. Then, under her grandfather's orders, the young man moved the ladder again and fixed new ropes to the iron hooks beneath the crossbar. When he had finished, he replaced the shorter stomach chains, which he had disentangled from the skeletons, and hung them next to the ropes. Then, stepping off the cart, he gripped the rope between his legs and hung on it until her grandfather came up, carrying a black gnarled piece of wood about five foot long, shaped like a 'T' with a curved top. This the old man with difficulty lifted and, resting it against his assistant's back, pushed him backwards and forwards.

After this test had been carried out on four ropes, Sefchen saw, by the sun, it must be nearly time for their midday meal. Not wishing to be questioned, she slowly made her way home. Later, she noticed by the number of times she had to fill the jug that her grandfather was drinking more than usual, and also that his hand shook as he cut the bread. Once, through nervousness, she spilt some wine. He looked up at her and she saw that his usually lifeless eyes were shining. He wasn't alone in his excitement. The three old women were dressed in coloured skirts and had washed their mops of hair which, instead of sprouting out, now hung lankly down like thin grey string over their shoulders. This style made Aunt Fat's face look redder and fatter than usual. The old women emptied their glasses again and again and cackled with laughter as they put red scarves over their heads for their afternoon treat. The only member of the household who remained unaffected was Margaret, who, sullen as ever, slammed down a bowl of stew on the table before walking away with a black look on her face after Aunt Thin whispered something in her ear.

Sefchen did not usually pay much attention to Margaret's moods, as something or other was always annoying her and a meal seldom passed without her crashing the pans together or banging the door. But, today, she felt sorry for her, as while her cousins and grandfather seemed for once merry, instead of in their usual black mood, why could not Margaret be in a good mood as well? The meal ended by her grandfather standing up, and Sefchen saw to her surprise that he appeared to look bigger and stronger. When he spoke, she listened intently, as he looked as if he was about to say something important. But she was disappointed. He only remarked quietly: 'Don't forget to bring Bruno – he's a good watch dog.'

Aunt Fat nodded, turned to Sefchen and said: 'Now, my dear sweet child' – she had been drinking from the black bottle as well as from the barrel – 'remember what I said. Go where you will, but keep away from the clearing.'

She swayed, smiling. Sefchen nodded. She had no wish to tell a lie.

But twenty minutes later she was back in her hiding place, her eyes wide open with excitement as she watched the most amazing sights she had ever seen. On one side of the clearing stood a number of men, wearing gold-braided hats and carrying rifles with long knives fixed to their ends. She thought that they looked like pictures she had seen of French soldiers. They stood guarding eighteen men, some old, some young, but all with their hands tied behind their backs. Sefchen could not take her eyes off a young soldier in a smart uniform, wearing a beautiful hat and carrying a sword instead of a rifle. He stood apart from the soldiers and looked at ease and pleased with himself. He usually spoke to a man with a large moustache, who was the only other soldier not carrying a rifle. Sefchen thought the young soldier looked enchanting. Perhaps he was a real prince.

Standing behind the prisoners were three stooping, elderly men. Two of them led little donkeys with baskets attached to their thin ribs. The other had a basket strapped to his back. Each wore a little black cap above hooked noses and long dirty grey beards. Behind them stood another large cart with high wooden sides, guarded by two more soldiers. Sefchen tried to hold her breath as she wondered what would happen next. She soon found out as the good-looking soldier with the sword took a large silver watch out of his pocket, looked at it and said something to the burly moustached man, who immediately shouted loudly, speaking so quickly Sefchen could not hear a word he said. At once four soldiers approached the bound men and, nudging with their rifles, separated six of them from their companions and pushed them towards the gallows. Two more soldiers stood behind them, their muskets pointed at their backs. Then the six men's hands were untied and, to Sefchen's surprise, they were slowly undressed, and their boots, underclothes, smocks, coats and breeches carefully placed into separate piles. One of the six started to tremble and cry, but no one paid any attention, except for one of his companions, who said something to him with a coarse laugh.

She was amazed at the men's bodies, even though she was looking at them from behind. They had such thick legs, and some of them looked as hairy as dogs. When they had been stripped naked, they were turned round and told to hold up their hands, and Sefchen saw for the first time how much their bodies differed from hers. She was not surprised. Dogs and bitches had different parts, and so had all the animals in the wood. She was glad she was a girl. Their nakedness was soon covered by six long smocks of sackcloth which were pulled over their heads before their hands were retied behind their backs. Afterwards they were prodded, one by one, to climb and stand on the long cart, now harnessed to the four horses, which was driven round in a circle and halted under the gallows, where the assistant looped the new ropes around the six men's necks. To Sefchen's pleasure, four of them continued to laugh and joke, but the others behaved differently, one looking sad and dazed, the other frightened. As soon as all the ropes were fixed, the men about to be hanged burst into song, the young soldier with the sword gave a sign, the driver cracked his whip and the horses bounded forward. She heard some sharp cracks and, within a second, the six men were swinging, kicking convulsively as their arms jerked upwards behind their backs. Her grandfather gave a command. His assistant at once ran to each of the six in turn and, jumping into the air, swung for a moment on their dangling legs. Then the long cart was brought back beneath the bodies, two soldiers lifted the corpses upwards by the waist and the assistant, using an iron bar, loosened the ropes around their necks and the bodies tumbled heavily to the ground, from which other soldiers dragged them and, with difficulty, lifted and tumbled them into a high-sided black cart.

The scene was repeated twice with little variation, except once when a man screamed and tried to lie down until he was struck over the head with a rifle butt and then held up by two of the strongest soldiers to have the loop fixed round his neck. Otherwise, the rest made rough jests and laughed and sang

24

before their execution. Sefchen noticed how, on the third occasion, the chains which had previously hung unattached now played a part in the ceremony, as the assistant, before jumping up to seize the men's legs, placed against each one's back a small ladder and attached the dangling chains to an iron belt which he had already placed around their waists. Sefchen realized this was to ensure that the bodies would remain swinging. She had watched the hangings with interest, and when the man screamed with fear had remembered hearing one day in the wood a noise like a baby crying, which she knew was a fox killing a hare. The man reminded her of the hare. She had felt sorry for it, but then remembered how, if the fox had not killed it, her friends, the cubs, would have nothing to eat and now it seemed to her that it was perhaps equally necessary for this man to be killed. She was not shocked as she had been brought up to believe her family profession was just, while her knowledge of life in the forest made her understand it was necessary to kill to live.

After the last men had been hung and chained up, her grandfather approached the three bearded men with little black caps, and led them over to the eighteen piles of clothing and boots. They argued violently over each bundle, sometimes coming nearly to blows before the highest bidder at length stowed the effects away in his basket. While this was going on, the young man with the sword, without a word, led his men out of the circle. Then her grandfather walked in his dignified manner over to the driver of the log cart and placed something in his hand which closed over the gift. But as her grandfather turned and walked away, the driver made a face and spat at his back. Sefchen wondered why.

The clearing was now empty except for the six bodies dangling on the scaffold and the peasant patiently holding the horse which drew the black high-sided cart into which the twelve other bodies had been thrown. Without any warning, her grandfather's assistant began to walk in Sefchen's direction. She ducked her head in horror. What if he discovered her? Would the three aunts, who stood chattering excitedly on the other side of the gallows, be angry? But nothing happened, except for a rustling in the bushes a few yards away as he drew out a short ladder, which he leant against the black cart. He climbed on to the driver's seat and began to tread upon the dead bodies lying in the back.

Sefchen watched curiously, wondering what he could be doing. He held a little sack in his hand, and all she could see was his back. For half an hour, he remained bent, obviously moving the bodies and sometimes giving the impression of pulling them about. Occasionally, she heard a faint chip of iron. She could not imagine what was happening, but whatever it was it fascinated her aunts, for they drew closer and came and stood by the horse, shrieking questions which received no answer. Eventually the assistant stood up, climbed on to the driver's seat and climbed down the ladder, still holding his sack, by now half-full, wet and black. Her grandfather took it and gestured to the peasant to lead the cart under the gallows, where the assistant climbed up and, holding each body in turn by its iron belt, clipped off with his other hand

25

all the fingers and thumbs, the aunts jostling each other to collect them as they fell on to the ground.

At last the work was done and her grandfather placed something into the peasant's hand, which he also took without a word of thanks and, as he walked away, also spat at his back. Sefchen noticed how, once the cart had gone, her grandfather changed again and became no longer frightening, but a little old man for whom it was only possible to feel sorry. Sefchen decided to go home and say truthfully she had gone for a walk. Taking a farewell look at the hanging men, she noticed for the first time Bruno was tied up underneath the gallows, a bucket of water beside him. He was standing, wagging his tail and sniffing the bare feet above him. She thought what odd smells dogs liked, for several of the dead men's feet were dirty. At the same time, she wondered what on earth the dog was guarding, since the men did not even have their fingers left.

On the way home, she saw a hare standing on its hind legs and eating at the side of the path. To her delight (for she wished only to be treated as a sister by all animals), he gazed back at her without fear. She stroked his head, which made the animal lay back his ears as he continued to eat the black buds of a young ash tree.

That evening, Margaret produced in a large black dish a huge chicken pie with a human head sticking up in the centre, surrounded by four crossed swords picked out in pastry. Sefchen wasn't hungry, she didn't know why. The afternoon's work seemed to have exhausted her grandfather as well, but he drank so much that twice she had to go and replenish the jug from the best cask. The old aunts, merrier than usual, whispered stories to each other, including one about three golden hairs, which they started to tell when she was in the room, but then sent her off on a futile mission to the pantry to find some currants. While she was looking carelessly – she knew they did not want them – she heard their cackles of laughter, but not a sound from her grandfather.

After the meal, Sefchen plucked up her courage and asked Margaret for Bruno's plate, saying she would be pleased to take the dog's meal to him. It startled her when her grandfather answered, looking towards her but not raising his eyelids, 'He's on a chain which will enable him to find his own food. He's a good dog. I've taught him to howl should anyone come near, as there are those who will try and cut down the dead and bury them secretly in holy ground, and cheat the authorities who have stated they should hang as examples to others. If I hear Bruno, I will be there in a few minutes with my gun. Justice shall not be cheated.' And he added, speaking slowly, 'The robbers never come after the bodies have hung for three days. Bruno can come back then.'

He drank his whole goblet of wine and continued to stare at the table, and went on drinking long after it was cleared and the cousins had gone to wash and clean the fingers. Before Aunt Fat left, she had kissed Sefchen and said, blowing strong breath into her face: 'I shan't be able to come and kiss you good night, for we have work to do. Go for a walk, if you like, and then to bed,' and she hugged her so hard they both nearly lost their balance and fell over.

Sefchen was pleased, she was not usually allowed out at night, and was even gladder when she found to her surprise the roosting birds chattered at her excitedly. She put out her arms, level with her shoulders, and a robin at once came down and sat on her left hand. Very slowly, she looked around and saw hundreds of little piercing black eyes staring at her from every bush. The robin seemed completely unafraid as it hopped sideways along her arm. She felt she had at last entered the magical forest kingdom of which she had read so much, and was sure the robin was an enchanted beauty who might turn back again into a king's daughter if she wished hard enough. She dropped her arms and the robin flew off, but followed her, fluttering from twig to twig. She had never known the forest so full of peace, and, sitting down on the spreading root of an old beech, remembered the afternoon and wondered why all the men except two had laughed and sung before their death. She was certain they were happy now. Looking up thoughtfully, she saw a hind's head looking out of a clump of bramble and dead bracken fronds and two large trusting eyes gazing at her. Stepping carefully forward, she looked down and saw a fawn lying beside the hind. She longed to hold and kiss the fawn but, looking at the mother's eyes, saw fear and slowly moved away.

As she lay in bed, Sefchen thought again about the executed men, the doe and the fawn, the hare and the robin. She realized she loved animals more than men and women but did not know why. She realized she had not minded seeing the men hung, but while she could not kill an animal herself, she also had not minded when she saw the baby foxes eating a lamb. Confused, she fell asleep and dreamed she was a lamb playing in the fields outside the forest, and then a large fox came up and all her friends ran away. But she knew the fox to be a friend, and they ran round in circles. First she chased the fox, then he chased her, faster and faster they ran until she looked and saw his mouth was open and he was about to eat her. She woke screaming, sure nobody loved her, neither people nor animals, and she longed to hear Aunt Fat stumbling up the stairs so she could throw herself into her arms and sob on her large breasts. She cried herself to sleep at last, and luckily did not dream again.

When she woke up, the sun was high. She dressed quickly in one of the three brown smocks Margaret had bought her to wear when her old clothes fell to pieces, and tied it at the waist with a piece of green ribbon which she thought was the prettiest thing she had ever worn. Then she ran downstairs, only to find all the household in a bad temper, with Aunt Old especially cross.

After she had finished her bread and milk, Sefchen went to the kitchen waste bucket and picked out a large piece of tough ham, and ran all the way to the foxes' earth. She wanted to make sure the vixen was still her friend. Chickens' feathers lay around, and it occurred to her that she was no better, for hadn't she eaten chicken pie yesterday and ham often? She went and sat on the patch of earth where the young ones played, and before long the vixen appeared, squeaking and wagging her tail as she squirmed forward, her stomach brushing the ground. Sefchen offered her the hard piece of ham rind, and she sat crunching it up as the young ones came out, one by one, and all played together. She laughed as they chased each other round, and then, tired, sat on the bank, where one of the cubs followed her and went to sleep on her lap, only waking up when the dog fox came back and threw down a rabbit before disappearing into the hole. The little foxes ran to help tear it to pieces, and Sefchen understood killing was a part of life, and she must make the best of it, although she would never kill a thing herself.

4

For the next five years, until her life was interrupted by a disturbing event, Sefchen lived a half-human, half-animal life. Each morning after her eighth birthday, she had to read for three hours in her grandfather's room his favourite poem-play, *Dr Faustus.* After a year, she knew the book by heart, but if she ever made a mistake, he would correct her and make her read the sentence again. Her favourite part, and his, she soon found, was Faustus' adventures on Walpurgis Night, which never bored her.

He often said to her of Goethe: 'Ah, there's a great man. Not a hair of his would I touch if it cost me my life. He's not only the greatest German who ever lived, but the greatest man of any nation.'

Sefchen thought it was the longest sentence she had ever heard him speak, and Goethe was the only man of whom she ever heard him speak kindly. She never understood why he should have loved him, and doubted if he knew. All she knew was that she did not love her grandfather, who never said anything kind to her. The only occasion when he ever showed interest was on her ninth birthday, when he announced to Aunt Fat at supper, 'The girl is to wear her clogs in the wood.' Sefchen hated clogs. It was not so bad once May came, for then she could go for walks and, directly she was out of the house, kick off her wooden prisons and find a thicket and sit and listen to the nightingales. She often thought of trying to tame one, but something stopped her. The magic of their voices made her believe they should be little golden birds, but she knew they were in fact an insignificant brown, and that if she saw one, half the magic of the singing would vanish. And so she shut her eyes when she heard one of them, pretending it was a golden bird singing and never looked up. If the bird was silent, she would sing herself to try to make it answer.

In the same way, she made herself believe in her dreams, which usually had a deer in them. After a few years, she had many friends, and if she passed a doe on one of her walks, the animal would stand up, a new-born fawn beside her and walk up to Sefchen, who would look into their eyes and gently stroke them. Of all her friends in the wood, the deer had the coldest noses, and none colder than a young buck's with a golden fleck in his right eye whom she had known since he was born. She was sure he must be a changeling who would one day turn into a prince, for although he would approach her with a questioning look, he always backed off if she tried to stroke him, and stand a yard away, looking as if he was begging her to return him to human form. She would stare hard at the golden fleck and wish and wish, but it was no good. She always had to leave him looking sadly after her. Then, one night, she dreamed he walked up to her in the wood and she knew exactly what she had to do and lifted his right hoof in her left hand and his left hoof in her right hand and walked three times sideways around an oak tree. At once he turned into a prince, dressed in gold sparkling with diamonds. He smiled gratefully and vanished. For weeks afterwards, she searched for the buck with the golden fleck, but did not find him and was sure she had returned him to his kingdom.

Shortly afterwards, another dream persuaded her she was about to become a part of the secret magic kingdom of the forest which she had always believed existed. She was searching in vain for an enchanted castle, and found instead a broken-down old house with a collapsed roof standing above a square pond covered with water lilies, the water level with the old brick sides. As Sefchen approached, she heard a number of plops and wondered what made them. Soon she was uneasily aware someone was looking at her, but although she looked hard, she could see nothing except green leaves. Then, all of a sudden, she saw sitting on a leaf a huge green frog staring at her with unblinking eyes. At once she remembered the story of the Frog Prince and said to him: 'Prince, I know who you are. Come to me.' But the Prince didn't move and she didn't dare to tread on the water in case whoever guarded him had filled it with serpents who would wrap themselves round her legs and pull her under for ever.

Every day for a week she visited the pond, and each day felt sure the frog was the Prince, although sometimes he looked bigger and sometimes smaller, but always the same pleading brown eyes implored her help. On the eighth day, she remembered the fairy tale and knew the only way she could rescue him was by picking him up, giving him a meal and taking him into her bed. But as she leaned nervously forward, the frog jumped into the water, and she had to go home frustrated. But that night, in her sleep, she approached the pond again and out jumped the frog. Picking him up, she brought him home, fed him surreptitiously on her knee. Pretending her head ached, she went to bed and laid the frog by her, who instantly turned into a beautiful prince in another golden suit who, getting out of bed, bowed, thanked her, asked for her hand and kissed it so gallantly she was filled with happiness. Then he bowed again and vanished. When she woke up she knew she had, in her sleep, released another prince from a wizard's spell, and was happy, but sorry that, whenever she saved handsome princes, they disappeared at once. The next day, she walked to the pond, and, sure enough, the frog was gone, which confirmed her dream was true. But, again, she wished the Prince had stayed longer and told her what it felt like to be a frog.

As Sefchen grew older, she had to rely increasingly on herself and the books in her grandfather's library. In the house, apart from the occasional whispers of the old relations and the sentimental drunken outbursts of Aunt Fat, silence reigned. Margaret seldom spoke, and Sefchen's morning readings with her grandfather became each year increasingly distressing.

Her neglect by the family made her both imaginative and observant, and she noticed how, in the days before his 'absences', her grandfather became a different man and would sit in his chair trembling with excitement, wiping the sweat off his brow before walking over to his swords, examining them carefully and returning to his chair and his feverish thoughts. The day before he left he would eat and drink more than usual and stare furiously round at his household until everybody longed for him to go. Once he had gone, the house would be almost happy. The old women would drink less, Margaret would be less sulky and Sefchen would take her wallet out and spend whole days in the forest, which she gradually came to believe belonged to her. As it was no longer used for hunting, the few old keepers who remained lived far away on its northern edge, seldom venturing further than it took them to shoot a hare or deer for themselves. The foresters were more numerous, but always worked together in bands, so Sefchen could hear the falling trees and avoid them. As for the children from the neighbouring villages on the edges of the forest, they regarded the executioner's house and the gallows as haunted areas where skeletons might seize you, and Sefchen as a dangerous witch – a belief added to by occasional sightings of her talking to or sitting by a wild animal, whose form, it was said, she took at will. Later on, the costume she wore convinced even the sceptical that she was an enchantress. This happened when, in her twelfth year, her smocks finally dissolved into rags. Margaret told Sefchen's grandfather, who nodded but continued to stare at his plate. But Aunt Fat, in a defiant mood, said firmly: 'The child's growing. At her age she should choose her dresses. Let Margaret bring a roll of material, but let the child choose the colour.'

Sefchen thought and, since it was spring and the forest looked beautiful, said slowly, 'Green.'

Two days later, when Margaret returned from her weekly trip to the town, she brought back a roll of green cloth and, to the girl's surprise, said she would help her cut out and sew up her first dress. Sefchen, who had, without realizing it, become interested in her own appearance, thanked her, looked at the pictures in old books and discussed them with Margaret, who silently shook her head. Eventually they made a dress from a pattern which she never abandoned as long as she lived in the wood. It was copied from an old picture of a woman wearing a long green skirt, above which a jacket was laced upwards from the waist until it joined a square surrounding her neck. The jacket they copied exactly, but Margaret said Sefchen must have a looser, fuller skirt to enable her to run among the trees.

It was a strange, original garment, which would have caused astonishment in any town, as the way the jacket exactly fitted her long and slim body created a startling effect. When she wore it for the first time, her grandfather frowned and the cousins' mouths fell open, but none of them said a single word. Neither did Margaret when Sefchen thanked her, but merely turned her back and walked away. The dress made her happy, but the effect on the neighbourhood was startling, as villagers caught occasional glimpses of the 'witch' in green with the dead white face and long red hair. Daring children, picking flowers, would hide their faces and run home, and any woodman or keeper who saw the 'green girl', would simply cross himself and that evening tell his wife, who'd say angrily: 'What do you expect from such a cursed house? She is a child of wickedness and sorrow, as time will show.'

The fact that Sefchen's simple idea of adorning herself to match the spring had firmly established her in the locality as a witch was something she did not know and so did not mind. To her, the spring meant new life and joy, and each year she made a fresh generation of animal friends, while the old ones welcomed her with joy and she was sure the birds befriended the year before brought their young to perch on her arms. But it was not only the animals that entranced her. She could gaze for hours at the young green of the wood, the violets, anemones, primroses and bluebells, and would make garlands for young animals, who would indignantly rub or shake them off. She loved examining nests and sprouting ferns as much as observing how the uncouth young animals of the previous year became dignified. She was so happy she could not understand why, at the bottom of her heart, she was beginning to wish to see the world outside the forest.

One evening, when she was thirteen and cared no longer whether or not Aunt Fat came to give her a boozy good-night kiss, the old woman stumbled up the stairs and sat on a chair by Sefchen's bed, and said in a lachrymose voice: 'I've come because I'm missing my little baby, who I know cannot sleep without her beloved aunt saying good night, and she has remembered a story which she was told as a child, long, long ago, of two little sisters who lived in a wood . . . in a wood,' she repeated, '. . . who lived in a wood,' she said for the third time, as her head dropped forward, and she fell asleep, snoring loudly. After this, Sefchen could not get out of her mind the idea of two little sisters and how much more fun it would be to have a sister to whom she could introduce her friends, although, of course, she would have loved best a baby to talk to when she was lonely.

The next day out walking she pretended she had a sister called Gretchen, who she led excitedly to a small pool in a stream across which a tree had fallen, making a perfect seat, and explained to her exactly how she should hold her toes in the cold water, but only her toes, so that they gradually chilled the rest of her legs, and how, when she took them out and sat on the bank, it was pleasant not painful to feel the blood coming back. At that point, she heard a tapping and took the girl, who had obediently put her toes in the water, to show her a green woodpecker gripping a tree trunk with his claws as his head went *rat-tat-tat* faster than you could believe, and Gretchen had asked why banging on a tree didn't injure the bird's brain. Sefchen told her it was an intelligent question, annoyed that she had not thought of it herself. Later, when they found the young foxes eating a hare, her new sister asked another irritating question: 'How can you love foxes and hares when foxes kill hares?' Sefchen replied: 'Well, I just do,' and left it at that.

That evening, as she lay in bed, she decided that while it was very nice to have found a new sister, she did not wish to see her every day as she somehow intruded into her private world. On the other hand, it would, when she was lonely, be nice to ask Gretchen to come for a walk, but only when she felt like it. Consequently Gretchen in the future became not a constant companion, but one who only appeared when wanted, which was about once a month, or less in the spring and in the winter hardly at all, unless it was for a few minutes in the early morning to see the sun shining on newly fallen snow. But at the same time Sefchen decided she would one day have a baby who would be the perfect companion.

But her sister had made her adventurous, and once, when the ground was iron hard with frost and water frozen in the house, she suddenly had a passionate desire to walk on the Frog Prince's pond. She had never gone so far in winter, and as she went further from home shivered at the unexpected silence of the wood. She would have called Gretchen if she had not known she would only have said: 'Let's go home.' The forest was frozen in a cold sleep, but the pond made up for her doubts. With fearful delight, she stood on the side, gazing at the brown dead-leaf ice beneath, in which the frogs must lie buried by mud. Had the Prince spent a winter there? How odd he must have felt. Doubts crept into her mind, she pushed them aside and stood on the edge of the ice, terrified it might break. As nothing happened, she walked into the centre of the pond, and found it as firm as a road. She stamped, the noise echoing round the woods, and felt delighted that the guardian serpents should be trapped harmlessly beneath her feet. In the cold valley, the frost still clung to the trees. Her mood changed. It was exciting to be the only living person in the valley, and comforting to be treading on serpents prisoned and powerless beneath her feet. She was glad she had not sent for Gretchen.

Feeling cold, she decided to run home. Turning a corner, she would have crashed into a young stag if he had not taken three gigantic bounds down the ride. Having run a hundred yards, he stopped, turned round, pricked his ears, looked at her and slowly began walking back. Sefchen was pleased, but when he halted a few paces away her pleasure turned to astonishment. Surely, although much bigger, he had the same eyes and stood in the same nervous way as the buck she had two years ago turned back into human form. Yes, there was the golden speck in the eye of the enchanted prince. The stag pawed the ground, and she noticed the hot smell of his breath and body. No, the speck must be a coincidence. She tried to pat his head, but he backed away in exactly the same way as the prince had done. She felt shocked and tears came into her eyes.

That night, in bed, she wondered if her dreams were illusions and whether she had only in her imagination rescued the Frog Prince? If so, the forest could not be the enchanted land she had supposed. The idea left her doubtful and disappointed, and all the glory seeped out of her thoughts. She cried herself to sleep. But then help came in her dreams: the two princes appeared in their golden clothes and told her how she had saved them. Before she could thank them, they disappeared.

In the morning, she told herself she was reassured, although her doubts would certainly have returned if her doubts had not been put out of her mind by Margaret falling downstairs and breaking a leg. The event at once shocked and excited the three old women out of their cocoon of drink, and they clustered around her, placing herbs on her leg and pulling the bone straight so that the poor woman shrieked with pain until they pressed a wet pad strongly smelling of herbs on to her mouth until she fainted. Then they strapped her leg between boards and tied it up and made a rough bed for her at the side of the kitchen and grumbled all the time about who would have to do the cooking until she was better.

Sefchen immediately said that she would try, as she had watched Margaret and often seen a dish prepared which did not look too difficult. All she had to do was lower the simmering pot on to the fire and add bits of meat from the joints of venison which an old keeper secretly brought once a month. He never entered the house, and as soon as he got his money scuttled away without looking back. Confident, Sefchen went into the larder and cut the slices. Then she took the bread, cut it into slices and put cheese on the table. She changed only one of Margaret's habits, and cut the meat into much smaller pieces, as she had never known what to do with the huge hunks Margaret put on her plate. The housekeeper watched her balefully from her bed, but didn't speak and only nodded when Sefchen asked if, having lowered the pot, she should now stew the meat for forty minutes and replenish the pot afterwards with fresh venison.

That evening her grandfather looked pleased. He picked out and ate smaller pieces of the meat and congratulated her. Even the aunts thanked her. Sefchen looked nervously at Margaret, but her eyes were shut and she gave no sign of having heard.

Two days later, the bread, butter and milk were nearly finished and it was decided Sefchen should drive next morning out of the forest for the first time since her arrival many years before to do the marketing. She had no idea where the market town was and had only the vaguest memory of her life in Düsseldorf, and while she told herself untruthfully nothing in the wood frightened her, she was terrified at the idea of going to the market town, finding the right shops and paying the correct money. When Aunt Fat saw how upset Sefchen was, she limped over with her to the saturnine Margaret and said: 'Come now, you must tell the child of the shops and how they lie. How's the poor thing to find them? We can't go with her – we're too fat, thin and old. She has to go alone.'

Sefchen looked imploringly at Margaret, who replied in a cold voice without raising her eyes: 'The girl's watched me harness the pony. She's clever. She can do it herself. She needs no whip. The old pony knows where to go. He'll take her and will stop at the baker's shop where she can buy the white flour the master likes, and then at the butcher's, and beyond them at the dairy, where I put milk in our churn and buy the cheeses and the salted butter which the master will have. That's all she needs to know. The shops lie on the right of the main street. The pony will take her and follow her from shop to shop. But let her come home quickly. They would kill any of you three, but I don't know what they'll do to her if they realize who she is.'

Margaret's words added to Sefchen's fears, and filled her with gloom. It wasn't only her fear of leaving the shelter of the forest, but the reappearance of the stag with the golden fleck had shaken her and made her doubt her magical powers. Now Margaret said she might be attacked. She felt her heart thudding with fear and longed to confide her worries to someone, but who? Certainly not Gretchen, who would only give a depressing answer. In bed, she thought again about her fear of leaving the wood. She had spent years avoiding even the outskirts of the forest, and when, in winter or early spring, she had heard noises from the outside world or had glimpses of distant cattle or sheep, she had turned her steps towards the thickets and hidden valleys where she felt the magic of the forest protected her. Now, just as she had begun to doubt the truth of the magic protection, she was to be sent out alone.

Every time she was about to fall asleep, her thoughts became confused with fears. She even imagined the old voices in the Abbey, which the forest had silenced, calling to her, though she was not going to the Abbey but to a strange town to talk to and buy from strangers who Margaret said might hurt her. She never knew whether she slept or not, but suddenly it was time to get up. She could eat nothing, but nobody cared, and Aunt Fat merely repeated again and again what she had to buy. She went out of the kitchen without daring to glance at Margaret, to find the dumb man waiting and holding the pony, which backed itself into the shaft. She fastened him in from memory as the dumb man stood staring, making no effort to help. Having counted her money, she climbed up into the dog cart and, exactly as Margaret had said, the pony broke into a trot.

After half an hour of jolting along between trees, they came out of the forest and joined a larger road. Sefchen found herself trembling, especially when workers looked up in surprise. For the first time she realized her beloved green dress must look odd and stupid compared to the clothes which the peasant women wore. She did not like the way they gaped at her, and then stopped and stood, shading their eyes and staring as she left them behind.

At length, the cart passed a few large houses with walled gardens and then entered a large street. She shook with terror. What if the horse walked past the shops? She would never dare ask the way. But the animal had no such idea in his quiet head, and stopped at a little house with two curved white windows divided by pieces of wood into many squares through which she could see piles of loaves and the most beautiful cakes she had ever seen. She felt safer now, as before she left she had made Margaret write in chalk on three slates all that was wanted from the shops. It had seemed easy, back in the forest, but now, sitting in the little pony cart, Sefchen did not dare move. What would the people in the shop be like? For years she had seen nobody to talk to outside the household.

At last, she jumped quickly down and pushed open the door, almost falling into the shop, where a middle-aged woman with blonde hair in two pigtails and a good-tempered round face was serving a black-haired woman, beside whom a boy of ten, with white hair and red eyes, was carelessly tilting a large whicker basket already full of loaves and sugared cakes. All three turned and stared in amazement at Sefchen, who realized she must look a fool. Since it was summer, she wasn't wearing an overcoat, but had thrown a green shawl around her neck and shoulders, while on her feet she wore green painted clogs. For endless moments, it seemed to her six eyes bored into her brain. Then the black-haired woman, who must have just finished shopping, hissed with a venomous look on her face a few words to the woman behind the counter, who shook her pigtails, smiled and, turning to Sefchen, asked kindly: 'Are you from the house in the wood?'

Sefchen could only nod, wonder whether she was going to faint and hand the woman the slate with the housekeeper's orders. Then, as she passed it over, she remembered, to her horror, that she had left her basket in the pony trap and ran out again in a panic. It took her only a moment to pull it from under the seat, but as she turned back towards the shop, the door opened and the black-haired woman came out, stared at her and, as she passed, raised a hand as if to shield her son from an evil influence. Sefchen had time to notice that the boy had a red face and a mouth full of large teeth. In the shop, the shopkeeper gently took the basket and loaded it with flour, the fresh white bread her grandfather loved and the scones which the old women chewed, smiling at her all the time. She passed it back over the counter and said in a friendly voice: 'Don't tremble so, child. I've heard of you, you know. Is it true you've lived all these years with the old ones in that . . . that . . .' she paused, and ended lamely, '. . . house?'

Sefchen nodded.

'So what's become of Margaret?'

'Ill,' said Sefchen.

'What of?' asked the woman, speaking sharply for the first time.

'She broke her leg,' said Sefchen trembling, not wishing to irritate the kind shopkeeper.

'Ah, that's good, it's not catching,' said the woman, looking relieved. 'Now, little one, here's a cake for yourself,' and she gave her a small round white cake covered with icing.

'There, eat it now. You have no flesh on your bones as it is, and that red hair of yours, falling round your neck, makes your skin look deadly white. It dearly makes me long to fatten you, whatever they say you may be. Come again. It does my eyes good to see you, instead of that grim Margaret, who hasn't smiled in ten years. Here, my dove, take another,' and she put a second cake in the basket. 'Eat it on the way home.'

Sefchen blushed at the unexpected kindness, and the woman continued, 'My, but aren't you pretty when you colour up? I'm glad to see you've some blood in your veins.'

The reassured girl bobbed a slight curtsey, as she had been taught was

36

polite, and the woman laughed and repeated: 'Come by again. I'll keep a cake for you.'

In the street, Sefchen put the bulging basket in the back of the cart, lifted out another empty one and walked on, remembering Margaret's instructions. Sure enough, the pony followed her to the butcher's shop. She opened the door and found an empty room and the sound of chopping coming from a room behind a door. After waiting nervously alone for five minutes, she forced herself to peek through and saw a huge man, his hands covered with blood, hacking up a carcass of meat. He almost jumped into the air when he saw her, and wiped a bloody hand across his brow before following her into the shop saying crossly: 'Who are you, coming here like a spirit, frightening a man out of his wits! Where are you from? I've not seen you or the likes of you before.'

Trembling, Sefchen gave him her second slate, at which the man, having painfully spelled out the words, looked up at her sharply.

'So you're from the house in the forest, are you? Ten years ago, I was told to trade with you people would bring bad luck, and I nearly refused, but then, I thought, I've done a bit of slicing myself, ha ha. One thing I will say for Margaret is, she pays on the nail, and when all is said and done, someone has to do the old man's job. In my view, many more heads should be cut off, and he's a clean workman, they say. But I'll wager he can't slice a joint as neatly as I can. But why do you wear such clothes? There's some in the village who won't like it. Take your things, now, and get out quick. They're a funny lot round here, and the old man has enemies, many enemies. In these troubled times, there's hardly a man or woman in this village who hasn't lost a friend or relative.'

He nodded to dismiss her and she put the meat in the cart and carried the last basket to the dairy, where she found that the milkman had long white whiskers and she could not help thinking, despite her fears, how each shopkeeper looked like their own goods. The baker woman was homely and kind, the butcher big, red, with huge hands and blood even on his face, and the milkman tall and thin and white all over, his colour the colour of milk. Like the others, he looked at her in a funny way when she gave him the slate – her last – but said nothing as he filled the basket with salted butter and cheese as she helplessly thought of the milk churn. However would she manage to lift it? But there had been no need for her to have worried as he said: 'I'll give you a hand with the milk. It's heavy for one so slight. What age have you?'

'Thirteen past,' she said.

He nodded and looked at her keenly, but said nothing, then shook his head and picked up the full churn and heaved it into the back of the cart, before asking in a mild tone of interest: 'Margaret dead?'

'No,' said Sefchen, flustered. 'She broke her leg.'

'Ah,' he said. 'Badly?'

'Yes.'

For some reason he looked pleased. Sefchen got in and stowed away her last basket, but as the pony, without instruction, turned for home, she suddenly heard shouts behind her. Looking quickly over her shoulder, she saw six youths running down the street towards her, led by the white-haired, red-eyed boy she had seen in the baker's shop. As the pony started to trot, she saw them standing looking as if they did not know what to do next. Suddenly the white-haired boy seemed to make up his mind and shouted at the top of his voice: 'Witch!' At which the others joined in with, 'She devil!' and 'Devil spawn!' All of them then bent down in the road and picked up stones and threw them at her.

Sefchen sat motionless, asking herself what she could have done to be attacked, but luckily the pony, with a whisk of his tail, broke into his first gallop for many years, which excited the boys into a frenzy, and joined now by friends, they ran after the cart hurling away, but luckily only one small pebble hit her gently on the arm. When Sefchen was at last safe in the country, she burst into passionate tears. Gone was her fearlessness. The display of hatred had brought back to her the beheading of her doll and the unkind looks she had always had in Düsseldorf. Why were men so cruel? But since they were, was it surprising her grandfather had to cut off so many heads? Yet no logic could comfort her. She was frightened and, worse than frightened, wounded to the very bottom of her soul by the hatred which she felt the unknown world felt for her.

Once her storm of tears was over, she felt better and settled herself quite comfortably, or rather as comfortably as possible in the jumping, rickety little cart. What had happened should have been no surprise to her, after all. Margaret had warned her, and surely she should be relieved to have got away without being hurt. In fact, she had been more kindly received than she'd expected in the shops. The baker's woman was friendly and had given her one cake to eat and another to put in her basket. The remembrance made her feel hungry, and taking the iced cake out of her basket, she found a small stone embedded in its top. She removed it, dusted the crushed icing and ate away with enjoyment. The butcher hadn't been unkind to her either and had given her what she asked for and even said pleasant words. Neither in the milk shop had anyone treated her badly. It had only been that horrible boy, and, as she knew from tales, boys were always cruel.

At supper that night, her grandfather unexpectedly questioned her about her visit, saying in a quiet voice: 'Did you manage to buy the stores without any trouble?'

She paused. 'Yes, grandfather.'

'Nothing happen?'

'Some boys threw stones, but only one hit me lightly on the arm.'

'Ah,' said her grandfather, stroking his chin. 'Ah.' Then, turning to the old women, he said loudly, so Margaret could hear: 'It's not safe for her to go again. She's young and . . .' He paused. '. . . they'll chase her again. It would be a pity for a stone to spoil her face.'

The aunts began to whine, but her grandfather leaned forward and said:

'Silence. You go next week,' he said, staring at Aunt Thin, 'and until Margaret's well. You're the lightest, and you have no looks to spoil, while your sisters are too old and heavy.'

Sefchen looked at her Aunt Fat and saw she was actually blushing. She felt sad for her and, reaching out a hand under the table, gripped a plump hot palm and saw to her surprise tears come into the old woman's eyes. Nobody else noticed, and Margaret said: 'I'll go next week.'

Sefchen saw her grandfather's face whiten as he replied coldly: 'You'll go when I tell you. The matter's arranged. I do not like arguments.'

He spoke in such icy tones, Sefchen shivered and a frightened silence fell on the room. That night in bed, as she thought the incident over, she again found herself longing for more affection. Curiously enough, the words of the baker's woman had made her realize that kindness did exist outside the forest, and that perhaps she would not always be alone. At that moment, she heard the stairs creaking, and Aunt Fat, who could hardly climb them any more, came staggering breathlessly into the room and, sitting on the edge of the bed, hugged her and told her she was a brave girl. Sefchen realized she had come this time not out of drunken sentimentality, but because she wanted to give her comfort. Touched and pleased, she decided to ask a question she had never dared before.

'Aunt,' she said, 'why do people kiss each other so often in books?'

To her surprise, her aunt lifted up her sad fat face, her expression changed and she brayed with laughter, smacking her lips as she replied: 'You'll kiss when you want to, and when a man wants to kiss you, but you've no need to worry. There'll be plenty willing to kiss you.'

Sefchen was half-shocked and half-pleased, and later dreamed she was lying in bed when one of the princes in a golden costume leaned over and was about to kiss her. At that point she woke up and was angry and tossed and turned before she fell asleep again and had a very different dream. She had become a princess, turned out of her home by her wicked stepmother who put a curse on her. She and her brother wandered deep into the forest, passing many places she knew until she became thirsty, and stopping by the stream which flowed through the valley below the foxes' earth, she bent down to the running water and was about to drink when her brother said: 'Don't drink here, Sefchen, or you'll become a wolf.'

She went higher up the stream and bent down again, but before she could drink her brother said: 'Don't drink here, Sefchen, or you'll become a deer.'

She thought a while, and decided it would be lovely to be a hind and to have her own fawn walking behind her under the oak trees and a warm nest in the bracken to return to at night. So she put down her head and drank, and in an instant turned into a beautiful hind, and ran about the wood, jumping and kicking, as her brother disappeared.

Later, with a bonnet on, she went into the bread shop and the kind woman patted her on the head. But when she came out into the street, the boys appeared again, this time with dogs, and there was no room for her in the pony cart as it was filled with her three old aunts and Margaret who shouted at her to go away. She hung on to the back and begged to be let in, but they only laughed, left without her and the boys appeared and the pony cart raced off. She ran as hard as she could behind, hearing all the time the boys and dogs drawing nearer and nearer while her heart beat so hard she thought it would burst. What frightened her most was that the pony cart went much faster than she could run even though she was a deer, and soon became a speck in the distance, while the noise of the dogs grew louder and louder until her heart burst, and she woke up weeping.

She could not sleep again, and felt odd all next day, and nervous when she went into the wood. To her dismay, she kept thinking she was a hind, and had to look at her hands to reassure herself. And sometimes she thought she heard in the distance the baying hounds. For the first time, she was frightened of the forest, and ran home as fast as she could.

That night, her sympathetic Aunt Fat gave her another roll of green cloth, and over the following weeks her fears slowly disappeared, but the kindness and compliments of the baker's woman remained fixed in her mind. She began to look at herself in pools and to notice how her hair looked when it tumbled forward. She found it suited her best if she tied a ribbon in a way which brought her curls forward over her shoulders. She was also, for a fortnight, obsessed by a robin's nest in the ivy on the house, her attention caught by a number of dead bodies lying on the ground. She, herself, fed the single remaining baby, which was already bigger than its parents. It grew so fast that it was soon almost as large as the nest, and sat all day with its mouth open, squawking, never satisfied, making the little birds fly to and fro and carry food from dawn till dark, until they became thin and tired.

One night, when her grandfather was away and her Aunt Fat in an unusually sober state, Sefchen told her of the birds which had produced a baby twice their size.

'Ah, that'll be a cuckoo. They often kill the mother birds with their demands.'

After that, Sefchen made herself dig and pick up slimy worms and stuff the fat selfish baby with them until it was full and stopped squawking and allowed the poor parents to rest. She did not know why, but in making herself carry out this revolting task, she felt that she was revenging herself on the cruel boys by showing them how they should be kind. She was sure the shock of her experience had changed her, for afterwards she began to make up stories rather than imitate characters in books, and would sit on a rock, which she named her castle, and tell herself romances of princes and knights setting forth at her bidding to solve impossible tasks. Often she sent out her champions to kill the demon who lived on the other side of the forest, down a little worn path which led into a tangle of fallen trees and rocks surrounding a cave. Occasionally, she was frightened her romances might have outraged the demon and, to placate him, she left offerings of food. These always disappeared and she was pleased her apology was accepted.

5

About this time, her body began to change its shape, and every month Margaret had to loosen the laces on her chest a little more and say grimly: 'You'll need another dress soon.' No criticisms could persuade her, however, to discard her beloved style. And then, when she was fourteen, another landmark in her life occurred. Her grandfather, who had been unusually busy that year, now looked tired and old, and was, if that was possible, more melancholy than ever. One day he broke a long silence by unexpectedly remarking in a sad voice: 'Margaret, this day week in the evening, you're to prepare a feast for fifteen. That is to say, there'll be fourteen guests. If the weather is dry, we'll eat outside, under the old oak. You're to go into the town and order the finest meats and the best breads and cakes. All must be of the finest quality, for my honour is at stake. And you must make for the banquet the four finest pies you have ever made.'

He spoke so sadly that Sefchen wondered what had distressed him as he turned to the others and continued: 'All of you will clean and polish the silver, which you, cousin,' and he pointed to Aunt Old, who pursed her lips and looked knowing, 'will get from under the stone step in the stairs, of which none but you knows the secret.' He turned to the others. 'Then all of you must help Sefchen lay the table. Place two bottles of my finest wine on the right of each guest, but put no glasses, only silver cups. Give each guest two plates and four white rolls. At six o'clock in the evening, you, Margaret, will leave, taking my cousins with you, for your father's farm outside the forest. Four silver coins will be his for looking after you. But the child stays here. I fear for her, should she leave the forest, and she must set the final touches to the table and bring the cheeses out after seven, so that they do not become covered with flies. I'll not speak of this again. See all is done as I've ordered.'

It was by far the longest speech Sefchen had ever heard him make.

In the afternoon of the feast, Aunt Fat took Sefchen aside and said in an angry voice, her breath smelling rankly of the black bottle: 'Now, you know, I've cared for you when others have not, and have saved you by keeping the ghosts out of the house. Well, your grandfather's not always grateful, and he's sending us away today and, for some reason, leaving you here alone with him so I won't be here to protect you, but I want you to keep your eyes wide open. If you're sent to bed, look out of the window, for, loving your grandfather, I'm anxious to know he does nothing which might harm him.'

Sefchen nodded, realizing all her aunt wanted was to know what was happening behind her back, which was not surprising as she could not help feeling curious herself.

At six o'clock, the three old women and Margaret, who had for days been cooking in silence after making two journeys to bring back the special cakes, meats and cheeses, all set off in a bad temper, squashed together in the pony cart. As soon as they had driven away, a strange silence came over the house. When Sefchen went to the kitchen, she could hear vague muffled noises coming from her grandfather's sitting room, and she knocked at his door to ask if there was anything for her to do.

'Yes,' replied the old man. 'Go now and shut up the dogs. Close the door of their kennels, for there are things which even dogs should not see. When you have done that, come back into the kitchen and you'll find on the table the Neptune cup. This will be strange to you. I use it on a few occasions.'

Sefchen did as she was told, and when she came back saw a wonderful silver goblet shaped like a baby's cradle which she had once seen years before in Darmstadt. The bowl was held up by a large bearded man surrounded by mermaids and dolphins made of gold and bright silver. It was the most beautiful thing she had ever seen, and she could see her grandfather had tried to clean it himself as there was pink powder all over the goblet. She took it herself and polished it properly before knocking on his door and showing it to him proudly. But he only looked doleful and said, 'How it glitters,' which was disappointing. Then, in the same tone, he told her to place it by the right hand of his seat, the largest wooden chair, and he would come in a minute to inspect the table. When he came out, she saw he was already in his official clothes and, although the day was still hot, was wearing his sword and best red cloak.

Sefchen felt nervous. Surely he could not be asking fourteen people to supper so as to cut their heads off? He walked round the table, making no comment except to remark without emotion: 'Margaret has forgotten the screws. Place seven around the table, so each may pull his own wine.' He looked up at the sky.

'It will be a fine night!' he said, and, taking a large silver watch from under his cloak, added: 'Now, Sefchen, it's seven o'clock. Are the dogs locked in?'

'Yes.'

'Bring the cheese, climb to your room. Remember, close the shutters.'

As he spoke, he trembled, and Sefchen decided she had never seen him look so nervous and wondered what was going to happen. She went into the kitchen and slipped out of the back door having made up her mind she would see the meal and know what all the preparations were about and who the guests could be. Since not even the old aunts knew, there must be something very strange about the evening. Her curiosity drew her in a short circle back to the oak tree, and she hid not far from the table, by the edge of the forest in a clump of broom, confident if she lay still she would see and not be seen.

The first arrival was a man on a horse who, jumping off, went into the house as Dumb William led away and tied up his mount to a post driven into the ground in a way which allowed the animal to nibble at the grass. He was shortly followed by others, the last guest coming on a large, fat, white horse. He was a little old man in a red coat who was seated in, or rather strapped into, a basket saddle. As he passed within a few yards of the hiding girl, she saw his head slumped forward as he sat asleep, his short little legs hanging down on either side of the horse's neck, only a thick belt keeping him from falling. His horse, which was exceedingly fat, moved very slowly but seemed to know what to do as it stopped at the front door and pawed the ground impatiently. At this point, the old man lifted his head and began to shout: 'Come, Fritz! Come, Fritz! I am here! Come quick and help me down, please, for you know what a poor frail creature I am.'

The gentle murmur in the house ceased and her grandfather appeared with two tall strong young men who, without effort, lifted the little man down to the ground, where he stood bent, his long arms nearly reaching the ground. He limped between the two helpers into the house. When he had gone inside the horse looked in at the door before slowly walking to join the other tethered horses. Sefchen thought they must be a magician, and a magical horse and wondered whether, if she mounted him, he might fly away. But while he was clever, he was surely too heavy ever to get off the ground.

She lay and listened to the sound of voices in the house, followed by a period of absolute silence, and then, without warning, a solemn procession came out, all the men, wearing their swords and red cloaks, following her grandfather, who led the way, arm in arm with the little old cripple. The group walked to the table and, as soon as they were all seated, her grandfather asked a young executioner to get up again and light the torches in their iron holders, placed round the table by Margaret that morning. As the flickering flames lit up the red cloaks and the hard severe faces of the men, her grandfather raised his hand and called for silence. Then they all, for two or three minutes, mumbled strange words under their breath. What they were saying, or to whom they were talking, Sefchen could not gather.

At last her grandfather broke the silence by opening one of the bottles, which he emptied into the Neptune goblet and drained it at a gulp. She heard more corks being pulled as the goblet passed to his left round the table. Everybody, she noticed, drained the goblet at one gulp, the last to receive it was the old man on her grandfather's right. Sefchen felt frightened that if he drank so much wine at a gulp, it would kill him, but without a moment's hesitation he raised the goblet to his lips, tilted his head back, and while his Adam's apple jumped desperately, eventually banged it triumphantly down. Then the linen was pulled off the food and each in turn, with sad expressions, cut themselves slices of pie. Sefchen saw, for some reason or other, either the wine or the sight of the food had upset the old man, for he started loudly to sob and lament: 'Ah, God, this misfortune has lasted so long, so long. No human soul can stand it any more. Oh, God, thou art yet unjust!'

Sefchen had sometimes heard this word 'God' being used, and when she was very young had asked her Cousin Anna in Düsseldorf who was meant by it.

43

Her father had been in the room at the time, and the two adults had looked at each other before her cousin said slowly: 'He's the one for whom we work, but never mention his name. Do as you're told, child, and ask nothing of him, but so long as you do your duty to the family, it's our belief he'll look after you at the end.' She had looked at her father, who merely nodded. The answer had satisfied her at the time, although she realized later it had avoided telling who God was.

Following the old man's example, but in voices which Sefchen thought sounded false, all the others started to lament as they ate their food, and Sefchen shivered, unable to think what they were wailing about. At last, as the full moon rose in the sky, mixing its pale light with the red glare of the torches, they rose from the table one by one and came a few yards closer to her hiding place. Two of the younger men then lifted a pair of the iron torch holders and placed them in different positions before throwing off their cloaks. Immediately they began to dig like demons, and worked with such vigour that soon only the upper parts of their bodies could be seen as they stood in what Sefchen fearfully admitted was to be a grave. Gradually the pile of earth began to obscure her grandfather and his friends, so all she could see in the darkness was their deep-lined faces above red cloaks as they continually passed each other the Neptune cup. The scene looked, to Sefchen, like hell in her illustrated folio of Dante's poem. But, at the same time, her curiosity remained stronger than her fear. Why were they digging such a deep hole?

At last the procession re-formed and walked, two by two, behind her grandfather into the house, the last and youngest pair carrying torches. She lay enthralled. What would happen next? She hadn't long to wait, for the men, some now walking unsteadily, came out in the same order, but this time her grandfather was wearing a white silk shirt and carrying a long slim oblong package wrapped in a white sheet. Her heart beat and her hair began to stand on end. Surely this could not be a human being, for never could there have been such a narrow man or woman. Could he be burying a snake? Her terror became so great that she ceased to think and shivered as her grandfather carefully lowered the object into the grave and then, slowly, held up a spade and shovelled earth on to it. For a time, he was left to work alone, and then the two young men took the spade from him and completed filling up the grave. Once they had finished, her grandfather began, in a melancholy voice, to make another speech, but Sefchen had seen enough and crawled backwards out of the broom, not caring whether she made a noise as she was certain no one would hear for the old man's sobbing. Running round the side of the house, she went in the back door, rushed upstairs, jumped into bed with all her clothes on and buried her head under the sheets. After a while, her fears lessened. She sat up and heard them coming back into the house. A brief silence was followed by the splashing of wine and, afterwards, loud cheery proposals of health to her grandfather and his new friend. The sobbing old man was the last to speak, as he sobbed out a blessing 'from God or the fallen God, whichever we choose as Master'. Then the sounds became confused and spasmodic.

One by one, the horses went away, and at last her grandfather was left alone. When the door had closed, to her surprise – for she had never before known him to show sensitivity – she heard him lament the burial of his 'old friend', who had served him faithfully and well, and now lay under the earth by the laws of the brotherhood, 'for had they allowed me, I would have kept you, my old friend, for as long as we could do our duty'. Tired out, she had no idea how long the old man continued to moan about his old friend, of whom she'd never heard him speak before.

The next morning, when Sefchen woke up she looked out of the window to see if she had dreamed the events of the evening, but the remains of the feast still stood on the table and the long mound of earth clearly showed where the burial had taken place. Margaret and her cousins returned early, and Aunt Fat at once asked Sefchen: 'What's under that mound of earth? It's freshly turned, I see. Tell me quickly.'

Sefchen said calmly she had done as she was told and had seen nothing except some old men arriving in red cloaks, 'who looked so stern and cruel I thought they might . . .'.

She left the sentence unfinished, but Aunt Fat at once put on a knowing look and said: 'Ah, all in red cloaks, and a narrow grave. I see, I see it all now. But,' she added nervously, 'remember, don't say a word of this to your grandfather, there's a good girl,' and she gave Sefchen a thoughtless embrace.

Her grandfather's melancholy lasted for two or three days, but Sefchen still had to read to him every morning. He would wave his hand and she would take down a volume. At the time, she was reading to him a translation of *Robinson Crusoe*, which he had brought back from one of his absences and encouraged her to read, as he said 'the bookseller told me the book was a favourite of Goethe's as a young man'. Occasionally he would ask her to re-read a passage, but would soon stop her with a shake of his hand, and she saw he did not take the slightest interest in what she was reading.

Slowly, she found herself coming to hate him, although she didn't find him evil, for children brought up in strange circumstances think the bizarre perfectly normal. Sefchen had never thought her youth unusual, or doubted there were thousands of other children her own age who lived in a forest with an angry housekeeper, three old crones and a grandfather whose bloody occupation had drained him of humanity, leaving him an animated mummy incapable of kindness or love. Of course, she unconsciously missed affection and had been disappointed when she realized her aunt's hugs came not from love but from the square black bottle. She did not realize it was odd for her to walk barefoot in the woods, to summon squirrels from the tops of trees and stand and gently whistle birds down to settle on her outstretched arms. And it didn't enter her head it was wrong for her father and grandfather to cut off heads. After all, nature was no less cruel than man, and death was a part of life.

In the first years in the forest, she had been happy and confident she could enter her own enchanted world at will. If she felt sad, she walked to the beech woods and soothed herself by looking up at their silver trunks rising to the sky.

If she felt worried, she walked to a distant pine wood where the soft needles were reassuring beneath her feet, and the whistling of the wind in the trees became to her the music of the wood. But her contentment had vanished when she saw the stag with the golden fleck followed by her visit to the shops in the village. The effect of both events, coming so close together, broke her belief in magic and she had begun to wish to leave the forest and live in the world again, encouraged by the voices from the Abbey calling insistently to her to return. Although they had always whispered to her at odd moments, she had been able to put them out of her mind before, but now when she was unsettled and sad and when her old love of nature no longer gave her any pleasure, she longed to leave the forest, marry a prince and, above all, have a baby she could love.

One day her grandfather returned with a new volume in shining red leather instead of one of the old folios. He told her he had, for the first time in his life, bought a new book. He could not resist it as he had heard about the Brothers Grimm and how Goethe admired them, and this was a collection of legends by the two brothers. For weeks she watched him looking at the book, taking exactly the same time to read each page, except those which had illustrations, while she longed to read it herself. Once or twice she caught his eye, and realized that while he knew she wanted to read it, his look told her she should understand it was his prized book, he had not finished it, was not to be hurried and she must wait until he had done with it, even though she knew he could not read. At last he set out on one of his business journeys. As soon as he had gone, she rushed in and seized the book, finding to her amazement that she knew many of the stories as versions of nearly all of them had already been told to her by her cousin in Düsseldorf and later by Aunt Fat. The Grimms' stories had many additional details.

One of the first stories which her aunt had told her was about 'Cinderella', and how, although her ugly stepsisters tried as hard as they could, they never managed to squeeze even half a foot into the glass slipper. But in Grimm the story was cruelly changed. When the eldest sister was asked to try on the slipper, she cut off a toe and forced her foot in, the prince never noticing until a bird sang a song telling him blood was pouring from the slipper. How could the prince have been so stupid not to see the blood? And the younger sister had cut off her heel so as to be able to squash her foot in. Sefchen very carefully fingered her heel and immediately felt the bone, so this did not make sense either, while, at Cinderella's marriage, her pigeon came and sat on one of the ugly sister's shoulders and pecked out one of her eyes. Why hadn't she pushed the bird away? And then came the silliest part of all: when they came out of the church the pigeon sat on her other shoulder and pecked out the other eye. It was all so stupid and unreal, and spoilt the romance of the story, for she knew that not even the stupidest girl in the world would have let a pigeon peck one of her eyes out, let alone two. It was very puzzling. The cruelties of the Grimms, and the fact that their stories were written not spoken, bitterly disillusioned her. Often, in the past, as she had gazed into pool in the wood, she had imagined a bear would look over her shoulder and turn into a prince, but now she longed for the prince to come by himself and take her away. She also had recently got into the habit of gently singing sad songs to herself when she felt in low spirits. She found some in her father's books, and some Aunt Fat had told her. Despite their melancholy endings, they cheered her up. And that night she walked into the twilight, sat on a fallen tree and sang three songs. She felt her gloom lift and slept well.

6

When she was fifteen, an event occurred which made her determined to leave the forest. Often, in earlier years, she had caught glimpses of golden cornfields and heard, in August and September, the merry sounds of children shouting; while, in May, she had sometimes seen the reapers singing staccato songs as they cut the hayfields with giant sickles. After a quick glance, she had always turned and walked into the thickest recesses of the wood. Then, one autumn day, she saw, through a gap in the hedge, a bunch of corn ricks and a long table laid out, and although it was several hundred yards away, she could see the brown-armed men and women happily eating. As she lingered and watched, she felt sad and decided the time had come to go out of the forest again and sit in the fields, even if only for a short time. She knew it was important she had to grow up as on both the last occasions when her grandfather came home, he had looked sickly and frail, and Margaret and the dumb groom had to help him dismount and lead him to his bed.

His frailty made her realize he would soon die and her life as she knew it would end. The time had come to prepare herself for a world she neither knew nor understood, and she decided to walk next day to the eastern rim of the forest and carry out a plan. It would be a long walk, but she had made up her mind, and the next morning, filling her wallet with bread and ham and her little leather pouch with water, she set off, wearing, as usual, her green dress. It was a lovely September day, and as she looked up through the tops of the beeches, she expected to admire the sky and the first falling leaves, but found they did not please her. Neither did she admire the space under the chestnut trees, where, in spring every year, she had come to pick primroses; and, when she passed through the pines, their gentle whispering irritated her. She never spared a glance for the cracked boles of the old oaks which she had formerly often carefully examined to see if they had once imprisoned princesses. As she walked on despondently, she noticed a doe in the bracken who the week before she had seen feeding her two young fawns. She noticed the animal tilt her head, inviting her to come and admire them, but merely averting her eyes she walked on, careless of whether she had hurt the animal's feelings. Afterwards she kept her head down and almost broke in to a run.

At length, at midday, she reached her destination, the end of the forest. On one side, she could make out dark yellow stubble and patches of bare earth, on the other, sheep in grass fields. She turned towards the meadows and, as she drew nearer to the wood's rough palings, felt her heart beat and sat down, knowing that the trees which had been her companions for nine years were pulling her back. She knew that now she must climb the fence, but felt afraid. Why? Of what?

And then, her instinct told her, she was young and had to live. Jumping up, she ran, leaving herself no time to change her mind, and reaching the palings a gap appeared and she pushed through, feeling very brave, on to the meadow grass. Overwhelmed at finding herself in such an open and unprotected place, she looked nervously around and saw a view that stretched over miles of green and yellow fields. Excited, she looked backward and sideways and saw the trees reaching away into the endless distance. Turning from safety, she looked to her front and saw the sheep had closely cropped the grass. She sat on the ground, excited by this different world which disappeared towards an unknown sea, and wondered what would become of her.

As she looked carefully around, still overwhelmed by the distance, a movement caught her eye and she saw to her right a flash of colour beneath a hawthorn tree in the hedge. At first she thought two people were fighting, for she could see limbs threshing violently on the ground and it looked, to her, as if a naked man was on top: perhaps killing another? She shrank back to the hedge, and clambering back quickly over the paling, sat beside a tree and felt safe again. It was not that violence surprised her; only that it saddened her once again to see the cruelty of the outside world. She had heard of escaped murderers wandering in the forest. But she had never seen one, and had no wish to be killed now. Straining her ears in vain, she sat on the spreading root which enabled her to see signs of life through the hedge on the sunlit plain. She carefully examined cottages, surrounded by rose-coloured farms, haystacks, fields with cows, boys hitting pigs with sticks, and washing fluttering in the wind.

She was so interested by these sights and activities that she was alarmed when she heard voices. Quickly she moved behind a young beech and stood listening. The sounds grew louder, and she was reasssured only to hear a man and woman talking gently to one another. A young couple came into sight and, by chance, stopped in front of the gap through which she was looking, turned and faced each other. He was a working man, in foresters' brown uniform, with brown face, hair and hands. As Sefchen watched, he put his hands behind the girl's back and pulled her unresistingly towards him before putting his mouth against hers. She realized she was, for the first time, seeing two people kiss.

Confused, she turned away in embarrassment, but found her eyes returned against her will to the young couple. Not daring to breathe, she watched the young man stand back and take the girl's long pigtails in his hands and pull them under her shoulder towards him as he arched his back away from her and said: 'I've told you, there's no need to fear. I love you and always will. I've saved a little every year, and done up the pine cottage by the forest. It's ready to move into any day you choose. I'll tell the pastor we're to be married quick;

your parents shouldn't be angry. I'm steady, you know. The head forester likes me, the house is ready, and I will always love you.'

It seemed magical to Sefchen to hear such romantic words spoken by a common labourer. She stared at the girl, who flushed red and looked down before letting her head fall forward into the man's shoulder as she burst into tears. He stroked the back of her head with one hand while, with the other, he pulled her close to him and said: 'Don't worry. There's many done the same as us before,' and then kissed her again.

Sefchen thought the girl would be pleased but, to her surprise, she went on crying while the young man whispered in her ear. Then she suddenly backed away, wiped her eyes and, showing flashing white teeth, laughed and said: 'I don't mind, for you're a nice boy and I've never fancied another. So the sooner it's done the better. I'll tell my mother tonight. She's a funny woman. She's strict, but fond of me and has been a good mother. Sometimes I think she knows more than I think.'

He leaned forward and hugged her. They walked on. Sefchen burst into tears. She had never before seen two people making love. She had read of love, but it was something which had never happened to her except ethereally in her dreams. And here were two people, living in the world she feared, where strange boys threw stones at her and cut off dolls' heads, who were not a bit like her persecutors, but quiet and gentle. The way the man held the girl was completely different from the way her aunt had held her when she wheezed drunkenly, 'You are a good child.' Now Sefchen understood why she loved to see deer and foxes lick their young; it was because they truly loved them. As if reaching a decision, she climbed through the fence again and looked to her left, but the couple had vanished from sight. The view no longer interested her, and she turned back into the wood and walked home, again avoiding her friends, keeping her eyes on the ground.

That evening, as he was drinking his wine, her grandfather had a tremendous fit of coughing and Aunt Fat hit him on the back, at which he fell head foremost on to his plate. When they pulled him upright again, he was no longer breathing. Everyone started shouting; Aunt Thin blamed Aunt Fat and everybody, including Margaret, talked at the same time. Before long, however, the relief of his death brought them together, and they decided it was nonsense to blame anyone in particular, as his heart was weak and it was time for him to die. They all tugged and lifted him to his bed, and then the three women whispered together before Margaret was sent off in the pony cart to inform the authorities and buy certain necessities.

The next day, a black cart rattled up, drawn by a horse shaking a black plume on its head. A very important-looking fat man sedately descended and stalked into the house, still wearing his high hat. He was followed by a thin young man, who looked nervously about him. The fat man did not condescend to notice Sefchen, and disappeared into her grandfather's room but the thin man stayed by the black cart and helped the driver to carry in a long box and quantities of the most beautiful soft white material Sefchen had

50

ever seen. They spent a long time in the room, and when they went away gave the briefest of nods to the three old women. Sefchen noticed the thin young man looked fearfully back at the house, as if he was lucky to get away.

Then Aunt Fat took Sefchen by the hand and led her into her grandfather's room, where her two sisters were ransacking the drawers and pulling out and energetically shaking all the old folios. They had even taken up the carpet, and continued their search all the time Sefchen was in the room, while her grandfather lay with circles of black velvet covering his eyes. Only his head was visible, and it looked different as his cheeks had fallen in and his mouth gaped open with the top teeth protruding in the same snarl she had seen on her father's dead face. The one difference was that his head lay on the beautiful soft white material. She remembered clearly her own father's death, and felt sorry he could not have been buried in such pretty stuff.

She remembered him again next day, when a pastor appeared with a red nose, and she wondered whether all their noses were red. He brought with him no less than four men, who also looked nervously around, and nearly ran away when a dozen of her grandfather's colleagues appeared, with swords under their red cloaks. But at last they finished, and he was buried in the site he had chosen in the centre of the clearing not far from the gallows. But, before the coffin box could be buried, they all stood round the grave-diggers, who sweated with fear as the priest sprinkled the coffin three times, intoning in a language she did not understand. Then they all went away.

The next day, two other men in black arrived and asked the three aunts numerous questions in low voices, now and then looking at Sefchen while the old women stared at her and then back at the men and nodded their heads. Then one of the men sat at the table and wrote something on a piece of parchment with a red seal, and the three cousins scratched away in ink at the bottom of the sheet, which was then placed in an envelope and, to Sefchen's excitement, sealed with wax, which the official pressed with a gold ornament on his watch chain. They disappeared as well.

Late that night, when Aunt Fat crawled up to say good night, Sefchen saw she was drunker than usual and guessed she would be overflowing with sentiment. She was both wrong and right. The fat woman stood over her, leaning on a stick, and said: 'I'm drunk, child, but I'm your friend, and out of fear and fancy I'll remain so. I wish you to know what's happening in this cursed house. We have written to your aunt, the woman from Goch, and told her it was your grandfather's wish she should come to fetch you. He has left you gold, too, the others tried to say we shouldn't give it all to you, but I told them – and remember me always in your prayers – "If she doesn't receive every coin of her entitlement, he'll come back at night to punish your greed." They said no more, and crossed themselves. I have your share. I'll give it you when the woman of Goch comes to take you away. Ah, child, I'm sorry to see you go,' and she began to sob in her insincere way and, taking a little flat bottle out of her dress, tipped it into her mouth and sobbed even more. Sefchen rolled over away from her and could not manage to speak.

51

Three days later, Sefchen was told to pack her clothes in a basket as 'the woman from Goch' was coming the next morning. She did not have many clothes, since Margaret only made a new dress when a previous one was worn out. Again, she had to suffer hugs from Aunt Fat, but happily the other two only gave her little pecks. When she went to say goodbye to Margaret, she found to her surprise she was upset. As Sefchen held out her hand, she grasped it without a word before turning and walking quietly away, brushing her hand over her face. Sefchen was sure she was crying, and felt surprised and touched, but her heart sank when she saw her aunt from Goch. To begin with, she did not look as if she had changed her clothes for ten years and appeared to be wearing the same fustian cloak as when they had said goodbye at the Abbey years before. Her face also looked unaltered, with its brown wrinkles, coarse skin and, above all, the small darting eyes which watched keenly as Aunt Fat whispered: 'I've hidden your gold in the bottom of your clog sack, and with it, would you believe it, a little round gun-metal watch on a chain from Aunt Thin, who said reluctantly, "It was willed the girl by her grandfather, I can't think why." '

Sefchen saw she should leave quickly. The household, except Aunt Old, who was snoring by the fire, was clearly impatient to see her go. She carried her things to the cart and helped to pack them, which made her cry, as the woman from Goch said in a false voice as her eyes searched her with dislike: 'My, but haven't you grown! You're a pretty one,' and she pinched her cheek with fingers as rough as stale bread-crusts.

She slowly climbed into the pony cart and Sefchen jumped in after her as the pony broke into a trot. She could not help taking one last backward look, but the door was closed and no one was to be seen, only a whiff of smoke rising from the chimney showing any life existed in the melancholy house. She knew now they would all be turning her grandfather's rooms upside down in search of treasure, but still she felt hurt and her eyes filled with tears as she looked at the beloved woods where yesterday she had sat and cried in her favourite place, and stood in a clearing and held out her arms for the little birds to sit on, as she told them that, while she would never see them again, she hoped they would remember her.

7

As they drove down the rutted road, Sefchen was disconcerted by her aunt staring unceasingly at her. The shifty little eyes never left her face. And although she pretended not to notice and kept her eyes down, it was unavailing. As the wheel lurched into a hole, she was thrown against her and, out of self-protection, had to look into the face she had nearly hit and saw coarse skin round the mouth folding into dirty wrinkles, hair greasy and worse, black hairs growing under the nose and on the chin. Sefchen shuddered, and did not know what she would do if her face ever became so ugly. She looked down and kept her eyes fixed on her hands.

The weather was dry, the roads outside the forest smooth and the horse trotted along happily. Sefchen felt a longing to stop and look at the farmhouses which flew by before she could see them. Once they passed a long avenue of old limes behind great gates leading to a castle and she longed to ask, 'Who lives in such a place?' They trotted past soldiers with glinting bayonets, and herds of cows and gleaming horses with smart men riding them, unlike any she had seen before. Not to ask questions tortured her, but she knew that if she looked up and caught her aunt's eye, a conversation would follow which would be disagreeable. At length the woman from Goch could bear the silence no longer and burst out impatiently: 'My word, as I said when I saw you, you have become pretty. Are you sixteen yet?'

'Not yet,' said Sefchen. 'That's if I'm right in thinking I was born in November, but I never knew the date.'

'November, was it, child? Well, that's not far off. Have you any thoughts of marriage? Has anyone come to call?'

Sefchen blushed and felt quite faint with embarrassment.

'Look at me, child. I can't talk to you when you sit there looking down like a nun.'

When Sefchen had forced herself to look into the crafty black eyes under the bushy eyebrows, she would have given anything to be back walking alone in the wood. She clenched her fists. Whatever happened, she would not cry.

'Well?' repeated her aunt.

Sefchen shook her head.

'Ah, well your grandfather was always a selfish man, always thinking of himself and endlessly looking into those big brown books. He couldn't read, like your father. Not that any good ever came out of books that I know of, even for those who can read them. They're all lies. Life's the only thing to study and plan for, but, child, you're fifteen, grown up and a beauty. We must be thinking of marriage or . . .'

To Sefchen's surprise, her aunt looked down in momentary confusion, but soon fixed her piercing little eyes on her again and went on: 'Do you know your cousins?'

'I've never met any.'

'Tch, tch,' said the woman. 'Well, child, I shan't neglect you as others have done. We have cousins enough in all branches of the family to wed you. The pay is good, you know, although not so good now the Emperor's men have gone. On the other hand, there will always be those who have to be done away with, and always will be. It's a wicked thing, human nature, and our family's job's a holy one, as I see it. Well, I can think of four, if not more, men of property, and all under forty. My advice is to choose from among the oldest. They are steady, will work hard and save money. I shall ask them over next month,' and her aunt leaned forward, her eyes gleaming. Poor Sefchen blushed again.

'But I have a fancy you may be particular,' her aunt went on. 'You'll be, if your mind's anything like your face, as white as snow. Your skin and your hair, you know, child, are the colour to break hearts, although the last could also be said to be the colour of blood, so perhaps it's nature showing to which family you belong.'

She made a hideous grimace with her mouth, which Sefchen remembered her making the first time she saw her all those years before. Her lips had widened, showing her crooked broken teeth and, worst of all, she had clearly tried to please. At the same time, she made a strange sound far worse than Aunt Fat's cackle. Sefchen felt like crying at the idea of living with her as she already made her feel miserable. People were really different from how she had hoped they'd be when she had stepped out of the wood.

Sefchen had woken up early that morning, and although the cart jolted as it went along, there was something soothing in the motion. She found herself nodding off, only to wake up with her neck aching and her aunt pinching her knee, saying: 'We're home. Get down and open the gate.'

Sefchen, still only half-awake, stepped out and then stood still as she realized she was at the exact place where the boys had cut off her doll's head.

'Hurry, hurry!' shouted her aunt. Sefchen pushed the gate open, shut it again behind them, and followed the cart on foot until the ruins came into sight. As they passed across the back of the Abbey apse, she looked up at the remnant of the Gothic window above the rubble of the central arch. The cart turned the corner, her aunt got out, and Sefchen carried her things in, and was ecstatically welcomed by the voices who, reminding her of details she had forgotten, asked her to follow them up the steps to her bedroom, where they directed her to the window to gaze at the remains of the arch which had collapsed in the thunderstorm. It was as if she had never left. At once she remembered everything clearly, or rather, was reminded exactly how the curved path ran through the bushes down the nave and the loose stone hung over the door in the wall near the house, which itself sloped nearly down to the ground, the lowest point of the roof standing over the front door where she had sat reading as a child. She also remembered her father's room, with its big stone windows on the ground floor; and the first-floor parlour, seldom used, where, as it was the driest room, her father had kept his books on either side of the great stone fireplace opposite the large central window which looked down the nave. She whispered to herself, 'I have come home,' and both the voices agreed in unison: 'Yes, and you must never leave us again.'

Later she was silent when her aunt, showing her round, had asked her in a sweet voice: 'You remember your room, child?'

Sefchen nodded her head. Already she knew every inch of it, and longed to get into the wooden four-poster and pull the feather covers over her and cry at the unexpected happiness of her return. But she didn't because she knew she would then be expected to thank her aunt for fetching her home, which was the last thing she wished to do. When, at last, she was left alone, she put her things in her old chest of drawers, in which, to her surprise, her aunt had placed sprigs of lavender, and looked at herself in the old glass and tidied her hair with her hands before going down into the kitchen and turning instinctively through one of the side-doors, beyond which she knew stood a large wooden tub of water collected from the roof. This was where as a child she had always washed, and where now she splashed her face. It even seemed to her as though the soap by the barrel had not changed. She could remember clearly a little white bit with black cracks, and there, stuck to the barrel, was a tin bowl containing an identical piece of soap.

Going into the kitchen, she asked if she could help.

'No,' said her aunt. 'Before I left I put a hare in the pot high over the turf fire, which is a good one and has not gone out. The meat will be ready in half an hour and tender as a lark. Meanwhile, go out, child. Go out and see if that pet squirrel you cried about is still alive.'

But, of course, the squirrel wasn't there, and the voices, as soon as she went beyond the ruins, grew nervous, reproached her and disappeared. The birds weren't friendly either, and, when she lifted her arms, not one sat on them. She realized, with pain, when she left the forest she had also left her power with animals behind and would never again be able to charm them out of their holes or nests in the bracken. Her loss made her feel forlorn. How could she live without her friends, the animals and birds? All her dreams had to do with them. Would she, she wondered, be able to dream again? If not, what would she do in this house, which had received her with such affection?

The forest was growing dim and it came to her suddenly she had been called back as if she was a child. But against her wishes, as she wished to retain her freedom, not live in a prison from which some executioner would select her to be his wife. She had never thought of herself having to marry, except to a prince, and now, she was told, these executioners would be coming to examine her. She wondered whether bakers could only marry other bakers, butchers other butchers, woodmen other woodwomen. But the girl by the wood had said nothing about being a woodman's daughter. Sefchen did not know what to make of it. She did not know what marriage meant, or what she would have to do, except kiss her husband on the lips in the way the pair had done at the forest's edge. She knew she could kiss a young prince, and nearly had once in her dreams, but she could not even have kissed the young man with the girl, although he looked nice; and certainly none of the old men who had dined with her grandfather or his assistant; or any of the soldiers, except one; or any of the dirty, bearded, moustachioed men whom she had seen in the clearing, waiting to be hanged. But when she was back in the Abbey, she felt less worried, as if she had returned to safety, but then a revulsion against safeness and the ideas not her own which were being pushed into her mind.

The next morning was fine and she took a long walk beyond the wood which surrounded the Abbey, finding she missed the companionship of animals and birds which she had accepted as natural. When she saw a family of young partridges, they scurried away instead of running up to her, while the mother played the wounded bird and half-ran, half-fluttered off as if she had broken a wing. She stood still and called to her in the way she had learned in the forest, but this time the trick did not work and it depressed her the young ones were frightened. By the end of the day, her original pleasure had faded. Her aunt from Goch seemed to be always prying into her things, and she knew she had even looked under her mattress, though what for she could not imagine, and had shaken out her books to see if money or letters were hidden in them. She had asked the evening before about her grandfather's gold, and her eyes glinted at Sefchen's reply that Aunt Fat had hidden it in the wooden bottom of her sack.

'What's happened to it now?' her aunt asked in a voice reedy with excitement.

'Well, it's still there, of course,' replied Sefchen.

'How much gold?'

'I don't know. I haven't counted it.'

Her aunt was perfectly flummoxed by the simple reply and kept giving her suspicious glances as if she was being deceitful. At last she went on in a wheedling tone: 'Dearest one' – it was the first time she had ever called her that – 'don't you think your gold would be safer in a bank?'

'What's a bank?' asked Sefchen.

'It is where,' said her aunt, speaking very slowly and distinctly, 'your money is kept safe for you.' Then she added quickly, 'It can be in both our names, so I can get the money out if you ever need any. Where did you say it is now, dear?' she asked, with an expression on her face which she tried unsuccessfully to make pleasing.

'But, Aunt, didn't I tell you? It's in the bottom of my clog sack, unless it broke on the way.'

'Broke on the way? Why didn't you tell me, you silly child! You're so unworldly. You really do need me to look after you!'

Sefchen showed her the sack with its thick wooden bottom standing in a corner of her cupboard, and at once her face lit up. She carried it downstairs and placed it on the table, and within moments there was not a bit of wood or sacking to be seen. They had been hacked into a pile of rags and splinters. On the table was a collection of coins of different sizes, from which she insisted Sefchen took ten for emergencies. Two days later, she gave her a document to sign, which had all sorts of seals on it. Sefchen did so without reading it, and almost before she had finished writing her name, her aunt's dirt-engrained hands flicked out, seized the papers, pushed them into a drawer in the dresser and turned the key.

Their life proceeded monotonously. After breakfast, Sefchen would go to her father's old room and read for four hours. Then she would go for a walk or sit on a dead tree outside the nave, when her aunt would call her to have a slice of bread and cheese. Later she would go for another walk, mend her old dresses or read again until supper. This always consisted of a bowl of vegetable soup and a slice of wholemeal bread and jam or cheese. Afterwards, her aunt would make her sit in the kitchen and listen to her telling stories she did not wish to hear about the family. But at nine o'clock she would insist on taking a glass of milk and going upstairs with a candle to her bedroom to read before she fell asleep. All her days were lived in a mist of regret, sadness and an intense melancholy. It was not her relationship with animals alone that depressed her. After the sight of the couple outside the forest, she had expected life to change and to meet fresh people, who would be kind to her, as the two outside the wood had been to each other. But here she was, seeing nobody, only a mile or so from a large town. Even her love of reading suffered.

One morning, about two weeks after her return, she was sitting reading a folio on a cloth on the kitchen table as it was too heavy to hold upright. When the door opened she did not look up as her aunt was always running in or out, and she jumped with surprise when a male voice said: 'You must be Josepha.'

Leaping to her feet she saw before her, in the doorway, a man wearing a black coat in her grandfather's style. He had already taken off his hat, but as he stood with his back to the light, she could not see his face. They stared at each other but, however hard she tried, she could not make out his features against the light. She was too shy to ask him to come in, and he stood transfixed by the sight of this beautiful girl, her old green material still wrapped about her showing off her beautiful body. There was no knowing how long they might have looked at each other without moving if her aunt had not come bustling in through another door. She glided quickly up to the figure and, seizing him by the hand, declared: 'You must be Cousin Gerhardt,' before pulling him in and sitting him down opposite Sefchen, who she told to entertain their guest while she went to draw a measure of ale, for he had travelled from far away.

'It must be all of fifty miles,' she said as she left the room.

'Not so, not so,' he said, speaking to the door in a sonorous voice, which so startled Sefchen that she looked up and found herself fascinated by his face.

His skin was white, but not so white as her own, although three boils on the forehead and one on either cheek accentuated, by their bursting redness, the pallor of the complexion. His hair, the colour of carrots, was parted on the left hand and brushed across the head to fall down just over the collar, but it was his hands which fascinated her most. He had put one on the table in a self-conscious way, and then did not know what to do with it, which gave her a chance to see it was not only white but also covered with the same shade of upright carrotty hairs as his head. She could not help thinking he looked as if he was covered with a pig's bristles.

Her aunt brought in the beer and sat at the head of the table as he took a great swill and wiped his mouth with his sleeve. Sefchen could tell she was displeased. There was a note of tart criticism in her voice when she said: 'How fashionably your hair's been done. You must be prosperous.'

'Satisfactorily,' he replied, bringing out the word in the same pompous tones.

Sefchen, who, due to her past life, always compared people to animals, decided he was a pig, and could remember the very pig he looked like and how sad she had been when Margaret came in one day and calmly announced the sausages just eaten had been made of her friend. She had rushed out of the house to be sick.

After his last remark, the woman from Goch looked puzzled, and angry, and her face grew redder and redder until it seemed as if she was about to explode. At last she burst out: 'It's no good sitting silent. Cousin Gretchel informed me you wished to be married. If that's the case, speak and don't sit there occasionally giving us a word like a priest at a burial service. Ask the girl if you want her to marry you.'

She appeared to be about to add something else when Cousin Gerhardt, looking towards Sefchen, intoned, in the same monotonous sing-song voice: 'I have seen you, I am not disappointed. I offer you my hand in marriage. Here's the statement from my bank of the money I have deposited. Work slackened off last year, but has picked up again now as the Elector takes his revenge on those who betrayed their countrymen to the French. I've been told I'm as good a striker as your father was, of which I'm proud, for he was never known to take two blows, nor yet have I.'

Sefchen gazed at him with an intense hatred. His little red eyes shone and his excitement seemed to be encouraging his boils to burst, but nevertheless he appeared to be quite unconscious of her dislike and satisfied and pleased with himself as he droned on: 'My house has four rooms. My mother lives there now. She will go when you move in.'

Sefchen stood up and walked out of the front door. She went over the stile into the remnants of the forest and out across the fields, walking carefully beside the hedgerows so as not to tread down the late uncut corn. She walked, not as she usually did, with her head turning from side to side to see what was happening, but with her face down, looking no further than her next step, and several times she nearly walked into a cross-hedge. She was filled with a despair which she had never known, an unhappiness to which she knew no answer. Always, until now, she had the consolation of the forest and the pleasures of solitude to turn to. Now there was nothing for it but to walk blindly along the hedge and pass through gates across open country, avoiding farms, her sole purpose to take her mind off her life, which the proposal of marriage had brought home to her. How stupid her old comforting dreams appeared. She realized she had deceived herself. No prince would ever come near her, or even an ordinary man.

Did her aunt really expect her to marry this human pig with bristles on his hands? She had never minded her father's and grandfather's occupation. It had seemed to her that they were melancholy men who carried out their duty by doing away with bad men. The porcine figure with spots and self-satisfaction on his face, however, had spoken in a way which made her feel he would take equal pleasure in cutting off the heads of good or bad alike. How could she marry such a fat brute after she had seen, beside the wood, the tenderness of love, and when all her childish dreams and romantic fantasies had involved princes dressed in cloth of gold. Neither had she liked the way he had looked at her, with eyes that kept dropping to the top of her dress, where it clung tight to her body. She knew she ought to have let it out. Moreover, he had arrived at a difficult moment, because the day before she had thought she was dying and had run to her aunt, only for the woman of Goch to wink and laugh and go to a cupboard before offering her practical advice and telling her certain things which made her blush and understand that she was now a woman and could no longer dream.

She found this difficult, as the forest had been her own fairyland, where all living creatures loved her, a split tree had loosed an escaping princess and a frog was really a prince. Such an education had not prepared her to marry and have children by a bristling pig. She thought, again, of the couple by the wood, and how, when the young girl had laid her head against the young man's shoulder, he had gently stroked her shoulders and whispered in her ear. Sefchen longed with her whole heart for a shoulder to lean on, for a man to whom she could turn for consolation and kindness. How was she to live with the woman of Goch with her hateful little eyes, but how was she to escape from her?

The idea she would never meet a man she could love terrified her, and she imagined herself growing into an old unmarried prisoner on the edge of the town, knowing nobody, occasionally chased by pig men who planned to take her off to some house where her only consolation would be pig children. She thought of crying, but her sorrow lay too deep for tears as she lamented not only at her unhappy future but also the death of her past which, looking back, seemed full of a joy and happiness that could never return.

She must have walked for two or three hours before sinking down on a bank and lying with her head on the grass. Slowly her sorrow faded as she watched ants working their way over the thin new blades. How often she had seen them in the forest and noticed how they never rested, and even when they stood still, the things which stuck out of their foreheads constantly waved as if their brains were wondering what to do next. Then they would scurry away and find a dead fly five times as big as themselves and push it and pull it, overcoming all obstacles until it had been carried into their nest. Somehow the sight of the insects was a comfort. Feeling better, she walked home with a fixed determination to tell her aunt that under no circumstances would she marry such a suitor, and if she was only allowed to marry into this executioner's family, then she wouldn't marry at all. Instead, she would learn to paint. She knew the details of every little flower: the stamens, the petals, the juncture between flower and stalk. And the night before, when she had been looking at her father's books, she had seen illustrations of flowers in black and white, with two or three of them coloured in by an unknown hand. She would do the rest, for she could see that they had been painted by one who understood how it felt to be a flower, to drink water and expand in the sun. Yes, she would spend the long evenings painting. But then, gazing about, she thought how flat and ugly the country was and wondered if she could see the forest, where she had always been so happy. She put her hand over her eyes, knowing in which direction to look, and stared towards the horizon, but a haze of mist was her only reward. Depression returned as she walked slowly home.

It was five o'clock when she reached the Abbey. Her aunt was watching from the upper window as she walked into the nave. A meal had been prepared with boiled white sausages and the hot drink she enjoyed, of old lime blossoms kept in a large jar, mixed with the young shoots of nettles. Her aunt swore it was a great pick-you-up. She felt better at once and finished the sausages, and then, unexpectedly, her aunt produced for the first time a soft cheese, which Sefchen ate as well.

Her sly aunt waited until she was finished before saying: 'My dear, I'm so sorry. They told me he was a steady young man, but no one said he was a pig covered with spots. Don't you pretend now,' she said, surprising Sefchen, 'that you didn't think the same. Money's not everything, and it's no use living in a sty.' She stopped and closed one of her little eyes.

Sefchen felt relieved, but at the back of her mind a little frightened. If her aunt understood so much, was nice when it was necessary and knew how to win her over, could she fall under her influence?

'But don't you worry, child,' her aunt continued, 'for you're a lovely lass. I'm not one for puffing, but you're a beauty who can take your pick and choice. And then, you know,' she said, closing her eyes and looking at Sefchen in a confidential way, 'you don't have to marry into "the family", even though none else will marry you. Marrying's not the be-all and end-all, you know, but that's enough for the time being. We'll talk more of it later. I hear that two more of "the family" are to call in the next couple of weeks, but if you don't care for them, your old aunt won't make you marry, that I promise.'

She horrified Sefchen by kissing her on the cheek. Only with difficulty did the girl stop herself from jerking back at the touch of her aunt's wet lips and bristly skin.

Three nights later, as Sefchen sat reading by candlelight and her aunt was rummaging around with her odd boxes and writing addresses on little parcels she was sending to the valley of the Rhine, the dog began to bark and hurl itself at the end of its chain. Her aunt ran about the room and, with a worried face, checked the front door was locked and bolted. Then she took the key and rapped with it on the wood before sliding back a little panel in the top of the door.

'Who's there?' she called out nervously. 'Who's there, disturbing folk at this time of night? Cousin who . . .?' Sefchen heard her ask. 'Ah, but just like you to arrive at such a time, causing inconvenience. Since you're here you may as well come in. Not that I think any good will come of it.'

Opening the door she went out and shortened the dog's chain, so it could not bite the visitor, and came back, pushing in front of her a tall, gangling, bent man of about forty with pallid cheeks, bent shoulders and huge hands on long stringy arms which not even his coat, which hung down to his wrists, could disguise. He had a pointed nose, and his chin fell away into his neck.

Sefchen got up directly she heard the word 'cousin', certain this was another of her suitors.

'Dear girl,' said her aunt, 'here's your cousin Engelbert, come many miles to see you, although he's not even dressed in the uniform of his office,' she added with some disdain.

'Oh, no, no. No need to cause offence when it's not necessary. Oh, no, cousin, no.'

As Engelbert spoke in a high-pitched voice, his huge hands fluttered about his knees, making his legs seem uncommonly like sticks.

'If you're travelling by day, there's no point in exciting animosity. I am all for a peaceful life. But you can't deny, cousin,' he said, turning to her aunt, 'that I'm a good workman.'

He appeared unable to make up his mind whether to sit down or stand up, or how he was going to greet her. Determined not to help, Sefchen stood still. The scene seemed to amuse her aunt, who, instead of aiding Engelbert in his dilemma, turned to Sefchen and said loudly: 'He wants you to know he's a good executioner. I can't tell you anything else about him. You can see for yourself, away from the block he can't make up his mind what to say or do. Unless I say it for him, he'll just diddle-daddle all night and I won't be able to rid us of him. There's no bed for you here,' she said, addressing Engelbert, 'so either say what you have to say quick, or I'll say it for you.'

'Oh, that'll be better, cousin, far better. I'm no man for words, no man at all. Tell her, first, that I make good money. Tell her, second, I have saved good money. Tell her, third, I am cautious and have no taste for adventure. And tell her, last, that since I've seen her, I'd like her to wed me.'

He finished this last sentence with a gasp which shook his whole body, except his hands, and for the first time he looked straight at Sefchen. She expected him to have the same pig eyes as his predecessor, but instead they were large, blue, innocent and kind. For a moment, she was moved, but as soon as she examined his thin receding hair, his long, protruding and lobeless ears, his chinless face and spindly body and legs, she felt nothing but disgust, and realized his eyes were a mistake which had nothing to do with the rest of him.

'Well, Sefchen?' asked her aunt jovially. 'Do you accept his offer?'

'Tell him,' said Sefchen, 'that I shall never marry him, and that it's my intention not to marry at all.'

'Ah,' said her aunt thoughtfully, adding sharply to her cousin, 'Well, Engelbert, you've had your chance. You'll be moving off quick now, I suppose. I can offer you a glass of ale before you go, if you wish it.'

'No, no,' he faltered, almost in horror.

Sefchen could not understand why his voice showed no sign of anger or disappointment. It was as if he was used to having requests refused and had asked almost as a formality, expecting a rejection.

'Well, I'll be on my way, cousin,' he said, his eyes downcast. Without daring to approach a step closer to Sefchen, he backed away to the door, turned and ran out.

Her aunt followed to untether the dog, which started to bark furiously at the end of his chain, as if baulked of his prey. When she came back, she paused again by the table and said in a satisfied voice: 'Well, child, your two richest cousins have come. I see you fancy neither, and I can't say I blame you. There's but one more yet, and I expect him at the end of the week. I must warn you he's a braggart, feckless with money, who plays the fool and talks big. Yet there's no doubt he's a fine-looking fellow, and while he may spend money, his mother's a shrewd businesswoman. We work together often, and I've her promise, I have it in writing – and may the Devil's curse be on her if she breaks her word – that if you'll marry her son, all her gold goes to you. You see,' she said, in a confiding tone which made Sefchen's stomach turn, 'your old aunty looks after you, dear,' and, holding her lantern high above her head, she went into her room and, as usual, slammed the bolt home.

For the next few days, Sefchen's unhappiness depressed her. She read more than usual, and when the sun was out, took her books to sit on the bench before the Abbey. She had asked her aunt to teach her to cook, for Margaret had never let her interfere, except at the time when her leg was broken, but her aunt, fearful of waste, allowed her only to watch. Yet over her life hung a deep, dark feeling of disappointment, which neither reading nor household tasks could dispel, although the voices talked kindly to her every day.

One morning, the week after her encounter with Engelbert, Sefchen was walking up and down the nave when, as she approached the far end, she heard the rattle of wheels along the path and guessed this to be the third supplicant. Her first thought was to walk away and stay in the fields until he had left. She was afraid that his was the man whom her aunt had decided she should marry, as she had so carelessly dismissed the other two. In that case, however, he might be asked to stay the night, which would be dreadful. She turned and walked back and reached the house at exactly the same time as a tall man with a hooked nose, thin mouth and a firm chin walked in at the side-door. He was between thirty and thirty-five, and looked very conceited, but she found there was something compelling if embarrassing about the way in which he stood looking her up and down without the slightest sign of awkwardness, as if estimating her value. His dress gave no hint of his profession, but while Engelbert, in his old black coat that ended at his ankles, black breeches and dowdy waistcoat had looked odd and unromantic, her new lover was quite different. He looked like a hero in a portrait, and wore a long blue coat perfectly fitting his strong figure which ended below his knees, over gleaming polished brown boots. She was also impressed by the eight gold buttons of his coat, and noticed with pleasure his velvet collar above a fine silk white cravat. As he took off his high hat and made a low bow, she examined him carefully. He was clearly no peasant. For a moment, a wild hope surged through her that he might not be a member of the family, but her saviour. His first words, however, spoken in a harsh and, she thought, cruel voice, swept aside any misconceptions.

'I am your cousin Wilhelm. My man's driven me here to meet you. Let us discuss the matter without delay.'

Her aunt came bustling in at that moment. He looked at her coldly, lifting his hat a fraction off his head and put out his hand formally, as if to ensure she kept her distance.

'Come up,' she said, 'come up to the parlour. I have some wine for you from Schloss Metternick, which I am told you prefer, and there's cold venison with jelly. I would have made something hot, but could not tell what time you'd arrive.'

'Thank you,' said the man precisely, and, ushering Sefchen before him, followed them upstairs to the parlour, where to her surprise he told her to sit down and threw his hat and fawn gloves on a chair before taking the place at the head of the table. Before him was a bottle of wine and a silver plate covered with thin slices of venison and bilberries, an old silver cup stood beside silver knives and forks.

'Forgive me if I eat at once,' he said in an arrogant voice, 'but I've driven some distance and can . . .', he pulled out a watch on the end of a gold chain, '. . . can spend only a few moments here, but that should be enough to conduct the present business. Sefchen, I will speak plainly. I'm thirty-three years old and have not yet thought of marriage. Having heard of your beauty, I decided to come and see it myself. I confess, the journey was not wasted. I understand you read and can therefore entertain yourself when I'm absent. I keep a housekeeper and servant. I have a small vineyard. It only remains to arrange the marriage date.'

Sefchen felt breathless and was glad she was sitting down. But she noticed he obviously did not think there was any need to show kindness or affection since she was his for the taking. His behaviour revolted her. What sort of man was he? She remembered the callous difference between his greeting to her and her aunt, and noticed he had not said a word of thanks for the wine, venison and red berries. On top of that, his view of herself as a creature without opinions, who was there merely to serve him, made her feel frightened. She looked down at her dress and wondered whether, if he had stared at her kindly, treated her with respect and asked her to marry him as he knelt before her gently taking her hand, she would, despite his profession have said yes. She certainly had to admit that she had, for the first time in her life, met a man who made her weak and who she feared could have made her follow his wishes against her own. But she had no wish to marry a man who treated her like a piece of furniture, who was hard and cold and lacked kindness and would never think or speak of love. At the same time, she realized she was unable to stand up, and he could probably make her say, despite her doubts, whatever he wished. She felt helpless, and silently longed for him to say one kind word. Her silence only annoyed him.

'Well?' he asked roughly. 'You are not in disagreement?'

She did not answer, and he impatiently flung out his right arm and knocked the bottle of Schloss Metternich on to the floor. Her aunt gave a cry of dismay and lifted her hands to her cheeks, but Wilhelm, unperturbed, pushed the broken glass away with his foot and curtly ordered: 'Bring another bottle.'

'Alas, cousin,' said her aunt in confusion, 'I only bought the one. It's so expensive, you know,' she ended apologetically, 'but I can fetch you a tankard of the wine I get from Düsseldorf.'

'I'll not drink the filthy stuff,' he said with an angry sneer. 'If your plans succeed, and I agree to marry this girl, I'll need more than one bottle of wine to celebrate, won't I?'

While he was speaking, Sefchen noted the precise movements of his thin lips and the way in which his eyes turned on the old woman with a venomous look when the fault was surely his. Her sense of fairness revolted at his unkind nature, and she heard herself saying: 'Sir, you presume I shall marry you. I'll do no such thing.'

She wanted to run away, but realized she must stand and face him. He looked at her, raised his eyebrows, before saying in a cold voice: 'I admire your spirit. I'll not be distracted by your momentary stupidity.'

She said nothing.

'Fortunately,' he continued, 'my business affairs will make it possible for me to return in three days. I expect you, by then, to give a positive reply. As you must realize, there's none of our family who equals me in appearance and character, you would be a fool to dismiss your one chance of marrying a man who's not an animal and who will soon have enough riches to forsake this tedious trade. When I come back, I expect you to have thought these matters over and to have changed your mind. I shall expect your favourable answer. And, cousin,' he said, turning to her aunt, 'make sure to order a dozen bottles of good wine. I may need to break some over your head the next time I call.'

He laughed, opened the door, clattered down the stairs and out of the old house. The woman from Goch burst into tears, and Sefchen, going over to her, said: 'Please don't worry. You've done all you can for me, but I can't marry a brute, and won't marry him now, whatever he says or does. I'll not be in when he returns,' she added, 'but will leave a letter outside on the bench, and,' she said, not trusting her own strength, 'lock the door and let the dog have full run of his chain.'

Her aunt gripped her hand and stopped sobbing, but as she went out of the room turned and, looking slyly at Sefchen, said: 'Well, child, there are other options I've not mentioned, but we'll need to consider them now.'

8

As the winter was long and cold, they led a quiet life and Sefchen read and helped her aunt about the house now she knew she could not be forced to marry. She felt happier when spring came at last. One day her aunt said: 'Come now, child, we must sit and discuss your future, for women can't live alone and the lot of our family is hard. Since you came here, I've done what I could for you,' she said, putting on her wheedling tone, 'but . . .' and her voice changed, the words coming out in clipped hard tones, '. . . but no woman can live alone. If there's no one to care for her, she becomes a poor dependent thing like myself. But I was once married, at least, and the fate of women who are not is sad. All others look down on them. Now, as you know, child, you can only marry into the family, and last year I brought to you the three fittest. Two had money, which is the best reason for marrying, as it means comfort. The third breaks hearts wherever he goes. But you spurned them all. So what is to become of you? You are sixteen now, and it's true you have at least four years of beauty before you, but I'm a sickly, crotchety creature, and what if I should die? Where will you go then? You won't mix yourself up in my business, you know, although I sometimes wonder whether the colour of your hair isn't to remind you to stop having fanciful thoughts. However, child – and this is what I've been coming to – there are other ways a girl like you can live, especially if she's as beautiful as you are.

'You know little of life yet, but your knowledge of animals should make you understand what I'm talking about. It's no use blushing. There are facts that need to be understood. Those who don't face facts become unhappy, but facts are truths. Now, child, apply your mind to the mating of animals, and realize that humans are the only creatures which wed and put on a ring. In your case, there will be many men, old and young, who'll want to mate with you. I know, I've made inquiries already, for you're a fine girl, the type men like, and money's to be made . . . much money. Now don't change colour so, child, and think that I plan to sell you to some old man. I know your feelings. You're as full of fancy as a cow's of grass. We all are when we're young. But be sensible and realize that, since you've shunned the family, you won't, despite your looking glass, find others to marry you. That you must understand. But you can still do well, you know. Now, I'm not pushing you. You're young yet. But there's a young man coming today to call on me. He belongs to one of the town's best Jewish families. His father sells the finest velvets you ever saw, and his uncle in Hamburg lives, they say, in a house of gold.

'I want you to consider what you think of him and realize that, having turned away the family, you cannot be pernickety. You have got to realize, child, that, with your beauty, you might live with a man for ever better off than if you were his wife. Don't think I'm trying to push you away, dear one. I only wish you to lose your shyness and to study young men. This boy's like you – good-looking, all fancy and no work. He was brought to me years ago by his old nurse Zippel because a lady had called him beautiful in front of others, which, as you know, was to put a curse on him. They arrived, Zippel all upset, late one evening, and I touched his head, and shaved a patch, spat on it and rubbed in the spittle. No harm came to him, and he was interested, and so has come to see me ever since, and writes songs like yours. Therefore sing to him, for, since you have spurned the family, I want you to have a nice young friend.'

And now her voice changed from a confidential to a hectoring tone as she continued: 'If he asks anything more from you, refuse it. Allow him friendship, nothing else. But remember, his family has piles of money. He's calling here this morning and should be here in two to three hours, so wash your hair and put on the new silk dress I made for you.'

Sefchen shook her head.

'Well, at least tidy your hair and draw the red curls around your throat. For done that way in your strange fashion it makes you beautiful in a cruel way, and may appeal to such a fanciful boy. When he arrives, I will go into Düsseldorf, and you can sit and talk. You'll be safe in his hands. He's as innocent as yourself. But remember, talk and nothing more.'

Sefchen listened, her eyes cast down with embarrassment and worry. She had not forgotten the Jews bargaining for the dead men's clothes in the clearing after a hanging, and conceived them as a nation of ancient hunched men with hooked noses and black greasy hair. The boy was sure to look like them, which could only mean more unhappiness, a further reason for sobbing at night and confirmation of her fears she would never be happy.

After she had washed her hair she sat outside as she could tell already it was a beautiful morning and she knew that the sun would, for an hour or two, shine down on the house. She took out *The Ossian* and began to read and stopped to learn lines which she thought so beautiful they made her feel like weeping. 'But behold her love when his robe of mist flew on the wind. A sunbeam was on her skirts, they glittered like the gold of the stranger. It was the voice of my love, seldom comes he to my dreams.'

She liked to learn verses, and in the forest had had special ones for all the trees. The oak and beech had been the king and queen, but the mad beauty of Ireland kept intruding, and she shut her eyes and sank into her romantic Celtic world. She saw herself as a heroine from the olden days receiving suitors, who, having asked her hand in marriage, went away to be slain, which sad news the west wind would later bring to her. She felt comforted to think Malvina was as unhappy as herself when a strange voice said: 'I hope I'm not disturbing you. Good morning. Is the Meistereen in?'

She raised her eyes and saw before her a slight, neatly dressed young man of the same age as herself, with striking wavy brown hair, a fine aquiline nose, red lips and a finely pointed chin. That his head was too large for his slim body did not occur to her then or ever. All she could look at was the face, in which she saw the personification of the heroes of her fancy. There, in front of her, stood the frog turned prince, the snake turned prince, the cat turned prince: the embodiment of all her dreams and desires. She gazed in amazement at a man who spoke so kindly and gently she could not understand his words. He, in equal amazement, gazed back at this vision on a wooden bench, a huge volume of Ossian before her, wearing an extraordinary green silk dress, unlike any he had ever seen, which clung to her beautiful young body while, out of the tight sleeves, projected the most beautiful long pale fingers with pink nails. To add to his wonder, from beneath the skirt emerged high-arched, long beautiful white feet. But it was on the square top of her dress that his eyes eventually settled in wonder. He had known fair-haired girls in the town, and sometimes they had allowed him to give them kisses on the cheek, and once or twice on the lips, and had often called him a pretty boy. He had admired their red cheeks, full red lips and strong limbs, but here was a girl who belonged to another world, with her dazzling white skin, and shining, dark red hair which flowed like blood from the pointed widow's peak in the centre of her white forehead to the curled ends clustered around her throat.

Next he looked from her hair to her black eyebrows, so strange in a red-haired girl, but as a shaft of sunlight struck her face, he realized they also were red, but a darker red, the darkest red imaginable, while below them were set the profoundest deep green eyes, the colour of emeralds, although, he realized, he had never seen one. All he knew was that they could not have been more beautiful. Her nose was slightly aquiline, her cheek bones high, her mouth wide, her upper lip a Cupid's bow. Her face was oval, her chin rounded and covered by skin which, once it ceased to dazzle, amazed him by the purity of a whiteness enabling him to see the shape of perfect bones, the faintness of blue veins. As they gazed in silence, their eyes adoring, he knew his heart had reached out, and hers reached back to his, establishing a bond which never could be broken and which he would, that evening, record in verse.

She stared at his face, wondering whether she was asleep and would soon wake up to another tiresome day. The idea made her wince with unhappiness, and he saw how her breast rose and fell under her extraordinary green costume, and how a faint pink appeared like a soft bloom on her cheeks before disappearing again, leaving him to conceive he had imagined it. Then he noticed, with alarm, that even though she was sitting, she seemed taller than he was, so he sat down quickly and straightened his back. This alarm made him the first to recover his senses and say: 'You must be the Meistereen's niece. She said you were coming to stay. So tell me,' he continued, his absorption with literature breaking through his emotions, 'since you are reading the tales of Ossian, which one do you like the best?'

When she said 'Temora', he was astonished. She was the first girl he had met who liked reading. His delight was increased when she told him her other favourite books, and looking quite startled he said in a surprised voice: 'But those were the books which, Goethe says in his autobiography, formed his earliest reading.'

'I know,' she said simply. 'My grandfather told me. He admired the poet above all men.'

'Then where did your grandfather live?'

'Oh, in a forest miles away.'

'In a forest?' he asked in amazement, then added quickly, afraid he might have been rude, 'In a fairy castle?' as it occurred to him, as she was the Meistereen's niece, she must belong to the 'unspeakable' family. He thought, with pleasure, of how annoyed his mother and astounded his school friends would be if they knew who he was talking to.

'No, no,' she said. 'We lived in a house in a clearing not far from the gallows. My grandfather was the executioner who attended to the death of the cruel and bad . . .' She went on, reciting like a parrot, '. . . who preyed on society.'

The young man was both delighted and astounded at her honesty and found her even more fascinating. Ever since the publication of *Young Werther*, it had become the fashion for the youthful intellectual and poetical to dwell upon death and love, and here was a young woman of such beauty he could not take his eyes off her who actually belonged to the world of death, the shadow world which was the stimulus to his own poetry. It excited him that her grandfather should, in his red cloak, have removed so many heads. 'Have you read a great many books and poems?'

'Oh yes,' she said. 'I often had to read poetry aloud to my grandfather. He liked sad songs.'

'Which sad ones?' he asked, leaning forward and staring intently.

'Oh, well, there was "Tragig and Otilie". I was singing the words only yesterday. Do you know them?'

'Ah,' he said, 'so you know that song. How strange,' and he stood up and walked about before sitting down and continuing, 'Yes, I know it. My nurse Zippel taught it me. I'd pace up and down, imagining the scene in the forest. Let me hear you sing it to me now.'

And then he blushed scarlet, for how could he ever have been so unkind as to ask an executioner's daughter to sing such words? But she did not seem a whit distressed and sang, in a clear pure voice:

'TRAGIG: "Dear Otilie, dear Otilie,
                     Thou, sure shall not the last one be –
                     Say, wish you to hang on the lofty tree?
                     Or wish you to swim in the dark blue sea?
                     Or would you kiss the naked sword,
                     Given to us by our Lord?"

'OTILIE: "I wish not to hang on the lofty tree;
                     I wish not to swim in the dark blue sea;

I wish to kiss the naked sword,
Given to us by our Lord." '

The young poet listened, astounded by the naturalness of this girl who had
lived fearlessly with death and made no attempt to hide her relationship to the
abhorred family. At once he knew fate had thrown her into his path to
stimulate a muse he had thought of abandoning. He turned to her, bowed and
said: 'I feel at this moment that we are both above the mundane world. I knew
something strange was going to happen as I came through the wood, for the
trees bowed down their branches. They only do this to me when I am about to
write something worthy of a poet of my age, for I must tell you that one day,
when I am older, I shall be the king of poetry, the greatest poet Germany ever
had, except Goethe, for no man can hope to compare with him. He's
incomparable, and I shall be satisfied to stand behind him.'

She looked at him with a puzzled astonishment which drew her out of the
dreamy mood into which the song always sent her. Why was this boy so
surprised? The songs which appealed to her from her grandfather's books had
always been sad, telling of broken loves and violent deaths. For the first time,
she realized this could have been a consequence of her grandfather's
profession, but what did that matter? So she sang to him again, a sad old song
which told of a young man who had fought and died for love for a girl he found
weeping over the grave of two lovers. It was melancholy, but the young poet
listened with excited amazement and, when she had finished, asked: 'Did you
read *The Young Werther*?'

She nodded her shining head. 'I understood him killing himself, for I did not
think the woman he loved was truthful.'

He seized her hand for a moment before re-starting his excited pacing and
saying: 'Werther brought death to many young Germans. They read his book
and decided that they, as members of the most stolid race on earth, should be
romantic, fall in love and marry for love's sake instead of for cows and
dowries. But, of course, it did not work, for they could not fall in love, and so
shot themselves, not because anyone had jilted them, or because their hearts
were broken, but because they realized they were so dull they could never fall
in love. Therefore, pathetically to prove to an unbelieving world that they
were romantic and broken-hearted, they killed themselves . . .' He paused. 'I
don't think it matters when stupid people kill themselves, do you?'

Sefchen replied gently: 'I don't know. I've never thought of it. But then, you
see, death has always been near me.'

'Yes,' he said excitedly. 'Will you tell me your story?'

'All right,' she said, and tried to remember as much as she could of her
upbringing, of her father's death, of the journey to the forest, of the entrance
into her new home to be greeted by the hard-faced Margaret while the three
old women sat spinning by the fire. At this point he could hardly contain his
excitement.

'It can't be true,' he said wonderingly. 'It's all too Gothic, too magnificently

Gothic. I've recently, following my master, been devoting myself to the ancient world, to the Greeks and humanism, but they and their philosophy seem dead, stone dead,' he said in a reflective voice, 'compared with your trip to fairyland. For it was fairyland, wasn't it, with the three women spinning? But be sure not to leave out a thing,' and he put his face close to hers, passionate with interest.

She had never confided anything to anyone before, but as she began to speak, to her surprise the words came out and she found herself telling him of her grandfather's superintending of executions, of the hanging of the eighteen men, of the cutting off of the fingers and the dispatch of little parcels to wine and beer merchants all along the Rhine. At this he positively clapped his hands in excitement and, pointing up to a tree which swayed over the Abbey, said: 'See, nature's bowing to your story, not to me. Imagine!' he said. 'Imagine!' he added, in an ecstatic voice, and ran his fingers through his hair, making it, she thought, look more beautiful than ever.

She told him, without affectation or sense of guilt, of her fascination for the clearing where the dead bodies swung, and how she often sat, carefully choosing an upwind position, to watch them swing to and fro, and how, when they had been hanging some weeks and the bones were picked bare, she found their rattling a soothing sound which often lulled her to sleep. And at this point she stopped and became embarrassed, for how could she tell him how she had once dreamed of a frog who turned into a prince? Her embarrassment made her lose confidence and she hesitated to tell him of trees forced asunder to release princesses, or of the deep holes in the ground where witches held victims to whom she had sometimes called and thrown food. Thinking he would consider her a silly liar, she blushed and, instead of telling her story clearly, spoke out in fits and starts of the animals and how she had realized nature's cruelty was necessary and that, although she was friendly with the hares, when she saw the delight with which the foxes tore them to pieces, she realized nature lived on nature.

Gradually she recovered her confidence. Her voice grew sad as she told him about the deer and badgers and then, leaning forward laughing, how a clever partridge mother at first deceived her but how, later, the chicks ran over her hand. And afterwards – and she did not know why her memory kept jumping about in such a peculiar way – of the feasts her grandfather held with his colleagues before local executions, and of how one night, when a terrible storm raged in the forest, she had heard scratchings at the window, and her fat aunt had come up to her room, reeking of the black bottle, and told her on such wild nights the wind would lift the dead men off the scaffold. And they would come to the house to try and get their fingers back, and if they found them, steal them, and if not, would take linen to warm their bones. The next day Aunt Fat had told her: 'They got in and took our linen, and I had to run after them and only caught them as they were climbing back on to the gallows and tore the stuff out of their hands. It wasn't difficult, you see, for they have no fingers.'

At these stories, the young man pressed his hands to his temples and closed his eyes as he muttered delightedly. Sefchen was pleased at the effect her words had on him. She had never known anyone who listened to her sympathetically before. Encouraged, she continued to tell how, on another stormy night, her Aunt Fat led her downstairs by the hand and, lifting a key from a secret place with a chuckle, entered her grandfather's room and came out with a huge sword, which she carried all round the windows, waving it to frighten the men from the gallows away. Afterwards she had told Sefchen if ever the fingerless hands were to come pawing at her window she was to think of her grandfather's sword and the wretched things would shrink away.

The poet watched her face faintly flush and come to life at the memories of events she had never dared remember, and was filled with ecstasy. Never before had he seen a girl so romantic, so beautiful. But one thing had puzzled him, for whenever she told a curious story about some animal or member of the strange household which was faintly ridiculous, there was something lacking in her story-telling. He wondered why. And then, all at once, he knew what was wrong: she laughed but never smiled. He gazed at her, trying to remember every expression of her face, and only half-heard her describing the escape from the village when the children stoned her. And while the half of him which listened was interested, the other half was longing to break in and ask her how she could laugh without smiling. Had she ever smiled? At last he could bear it no longer. He had to know. And as she was describing to him her emotions in the butcher's shop, he seized both of her hands and shouted: 'Why don't you smile?'

'How do you mean, smile?' she asked.

'Well, it's the widening of the mouth before you laugh, the polite way of saying good morning without speaking, the way to tell another person that you share their amusement, a sign of pleasure. Oh, I could go on and on. What is so extraordinary is that you laugh but do not smile. It seems impossible, yet I have watched you and it is so. Why do you contradict the natural movement of your mouth? Why, why? And how? It is almost impossible for me not to smile before I laugh. You laugh alone.'

She flushed and said: 'I do not smile because my father never smiled. The Meistereen, as you call my aunt, laughs but never smiles. No one in the forest ever smiled. Once, I remember, when I was very young, when Margaret was carrying the dishes away after a meal she fell over. Her heels flew into the air and the china was smashed and the aunts all cackled. But I could not laugh, as I had seen the hurt look on Margaret's face, and so, I suppose, I smiled, and my grandfather looked at me so coldly that, I remember, the look faded from my face. I realized I must never look like that again, and stopped making that face, although I knew it was all right to laugh. But I think that, for many years, I have not even thought of smiling, and when Aunt Fat mentioned the word in a fairy story I asked her what it meant and she looked at me sadly and said: "It's not necessary for you to know, little one. There's nothing to smile about in this house." She said it in such a dismal way I never dared ask again.'

Sefchen's colour changed faintly, which he supposed meant she was blushing, as she asked: 'Is a smile like this?' and made such a funny face that he could not help laughing. His laugh broke the thin ice of formality which remained between them, and they laughed like children as she realized he was still holding her hand. At that moment, her aunt came up behind them so silently they knew she had been walking on tiptoe and jumped to their feet in confusion. Sefchen blushed, but her aunt did not look at all displeased and smiled slyly. Sefchen looked in the young man's eyes, he seemed to understand, and they laughed together, at which a puzzled look came into the Meistereen's little eyes, although she too pretended to laugh heartily as her eyes darted rapidly from one to the other.

The young man bowed and said how grateful he was to his old friend, who had, in his childhood, saved him from perdition, for allowing him to call and have the honour of meeting her niece. Then he stood up and said, 'Alas, it is time to be gone.' Then he took Sefchen's hand, stepped back and drew it towards him to kiss. She felt herself blushing, for he was touching her in a different way from when he had asked her questions. As his lips brushed her fingers, she felt the blood course all the way up her arm and on to her cheeks.

That evening, Sefchen felt peculiar. It was exactly as though a spell had been cast and she would, from now and for ever, be chained to the slight young man with beautiful wavy hair. She tried to remember his face, hands, hair and everything about him, and only needed to remember the way he had kissed her hand to feel him touching her again. She could not avoid the idea, despite telling herself it was silly, he was the only man she would ever love. The thought frightened her, for why should he, in return, love an ignorant girl whose life had been spent with animals? To think that she had not known what a smile was! Perhaps she was stupid, for she had sometimes noticed a slight change in the shape of Margaret's mouth, and the Meistereen often twisted her lips into a curious shape. Why hadn't she realized that they were smiling? Yet perhaps it had not been her fault, for certainly her grandfather had never smiled, nor her father, nor the three old women; and when they had cackled with laughter, it had been noisily, with open mouths, usually because of misfortune.

Lying in bed, she tried widening her mouth, but she felt so silly, self-conscious and stupid she soon stopped trying and wondered whether her love for the young poet who had never even spoken her name was swamping and burying her. It was frightening, for he lived in a world of which she knew nothing. How could he even think of marrying her? But she was sure, as they had sat outside the Abbey that afternoon, that he had given her his heart, and knew if she had dared to lay her head on his shoulder, he would have comforted her. Surely, even in the hard world, that was what mattered?

9

In his bedroom in the family home in Düsseldorf, the young poet, Harry Heine, tossed and turned all night, finding it impossible to get out of his mind the image of the red-haired girl and her singing of the sad song which his nurse had taught him as a child. She excited his imagination, as what could be more symbolic of the dark past of Germany than a beautiful red-haired girl resting near a scaffold lulled by the clanking of dead men's bones?

All night he worried about the future. He knew his mother would disapprove of his new friend while his kind and gentle father would pity her as he had pitied him when he had gone to school for the first time and had been greeted by his schoolmates with screams and yells of laughter when he proudly told them his grandfather was a little Jew with a black hat. Even now, they still never let him forget he was an outsider unassimilated into the German nation, of which he regarded himself a part. His mother was still anxious for him to triumph in the world as a soldier, which was possible since the Emperor – ah, now there was a great man, the greatest soldier since Alexander the Great – has insisted that, in his conquered territories, Jews must not be treated as outcasts and could serve, like any other German citizen, in the army.

She saw him as a second Napoleon, but the idea bored him. Imagine the marches, the times of peace which would follow when the Emperor was once more victorious, for such a demi-god must triumph in the end. What he wished, with all his heart, was to be a king of intellect, transcending by his writings all rivals except the sacred Goethe. He had no wish to exceed him, but to stand just beneath him on the mountain top of the world's intellects. But sometimes he was doubtful, without confidence, and would be filled with doubt and wonder whether he was merely a wastrel who would daydream and read his life away. But Sefchen had inspired him, and he knew she could make him write a ballad of death which was already haunting his mind with strange images.

He knew she could be the goad he needed, and that they would love each other. She would teach him the grotesque secrets of the black past of his own country, unknown to him, although his family had lived in Germany for generations, advising rulers, guiding finances, evading persecution. The German past was his as much as it was that of any of the beastly little boys who teased him at school. And now, by some extraordinary turn of circumstance, he had the chance of understanding why anger lay, like a patch of black fog, in the back of every German's mind, moving them to violence and hatred; and to find out why they despised Jews with all their hearts and had persecuted them for generations. If she could lead him to comprehend this mystery, could he bring the nation together? He remembered her with such intensity that he could clearly see her and study every inch of her beautiful face. In her eyes he saw the passivity of goodness and the acceptance of cruelty. How she inspired him!

He jumped back into bed to start writing, but then, looking at his watch, saw it was time to get up for school. As he sat waiting for breakfast he made up his mind to go and see her that evening and throw himself at her feet. But no, he decided, he would be dignified and wait. Yet the whole of that day she never left his mind, and his schoolmaster, the hateful Dietrich, who had once beaten him, warned him he would be punished if he did not pay attention. But still his mind strayed and his work was poor. He did not care, he was counting the minutes to seeing her, until he changed his mind again and determined not to see her until the next day.

All day she sat waiting for him on the bench by the front door, and when she tried to read a book, the letters changed shape and formed themselves into his face. At last, she laid her head on the open page and wept. What could life hold for her? She knew nothing, was an exile, an outcast, who had, alas, given her love to one who came from a world to which she could never belong. She wished, with all her heart, to be back in the house in the woods, from where she could have gone to see one of her animals. There lay the only world she would ever understand and in which she could love and be loved.

As she lay weeping, her face on the open book, her aunt came out and, after looking at her carefully, sat down opposite and said: 'Now, child, cheer up, cheer up. So you fancy that young man, do you? Very well, but listen *to me.*'

The last two words came out so like the hiss of a snake they startled Sefchen into drying her eyes and looking at her aunt. Was it possible she could help?

'Listen and don't weep. It wastes time. Leave the planning to me, as I told you before. You're too good for the family to which you belong, and there's none that's seen you who'd deny it. I sometimes wonder if your mother . . . but there's no business of mine or yours. At all events, I've been making inquiries about young Heine. His father's business is not so good as it looks, not good at all. No sound foundation, and that's not surprising, the way he throws money about. As you may have heard, the old man's responsible for doling out to the poor the pittance the town gives them, and what does the old fool do but add a larger sum from his own pocket? You can't do business like that. The poor will grasp as much as you give them.

'On the other hand, his Uncle Salomon in Hamburg is, I've heard on trusty advice,' and she leaned forward, the hiss coming back into her voice, 'the richest man in all Germany. They say he lives in a palace, owns millions, and could buy up Düsseldorf without quartering his hoard of gold. Ah, now that's money, child, real money. But then the Jews are a funny lot, and proud, very proud of their race. They'll do anything for one of their own, so long as they think the help won't be wasted. But if they think the money will be ill spent, they won't throw good after bad. So, child, you must find out what your young friend thinks of his Uncle Salomon and what the uncle thinks of his father. This will help us to know how to approach the matter. But I fear there's not much to be got out of the uncle as I hear he thinks his brother's nothing but a fool to give extra money each week to those who can't make it themselves.'

She continued talking about Harry's father's decline, and went into detailed assessments of hardware and velveteen which caused Sefchen to stop listening and try instead to remember everything the young man had said to her. She jumped when her aunt, having at last finished talking, asked her sharply whether she would find out for sure what Harry thought of his Uncle Salomon. She replied vaguely that she would ask about Harry's uncle if it pleased her aunt. The Meistereen muttered something angrily under her breath about 'wasting time on idiots', and disappeared into the house, banging the door after her.

The long, wretched day eventually dragged to an end, but next morning Sefchen woke up early to hear the birds singing as the sun rose. Instinctively she knew Harry would come that day and was sure he was lovingly at that moment thinking about her. Pleased, relieved and full of gratitude, to everybody in the world, she at once ran to ask her aunt what she could do for her. The Meistereen peered at her from the corners of her eyes and said: 'Yes, dear child. I'm always grateful when you lend a hand. One of my old lilac silk dresses is in need of a little attention.'

Sefchen knew that her aunt had all sorts of unworn, curious dresses hanging up in a cupboard which stank of camphor, and that they often needed attention, since the moths were continually getting at them. She liked this soothing, peaceful work, and followed her aunt to the locked cupboard, from which she was given a silk evening gown which must have been made a long time ago as it had an extraordinarily slender waist and the Meistereen had not a waist at all. She sat in the sun while her aunt produced spools of silk in soft colours and told her to pick those she thought matched most closely the colour of her dress.

'You never know when I might need to wear it,' she said, and Sefchen nodded, wondering when Harry would arrive.

She sewed for three hours. When her eyes began to ache, she went to the front room and then decided to wash her hair again as it was something to do. Her aunt said she had a wonderful preparation, but since Sefchen never knew what she put into her concoctions, she accepted politely but secretly used her own soap. Having plunged her thick hair several times into the rain barrels, she shook herself like an animal and went and sat in the sun, kneeling with her head resting upon a chair and slowly combing the thick mass forward until she felt the sun's warmth. It was intertwined after the washing, and sometimes she had to use both hands to untangle a knot. As she knelt with her head forward and hair streaming downwards, she began to feel faint but lacked the willpower to move or stop gently combing and parting. Now and again she would put her hands up to feel if her hair was still wet, or move her head sideways so a different area caught the sun. At last her hair felt reasonably dry, except for the back of her head, and this she could only get warm by leaning her head downwards and letting the cascade fall tangled on to the grass. The rush of blood to her head made her feel even dizzier, but being obstinately determined to dry her hair, she ignored her increasing sense of unreality until a voice said: 'Good day. I see why they call you Red Sefchen.'

She leapt up in confusion and staggered unsteadily. Dropping her comb, she threw her hair back over her shoulders and, as if for protection, pulled the red ringlets round to the front of her neck. She tried to look at Harry, but could not make her eyes meet his. What must he think of her?

In fact, he was enchanted by her confused and dramatic beauty. Wandering up the nave, he had tried his hardest to conquer his nervousness and appear calm and collected, when all at once he saw a pair of deathly white hands caressing what his eyes told him was a mass of dark red snakes. He forgot his shyness and stood transfixed for a moment, wondering what necromancy the Meistereen was up to until he realized the beautiful tangle was Sefchen's hair.

When, at last, she could make him out clearly, she was surprised to see he was dressed in black clothes – a black hat, black gloves, and even carried a black stick and, strangest of all, wore a velveteen black cravat. His nose was pointed upwards and he looked the colour of white paper. She sat down quickly. Something terrible must have happened.

'What is it?' she asked, putting her right hand to her heart.

He sat by her and placed the stick on the bench beyond him before turning and saying in a hollow voice: 'You've not heard the news?'

She shook her head, and he looked even sadder. 'Last night I was happy. We heard rumours the great Napoleon had trounced the English. I at once went to bed early, for I had not slept the night before and walked many miles yesterday,' he said, looking her straight in the face as if to emphasize the fault was hers. 'As I lay half-awake, half-asleep, I thought I heard a horse galloping through the street, which was odd since the gates are shut early. Then a voice shouted, and everybody was shouting out of the windows, and I heard many times the name, "Napoleon!" I thought with pleasure, "Ah, so he's taught those smug English a lesson at last," and fell asleep to dream I was a general walking at his side after another great victory we had won together. For, you know, I did see him once, on the way to Moscow. I'll never forget those eternal eyes set in the marble of his imperial face, and the way his grenadiers looked up at him with devotion in their eyes. He, unmoving, looked back, accepting their adulation as his due. But I understood him and would willingly have gone to my death in his service.'

Gradually, as Harry spoke, Sefchen saw how he was re-enacting the whole scene and unselfconsciously and dramatically re-living his memories. He continued: 'I was woken this morning by my mother opening my door. Since she never comes into my room at that time, I knew something had happened. I haven't told you much about her, but she's a strong woman and once, as I told you the other day, wished me to be a general. She looked tired, lifeless and pale as she leaned against the doorway, her left hand on the knob, her right against the wall, as if to steady herself. "My poor boy," she said, "my poor boy."

'I listened carefully as she went on in a flat little voice. "I had such high hopes for you." The words dropped slowly and bitterly from her mouth, and then she repeated herself, but even more sadly. I was beginning to think she had gone mad when she said: "I had made plans, despite your opposition, for you to enter the military academy and fulfil your promise and become a great soldier, but yesterday . . ." and here her voice broke, ". . . Napoleon was beaten near Brussels, beaten, they say, completely, his army destroyed, and no one knows if he's alive or dead. Our Blücher," she said, pride breaking through her sorrow, "won the battle and saved the English who had run away, but woe betide us, for, you know, it was Napoleon who gave our people freedom, and now that he's gone, they'll take it away again, and you, poor boy, will I know have all your opportunities frustrated. Ah, I had hoped for so much for you, for so very much," and she put her hands to her face and pushed back her tears.'

Sefchen had thought for a moment he was acting, but saw he was also looking unutterably sad and that tears came into his fine eyes as he said: 'Please don't think I'm pretending. I lament Napoleon with my whole heart. He was a great man. He gave us hope and freedom and opportunity. Now all the burghers will confine us again, and bully the poor.'

Harry looked at her to see how she had taken his display of sorrow and realized how beautiful she looked in her green dress. Forgetting his black clothes, play-acting and Napoleon, he stared at her and decided that her bosoms had swelled, adding perfection to her beauty. He longed to stretch out a hand, to take her red curls in his fingers and twine them around his, but feared the Meistereen might be peering out from behind the shutters. So, instead, he sat beside her and said: 'Yesterday was like a year to me. I could not get you out of my mind. I tried to read Hegel, but could not understand a word he wrote. You kept coming between my eyes and the page. When I was with you two days ago (or was it two years?) I think I behaved in a hasty, superior manner, but afterwards – and I've been thinking of you all the time – I realized I'm only your equal and we are brothers and sisters in misfortune. You have no idea how I have been persecuted at school. Do you know Dirty Michael?' he asked.

She shook her head. She knew no one in Düsseldorf.

'Well, he's a filthy fellow who, early every day, drives through the town in a little donkey cart. At least, the donkey walks along and he follows, stopping outside every door where all the muck from the houses and streets has been swept into neat little hillocks. These he throws into his cart, which is more like a boat on wheels, and when he has finished collecting the stuff from one house cries out, "Haaryh!" and his donkey moves on to the next pile. And do you know, sometimes my friends even today creep up and shout, "Haaryh!" in my ear, but make it sound like "Harry!" Years ago, when I was shy and sensitive, all the boys would come up one after another and ask me seriously whether I was Michael's son, and how was my donkey? They made me cry, even in public, and had a cruel riddle which each boy would ask me in turn: "What's the difference between a zebra and the ass of Balaam?" The answer was always: "That one speaks Zebrew." '

He looked as if he was going to faint, and she longed to hold his hands as he went on: 'They painted a picture of me with a donkey in the school yard, and I cannot tell you all the jokes they played on me. The worst of my tormentors was called Jupp, and he would throw manure at me, though at times he had to be polite, for my father was the city almoner and Jupp's mother received the dole from him, to which my father added his own money. Anyhow, one day the horrid old woman said how good-looking I was in front of my old nurse Zippel who, believing an old legend, said that if a child is flattered to his face, evil will follow, rushed forward and spat three times on me. I was disgusted, and so was my father, although he said nothing and only put a hand over his eyes to blot out the vulgar action. Zippel was still terrified, and did not think her spitting was enough. She had got it into her head the woman Jupp was a witch, and said, "Only a witch can take off a curse laid by a witch." That was the first time I came here. Your aunt, when she heard, looked very grave, shook her head and cut some hair off my head in three more places. Then she put her thumb in her mouth and rubbed her spittle into me.'

He was leaning forward and whispering now, his face close to Sefchen, who stared at him with wide-open eyes, which had shed tears twice as he told of his youthful tortures.

'Well, I must say, I didn't like it either when your aunt rubbed saliva on me, and really hoped that no one would ever praise me again if the only result would be Zippel spitting all over me and this . . . this . . .' He stopped, embarrassed, '. . . this Meistereen rubbing me with her wet thumb. But, at the same time, your aunt spoke magic words over me, and I was fascinated. For, it's true, I had a great-uncle who was once a bedouin chief and then doctor to a king whose name I'm not allowed to mention. That is a story I'll tell you another day. Anyhow, the Meistereen fascinated me. Years afterwards, I asked my father whether I could come back here and see her alone, even though I was afraid of the Abbey and this house, which I knew was all dark and dirty. He looked at me a long time before saying, "Yes." I came back often, and she has told me many things, and without knowing her, I'd never have met you.'

Sefchen thought it was odd how, when her aunt had told her the same story, she hadn't found it interesting, but when Harry told it her heart beat and as she understood how the poor little boy had been bullied and persecuted. She thought how fortunate she had been in comparison and how brave was the spirit behind this beautiful face, and how honest and clever he was to be able to put into words his sad sufferings.

'In any case,' he went on, 'before the news of the great man's defeat put everything else from my mind, I intended to come and tell you that we have a sad past in common and I am sure that as a result we will be close to each other, and do you know, I have thought so much about the stories you told me of your strange woodland life that I must know more about it.'

And he put out a hand gently to take hers. She felt helplessly weak and tender, and although she thought she ought to take her hand away she could not do so, as she felt as if she was chained to him. But gradually, to her astonishment, she began to feel secure and confident in the company of this strange young man.

'Would you mind,' he went on, 'if I ask you more questions?'

She shook her head. At that moment, she could think of nothing which she would have minded him saying or doing.

'Well, did you attend executions?'

'No, I never saw him cut any heads off, but as I told you, some of Napoleon's men, I think eighteen men, were hanged in the forest and I crept round and watched them.'

'What did you see?' he asked, his face glowing with interest. 'Tell me again. I was looking at you so hard I did not hear.'

She told again, without emotion, of the execution of the eighteen men, of the finger clipping and the onlooking figures, of her understanding of the necessity of death. He listened in silent fascination, paused and asked abruptly: 'Did you ever clip off fingers yourself?'

She shook her head. 'I was never asked to.'

'And would you have done, had you been asked?'

'No, I don't know why, but no.'

He looked disappointed and paused again. She saw he was summoning up courage to ask another question, and she did not mind. She had nothing to hide, and was delighted he should want to know about her life.

'And did you,' he broke out, speaking more rapidly than usual, 'did you ever see your father or grandfather cut off a head? In private I mean?'

He remained motionless, holding his breath.

'No,' she said. 'They both carefully dressed themselves in red cloaks and went away with their assistant. They would always be in good spirits before they left, but sad when they came back. I remember my grandfather often sighed as he looked at the new books he always brought with him.'

Harry let his breath out with a rush, then began to ask questions again as if he had been running: 'You never saw them use their swords?'

'N-n-no . . . I've told you,' she hesitated.

'Why do you pause?' he asked.

'Well,' she said, 'well . . . I'll tell you, as I know something about it and was going to tell you the other day when you started talking about my never smiling.'

And she began her story of the melancholy dinner and the burial of the oblong object and, lastly, how her grandfather had sobbed and sobbed as he sat alone in the empty kitchen. And then she told him, unconsciously gripping his hand, how troubled she had been by the burial, which for some reason had haunted her and made her long to know what had been so sadly and ceremoniously buried beneath the earth. At last, she could bear it no longer, and one evening last month when her aunt was in an unusually good mood, she had told her what happened and asked for an explanation.

'The Meistereen laughed and clapped her hands and said she knew what it was and there was no harm in my knowing either. It was quite simply that they had buried a sword which had cut off a hundred heads, as after that's happened, the weapon can't be controlled, as it has a taste for blood. No executioner is allowed, by the brotherhood, to keep such a weapon in his house, as at midnight every night it will rattle hungrily on the wall, while those who have stupidly used such a sword have often had it turn on them or one of their friends, for it seems the devil owns it once it has done so much work. And then she said: "There's magic in that sword, great magic. I shall go and dig it up. It'll be of great value to me." And, you know, she is actually going to the forest tomorrow to dig it up with a spade.'

'Ah,' said Harry, and sat back, shut his eyes and looked weak with delight as he murmured: 'I think you really should live in fairyland. How you stir my imagination! You know, I'll write a ballad for you and I won't come here again till I've finished it, by which time,' he went on, pacing up and down with excitement, 'the sword will be here. Take care to watch where your aunt conceals it and, please,' he said, leaning forward, 'go and listen to see if it rattles at midnight.'

Sefchen didn't reply. She longed to do everything he asked, but was not sure whether she would dare to creep down into her aunt's room, for what if the sword rattled and tried to kill her? She asked Harry not to be angry if she was too frightened, but already he had forgotten his request and was repeating her story to himself. He continued to pace up and down and suddenly, without warning, stood up and in a sad distracted way walked off leaving her unhappy and disappointed without even kissing her hand. She could not imagine herself leaving him coldly without a sign of affection.

10

Harry was true to his word and, still excited and inspired by his thoughts of Sefchen, worked unceasingly until his ballad was finished. At the same time, his love for her, which he excitedly built up in his mind as a great romance, came to haunt him. Every night he woke up dwelling on the three questions which appeared to be his only possible choices. Should he seduce her and make her secretly his mistress? Marry her secretly, abandon Germany and emigrate to the distant United States, where all men lived free? Or defy his parents and marry her openly? In the daytime, one or other of the alternatives would appear to him to be acceptable, but at night, after he had blown out his candle, simplicities turned into difficulties. He did not mind the idea of leaving his favourite sister, whom he would always love, or his brothers, whom he knew to be stupid. It was the idea of separating himself from his father or mother which frightened him, as he would be breaking the frame of his life.

The day after he had finished his ballad, as he was putting on his boots to leave for the Abbey, the maid came and told him his mother wished to see him in her sitting room. Such a summons usually meant criticism, and Harry went with a sinking heart. He found her sitting on a chair facing the empty grate, her hands resting on her knees – the position which, he knew, she always adopted when she needed to think or to announce a decision of great importance. He kissed her cold hand before taking a chair. Not knowing what to do with his own hands, he finally sat on them. His mother continued to stare gloomily into the grate before turning and saying in a small voice: 'It's as I thought, directly I heard of the defeat of the Emperor. Those who dislike us as a race are already banding together. There's no doubt that the same old people will soon resume power and your opportunity to have a career other than trade will be withdrawn. It is a great blow.'

Two tears gently coursed down over the wrinkled cheeks as she continued: 'I can only say again you are the only one of my children I expect to succeed, fond as I am of the others,' she added in a sad, half-hearted tone. 'You alone have inherited that ability which made both my father and grandfather advisers to the Duke. Now I shall tell you my thoughts, as you're almost a man and must face the truth. You will soon have no alternative except to enter the business. I've not mentioned to your father what I'm about to say, and must instruct you, as your mother, not to repeat this conversation. He, as you know, was a rich man ten years ago. Things have changed since then. The

English blockade since 1806 made the importation of materials, on which his success depended, a difficult matter. Last week I requested the head clerk to come here to see me. He's a man I have known and trusted for years, and sometimes he has, in the past, asked me to intervene when it was important to make your father alter his mind. He admitted your father's business is in a bad way. Affairs have come to such a state that, unless there's a change within the year, the firm will no longer be able to continue trading, so I suggest, when you leave school in three months' time, you should go to your Uncle Salomon in Hamburg for a period of two years. He'll teach you how to run a business as it should be run, and then, I hope, you'll be able to maintain your father and us all in the way to which we have been accustomed. Otherwise I fear the worst.

'I think there will be money to complete the children's education, but no more unless you make it. I ask you to put out of your head any fanciful ideas of making a living as a writer of verse. The reward of such a career can only be poverty. I hope, now, you understand the future of our family depends on your acumen. I asked to see you today to get your permission to ask your Uncle Salomon to commence your commercial education in three months' time. I expect, as a dutiful son, that you will give me your agreement.'

Harry was astounded. Even when he was small, she had, it seemed, bothered more about his future career than with loving him. He had always thought that she spoke to him as a stranger when what he wanted was a loving mother. The idea of parting from Sefchen for two years in three months' time at first dismayed him, but then, it occurred to him, three months was an eternity. Uncle Salomon was immensely rich and had two daughters. He thought of them romantically for a moment, then loyally pushed them out of his mind, replacing them with visions of himself mastering business and amazing his uncle by the unrealized Van Geldern ability of his brilliant nephew. He saw the two of them sitting together at a table, making momentous decisions and loans to kings, and himself jumping on a horse and riding off to some distant court to be honourably received by a grateful ruler as the welcome bearer of wealth. After all, business was in his blood. His Uncle Salomon, whose wisdom could not be dissimilar to his own, would realize at once the genius of his neglected nephew and gratefully make him a partner. He stood up, his fortune already made, and reassured his mother all would be well. As he bent impulsively to kiss her in parting, she held up her small brown capable hand to hold him off and said coldly: 'So you agree?'

'Yes, beloved mother,' he said as he clasped her, but she remained unresponsive.

Her last words as he turned away disappointed were: 'I must ask you again, Harry, to give up your dreams. Wealth comes through hard work, dedication, application and undertaking menial positions. Please, I beg you, do not immediately imagine yourself a merchant prince. You will, to begin with, have to lead a life of drudgery. Understand that, or you will be disappointed and deceive yourself and become, like your father, a hopeless dreamer. And all will be lost.'

Harry heard her words, but only half-took in their meaning, for already he was at the door, planning to hurry to Sefchen at the Abbey to tell her he was to be a merchant prince and that nobody in the world would then have the power to deny his right to marry her. He walked rapidly out of the town and was breathless by the time he arrived at the wooden gate. He stood recovering for a few moments, mopping his brow and running a bone comb through his hair before deciding that he was cool and collected enough to make a fitting and impressive entrance. Then he approached the arch at the beginning of the old nave and, declining to use the side-door, walked through the bushes towards the house. As he had stepped into the precincts of the Abbey, he felt, as usual, a faint burden of depression, as if he was entering an area of antagonism. He thought of all the stories of the ghosts he had heard in his youth and shuddered with pleasure.

The day was overcast and the house stood morose and unwelcoming. But he was pleased to find Sefchen in the kitchen, bending over a brass candlestick, polishing it with an intensity which enabled him to creep up and touch her before she knew he was in the room. The effect was gratifying. She leapt back, knocking over a stool, and stared at him with wild terrified eyes until she slowly realized he was not a figment of her dreams. Then, placing a hand over her left bosom, which was heaving up and down, she said: 'Please, never do such a thing again. You gave me a fearful fright.'

Looking into her face, he saw that her colour was more heightened than usual and wondered whether this odd paradoxical creature could become red with fear when others turned white. It was a curious idea. He took her left hand and kissed it, holding it a moment against his mouth until her arm trembled. Then, with a whirl, from behind his back he produced a sealed missive and offered it to her. She looked at it and sat down before unwinding the scroll. Turning the three sheets of paper over she asked: 'You wrote this for me, Harry? You wrote this for me? How good and kind you are.'

'May I read it to you?' he said, and went to the window to stand in the light. He read in a musical voice, surprisingly resonant for such a small man. As she looked at his profile against the window panes, and the hazy top of his wavy hair, she thought that she had never seen anyone look so beautiful, or heard anybody speak so beautifully. With delight and pride, she thought how he had written the ballad for her alone, and then felt afraid; for, while she loved him with her whole heart, she could never have written verses. She often did not understand what they meant, and knew she would have to pore over the words at length on her own. As he continued to read in a manner she could never match, she imagined the two of them walking together in the forest. She always, in her thoughts, associated Harry with the forest days, because he was the incarnation of the princes she had dreamed of there, although he had never been there and he would never go.

When he had finished, she turned to him and said: 'Oh, but it is beautiful. Thank you so much. I shall learn it and never forget it as long as I live,' and, walking over, took it from him without even a kiss of thanks.

The simplicity of her acceptance disappointed him, and there was something so naïve in her enthusiasm he could not help thinking she would have said the same thing whatever he had written. He found himself wishing she was cleverer and better educated, but then, as he looked at her with anger standing in the dusky light, in her usual green dress, her red curls falling over her shoulders, his feelings softened. She looked so beautiful, so ethereal, he realized all his early romantic dreams and saw her as a perfect work of nature which it would be his life's work to turn into a clever, cultured woman.

'Please, let me have my ballad,' he said, and when she held it out, gripped her left wrist with his right hand and her right wrist with his left hand, and held her tightly, their arms crossed, so that she could not move and swayed as if she was on the verge of fainting. He needed to exert his strength to keep her on her feet. The moment passed, and as they stared into one another's eyes he knew that, even though she was a lamia, he loved her. At once his mind leapt to her strange past and he asked abruptly: 'Has your aunt yet gone for the sword?'

She loosened her hands, as if he had broken a spell, and turned so that her back was half towards him before replying, 'As it has been raining she couldn't go until today in the pony cart. She'll be back by evening.'

But her feelings were hurt as she could not understand why, when she was conscious of nothing in the world but the touch of his hands and the love in her heart, he should have asked about the sword.

A little later he suggested they went for a walk, saying: 'I find the kitchen gloomy.' As they went out of the house, he felt again as if a chill wind had touched him. Without thinking, he remarked: 'Do you know, I always have a strange feeling of fear or cold in this Abbey. Do you as well?'

She seemed to give his question serious thought and replied slowly: 'I did as a child. I remember that when I was very young, I was allowed to go out and play in front of the house. Yet it always seemed to me as if there was somebody there I could not see who was spoiling my pleasure. Then, one day, I must have walked into the wood, and found that there was nobody with me, and that I could play with acorns and climb into the centres of the old trees and be happy as no one was bothering me. And so it went on, until I left, and it is true,' she said, turning her eyes to him with such effect that he was utterly convinced of this beautiful girl's cleverness and sensitivity, 'that when I came back, they welcomed me home, saying, "This is where you belong." '

She stopped, confused, unused to making such speeches, and remembering she had hardly thanked him for the ballad told him again how beautiful she thought it was.

He was pleased and thought, 'After all, she is intelligent.' They walked happily together in the wood, content with arms linked. Harry wondered whether he should kiss her, but decided no, it should not be a casual, careless action comparable to the three times he had kissed her hands, which had meant little or nothing. The next kiss must imply a meeting of souls, which celebrated their extraordinary relationship and tied him to this wild girl. It was pleasant to feel that she loved him and, he was practically certain, he loved her.

He thought of saying that now he would be leaving for Hamburg in three months' time, and in a year would be a merchant prince. Caution warned him, however, not to upset her. What was more, she kindled his imagination, and made him think of the great dramas he would write one day. No, certainly he was correct not to ruin his creative mood, and wise to do or say nothing except hold her hand as he allowed his teeming thoughts to wander far away to the Scotland of Mary Queen of Scots and the Granada of Muley Aben El Hassan.

Sefchen was now aware that, without him, she would be unable to live. Holding his hand, she felt happier than she had ever been. One thought alone troubled her conscience. He had told her the secrets of his childhood, while she had kept back a particular secret – why she did not know. It was as if a secret voice had forbidden her to speak, but now, with Harry holding her hand, she decided to be honest. The decision made, she squeezed his hand, which made him look at her with delight. It was the first time she had shown any physical response to his touches.

'I wish to tell you something . . .' she managed to begin, '. . . since you've given me a beautiful poem, and told me everything about your life, and how unhappy you were when the boys teased you at school.'

She breathed heavily, as if overcoming a physical restraint.

'It is this,' she said, speaking quickly. 'I don't remember how I felt when I left here, but I do remember knowing that one day I would return. When I actually came back and entered in at the side-gate, I felt as if someone welcomed me, and when my aunt opened the door and I carried in my baggage, I was sure there were two other people in the room. I was so certain I asked my aunt if anyone else was in the house. She only looked at me crossly and told me not to be fanciful, but I knew I was right, and that a man and a woman had welcomed me more warmly than she had. It was the only time I had ever known anyone to be pleased when I arrived anywhere, which was why I noticed it. Ever since I came back here, I have not dreamed I was an animal or a princess, as I used to in the forest, but these last few days I have dreamed of you often,' she said, turning her face away as she gripped his hand. 'But last night, you arrived in my dream with the couple, who then disappeared. He is a dark man with a strong jaw who looks at me in the same way you do. With him is a beautiful girl with long golden fair hair, who wears clothes I have never seen in any book. But since I wished to dream of you, I made them disappear, although I don't think they wished to go, and I could feel them wanting something from me. I don't know what it is, but I'm sure they expect me to help them.'

Harry mused for a moment and remembered the ancient legend of the couple who had died by the falling stones in the church. Was this girl, he wondered, one of those rarities who can get in touch with the dead? He looked at her with an increased interest, mastering his excitement with difficulty. The idea that she could clearly see and hear two spirits of whom he was only vaguely aware filled his mind with delightfully macabre fancies. When he was younger, he would get out of bed, excited to frenzy by the story of the *Castle of*

Otranto or the works of Mrs Radcliffe and stride up and down his bedroom, talking loudly until his mother came in and sternly told him to go back to his bed and took his books away. Bereft, he would lie dreaming of castles, secret passages and the call of death which had often excited Goethe as a youth.

How he wished that he could share her power to associate with the other world. Perhaps she would teach him! As the same time, he was pleased that he now understood the desperate love of Werther for the dull Lotte. Surely he himself was entranced by a nereid who had entwined him in inexplicable love? He looked at her out of the corner of his eye and wondered, for the second time, if she could be a lamia. No! But she was, without question, summoning him back into the Gothic past, and he knew he was too young to resist. Would he, like Werther, kill himself? The idea entranced him, and he thought with satisfaction of the sorrow it would cause his parents and his sister and brothers. Certainly his father would miss him. Tears came to his eyes at the thought of their sadness when he died. He looked at Sefchen again and knew she would join him. He could feel new poems growing, and in his mind the family of executioners had come to represent the avengers of Germany, the destroyers of the aristocrats, the precursors of a German renaissance. His thoughts confused and overwhelmed him and made him long to be alone.

He stood up suddenly and left Sefchen again sad and disappointed as he only kissed her hand in a hurried way and walked off without looking back, declaiming to the Abbey walls as he went. But that night he dreamed she was dead and woke broken-hearted. As the following day was a holiday, he practically ran to the Abbey and, as soon as he saw her, cried out: 'You are alive! Tell me, did your aunt bring back the sword yesterday?'

She shook her head. 'No, she's not coming home until tonight.'

'But she is bringing it back!' he repeated in ecstasy. 'We must examine it as soon as possible.'

He felt a flood of gratitude and told her how he loved her with all his heart, which brought tears to her eyes and which, in turn, made him decide it wasn't the moment to tell her that he was in a few weeks' time to be sent away. He could not face hurting her feelings and, looking round, saw that they were standing in a small square of undulating grass in what had at one time been the Abbey's cloisters. The area was now occupied by a colony of rabbits, who kept the grass cropped short, creating the effect of a lawn. Harry's spirit immediately soared. He hardly knew how to dance, but said: 'What a place to dance in! Can you?'

She shook her head. Six months ago the question would have confounded her, but she had read of women dancing, of girls dancing. Why shouldn't she do so?

'I can try,' she said.

'Well,' he said. 'See if you can follow these steps.'

She did not realize he was a poor dancer, and, to her ignorant eyes, his feet moved gracefully over the turf. She thought she could follow his movements. He paused, bowed to her and said: 'Will my princess of the woods grant me the honour of a dance?'

'Yes,' she said bowing, for that morning she felt possessed of a determination to live. His hand touched her waist and somehow she managed to follow his erratic, stumbling steps. To an onlooker, it might have appeared a graceless scene, but to Sefchen it was the most wonderful moment of her life.

'You are a marvel,' he said, and, bowing, stepped backwards into a rabbit hole and fell on his back. Her first reaction was fear that he might be hurt, but he sat up with such a comical look of surprise on his face that she became amused, at which his whole face changed and he jumped up, shouting: 'You smiled! For the first time, you truly smiled naturally, instead of showing your teeth!' and he whirled her round and about.

She could not help laughing and felt utterly happy as they leapt about until he sat down exhausted. Yet again Harry's mood seemed to undergo an instant change as he said: 'Last night I lay awake thinking of you, counting the hours, talking to the clocks, begging them to stay still. For each time I was about to sleep, their striking roused me. I thought how alike you and I are. Both outcasts: you in a forest and I among people. You remember how you told me that you used to talk to foxes and hares? Well, I used to speak to mice in my bedroom and explain to them my unhappiness. I don't think they understood, for they would only listen if I put down a bit of cheese. And when they had eaten it, however interesting my conversation, they would run away. The world has rejected us both, and I am happy with you because I am able to tell you shaming secrets which I have told to no one else, not even my father, who's growing old and muddled.'

He saw a chance of tactfully bringing up his departure without it seeming to be his choice, and he described how the dear old man was growing increasingly depressed, sometimes sitting by the window without even a book in his hand, thinking. He was about to add that this meant he must start to support the family, when his eye caught, through a gap in the trees, a number of iron bars sticking out of the back of the Abbey and leading up to the gap at the top of the Gothic window. At once, everything else was forgotten.

'What are those?' he shouted, getting up and leading her by the hand until they stood beneath the walls. On either side of the remaining window remnants, the rusty irons stuck out of the stonework, while, every few feet, holes had been made in the masonry as if larger irons had been placed there to bear heavy weights. As he studied their pattern, he saw smaller bars climbing up the building and ending at the gaping space at the top of the centre window.

Since Sefchen had known them ever since she was a child, she had never given them a thought. She shook her head and replied, 'I've no idea what they are.'

But he was trembling with excitement, and she could not help noticing how the least innovation set off in him a nervous reaction which made him concentrate with fervour on small and unimportant things.

'I cannot imagine,' he said slowly, 'what they were for. Ah, yes, I see!' he then cried excitedly. 'The large iron bars were for hauling up masonry and plaster. The small ones were a rough ladder to the top. Look at the holes everywhere – the irons have been moved many times. Yes, yes, it reinforces the legend told about this place, which, of course, you know.'

She shook her head.

'Well, I felt sure you must have been told. Anyhow, before I knew your aunt, I heard how, years before, the wife of the man who built the house was killed by a falling stone. To prevent the same thing happening to him, he planned to block up the arches, but before they could finish filling in the central window, where you can see the opening now, a stone fell and killed him. So, of course, it was left as it is. How interesting, how interesting. It proves the legend!'

He tried to dance with her again, but she only said: 'No, no. It's a dreadful story.'

'Well, yes,' he said. 'Of course, it was very sad. I wonder where they buried them.'

Sefchen, remembering her father's death, suggested: 'The priests' burial ground is on the right at the front of the Abbey.'

He looked doubtful. 'No, I don't think they'd have buried them there.' He took out his watch and said with alarm: 'I'll have to hurry home. My mother's bad-tempered if I'm late for meals, and even my father's bad-tempered nowadays.'

It cheered him that he had evaded telling her he must soon be leaving Düsseldorf, and he continued: 'I wonder, when will your aunt be back? I can't call tomorrow. Examinations. Try and get her to go out on the day after, and then we'll be able to examine the sword. How exciting!'

His eyes shone again with enthusiasm as he knelt, took her hand and kissed it. She felt a return of the intense happiness which made it an agony to watch him walking away through the trees, reciting to himself verses of his ballad.

Happy Harry was coming back in a few days, she started to read Goethe's *Elective Affinities*, which he had given her for her self-education. Several times she had felt, despite his denials, that he found her ignorance irritating, so she ploughed on through the book with determination, but found it very difficult to understand the characters of the baron and his wife, who seemed to belong to a depressingly artificial world. She wondered whether she would ever possess the intellect to talk to people untouched by the realities of nature. Obstinately she struggled on, but sometimes she found her mind straying back to the forests and the heroes of the fairy tales. But then she remembered how much she loved Harry and turned back to her book, but was secretly relieved when her aunt arrived with the rusty sword, which they spent the evening cleaning as it lay safely under a lead weight on the kitchen table.

11

When Harry arrived home, he found a letter written on thick white paper from his Uncle Salomon announcing simply, and he thought rudely, that instead of going to Hamburg, he was to proceed to Frankfurt, 'to learn by practical experience the principles of trading'. After Christmas, he would be expected in Hamburg.

The letter, which could, he thought, have been written to any clerk, sent Harry into a violent rage and he tore it into little bits and decided to write a rude reply. But, the next morning, all his plans were upset by an unexpected event. He told Sefchen what had happened in a note brought to the Abbey by a boy on the next evening.

This morning, when I went in as usual to kiss my father's hand, I saw to my alarm that he was leaning forward in his chair, a curious gurgling sound coming from his open mouth. Frightened, I ran forward and tugged at his arm to see if he was ill. My action must have upset his balance, and to my horror he fell forward on to the floor and lay on his back, his body twitching as foam appeared at the corners of his mouth. Horrified, I ran to my mother, who came into the room with an expressionless face and said shortly: 'Again.' She told me to go on to school and sent one of the maids to fetch the doctor. I shall never forget this morning and the uncertainty of whether my father was dying. I thought the day would never end, and although I am sure that I knew the answers to all the questions in the examination, I can't say now if I wrote them down. Directly our time was up, I jumped out from my desk and bolted for home. 'How is he?' I asked the little maid in the passage. 'Oh, the master's better,' she said carelessly. 'He's taking a dish of tea.'

Imagine my relief. I shall see you in two days.

Your loving Harry

As soon as Harry had heard the good news, he leaned back against the wall and placed his hand on his heart with relief, and went down on his knees to thank God, although, not being sure in which god he believed, he said: 'Thank you, all you gods,' which pleased him and made him smile. He ran into his father's room, radiant with happiness, to see the old man putting down his dish and gazing at him with kind eyes set in a placid face which bore no resemblance to the choking, slobbering wreck it had looked that morning. He asked Harry gently about his school work and gave him tea before he allowed him to slip away to ask his mother what had happened. She told him to sit down and looked at him severely, as she had done in the old days, when he knew he would get a box on the ears if he couldn't provide an adequate explanation for one of his crimes.

'Now, I must ask you to be good enough not to tell the younger children, for, you must remember, you are your father's heir and their support. Your father is what is called an "epileptic". He has these spasms occasionally, but soon gets over them, and the doctor has told me not to worry since more people than anyone could guess suffer from the same illness in this town. But, Harry, I do worry, and I'm glad you're going to Frankfurt, for your father's business is going from bad to worse, even if he won't admit it. He still insists on going into fancy goods which he himself thinks pretty instead of the fashionable materials folk wish to buy. The first lesson to learn in business is that you cannot be moved by sentiment or pity, as you will shortly learn. I beg you to work hard, for his attacks have increased in numbers over the past few months and his business sense seems more out of control than ever. I know you have to remain at school for another week, but as soon as you can, please go down to see the head clerk at the business and ask him to show you round, for you must prepare yourself to take your father's place . . . one day.'

'But will Father die?'

'No, no. There's no question of it. The doctor says he should live many years, but it may be that you will need to support him.'

'Oh, I would like that!' cried Harry. 'Mother, I promise you to work hard, even if I hate business, and I will buy a golden chair for Papa and anything he wants.'

'Enough of such nonsense,' his mother said sharply. 'You'll be as bad as your father if you go on in this ridiculous way. I despair of you. Oh, I despair of you both,' and she burst into tears.

On the day that Harry received the shock of seeing his father in an epileptic fit, Sefchen and the Meistereen had been setting out for Düsseldorf. The previous evening, after cleaning the sword, as they ate their sparse dinner of soup, her aunt leaned across the table and put on the look which, Sefchen knew, meant she was about to ask a favour, even if it was only a simple task such as taking the bread out of the bin or throwing corn to the chickens.

'Well, dearest,' she began in her whining voice, 'you know that I'm growing old and crotchety.'

Sefchen knew she was not, even though she would often put on a limp and talk about her poor leg, but directly anything caught her interest, her infirmity would be forgotten and she would run about without a twinge of pain.

'My leg hurts cruel sometimes, but as you know,' and the little beady eyes fixed themselves on her niece, 'I have to work hard and go to the shop four days a week, although it's a strain, a great strain. The cobbles are wicked on my feet, and I wonder, dear one, if in future you might serve in the shop twice a week, while I go on the other two days. I only open in the mornings, after all, and some days nobody calls. But my hours are known, and business can appear at any time, especially now all those who aided the French are unpopular. Anyway, if you agree . . . and I'm sure you won't refuse an old woman who's never done you an unkindness, for I never have, have I?' and she looked at Sefchen, who shook her head. 'Well, then, tomorrow we shall go and I will show you the way and tell you what's to be done. I promise you that working for me will be easy, especially as you like reading. There's a pile of books in the parlour which I've never looked at, but I'm sure they are valuable. You're free to read any time you like. We will start out at seven. A customer's due at nine and my bad leg makes me walk slowly.'

Sefchen woke up twice in the night, dreading the next day. She could not forget the last time when she had visited a town and was pelted with stones. Then she jumped and remembered, trembling, the boy at the gate who had cut off her doll's head. Her fears made her think of Harry, who had said she should smile at people, so she practised smiling, and was pleased at how naturally and effortlessly this gesture was beginning to come to her.

They set out at a sharp pace early next morning, her aunt's pains forgotten as she talked incessantly, as they walked along the verge of the dusty road, about how important it was for Sefchen to look her best, and added, 'I have to admit that, despite the fanciful way you dress, you're a beautiful girl, and beauty, like everything else, is not to be wasted, for it lasts only a short time and afterwards can never be recalled.'

When they reached the gateway to the town, she turned to deal with Sefchen's hair and combed out the ringlets, which fell round to the front of her neck, telling her meanwhile to wipe with a handkerchief the dust from the corners of her eyes, for 'men minded the oddest little things'.

'Now, there's nothing to be afraid of, child,' she said. 'There's order kept in this town, and you have nothing to fear here as you had near that savage forest. They may not like us, but they won't molest us, for they fear I'll put a curse on them if they do. Ah, if only I could! Although I'm not saying there aren't things I could do to make them think. There's plenty I can teach you if you want to learn, but you're young yet, and maybe somehow you'll get on in the world and not need to rely on craft to bring you a little money.'

Sefchen always noticed how, whenever her aunt spoke of money, she always said how little she had, or how little she made. She supposed that that was why they rarely had anything to eat except soup and dishes of eggs and vegetables. She had hoped the gold which she had given her aunt might have made her feel secure, but apparently it had not.

After Sefchen had been smartened up, they walked down a cobbled street with, on either side, houses whose top storeys of wood and plaster overhung the swept stone pavements. It was not yet eight o'clock, but now and again maids could be seen looking out of windows, shaking dusters. Some, she noted, shut the windows quickly as they saw them approaching, while others gave little waves. On one occasion, a maid in a white cap pointed in front of them, leaned out on the windowsill, and placed her forefinger to her mouth, suggesting silence, then pointed again. Her behaviour puzzled Sefchen, but not her aunt, who said: 'Ah, she's a customer. She's in love with a boy who ends his apprenticeship next year, and is anxious to know if he'll marry her, but she does not want to be seen, so we'll wait a moment beyond this porch. You see. She'll be down in a minute.'

And, sure enough, a plain girl with thick limbs and a worried look on her shining pink face came stepping cautiously out of the door and ran, her skirts held up, down the street towards them.

'Good day, fair one,' said her aunt, putting on her smiling face. 'All keeps well with you, I hope. I warned you your young man would be as difficult as all young men are. Has anything happened to cause you concern?'

'Well, he will talk of moving to Darmstadt,' said the girl with a blushing glance at Sefchen. 'I'd not mind if we were engaged, but if he goes and we're not, he's sure to be snared elsewhere, or so my mother says. She tells me never to trust men's promises.'

'Your mother's a wise woman,' said the Meistereen, shaking her head. 'There's many that's got into trouble for believing men's false words. Don't forget, child,' she added, gripping the girl's wrist, 'to tell your mother I say she's a wise woman, will you?'

The girl nodded and went on: 'Mother says as the first potion has worked and he says nice things to me, that I should bind him further by a spell, and asks can she and I come and see you some time?'

'Why, yes, of course, yes,' said her aunt. 'But not today, because my niece Sefchen, here, is coming to take some of the work off a poor old woman's shoulders. But tomorrow, come tomorrow. Do you do the shopping?'

'Yes.'

'Well, slip away then, and if you walk quickly down my street, no one will know. What time's easiest for you to be at my house? Between nine and ten?'

'Around half past,' said the girl.

'That'll be convenient. I'll see you both then. But wait. Tell your mother...' and she again reached out and caught the girl's arm in her bird-like claw hand as she whispered, pulling the girl closer, 'that the last time only silver changed hands, so bring gold this time. Then, my sweet, I will bind him to you safe, and eighteen months hence, you'll be carrying his child.'

The girl flushed bright red and, disengaging herself, ran away.

'She'll be there, all right,' said her aunt, 'and her mother with her. She has a comfortable time as her husband's often away, giving her opportunities to make money,' she cackled.

As they continued, the streets gradually began to fill with people leaving for work. The old men greeted each other in silence, gravely lifting their hats, but the women, with shopping baskets on their arms, collected in little groups and whispered into each other's ears. Nobody spoke to the Meistereen, and some, it seemed to Sefchen, slyly turned their backs on them, while watching them keenly out of the corners of their eyes as they passed. But this was bearable, and nobody looked as if they would dream of throwing a stone. Sefchen felt easier and started to look with interest at the big town, to which she lived so close but had never seen since she was a child.

She found herself fascinated, not only by the tall, overhanging houses, the glistening door knobs, the scrupulously clean streets, but also by the variety of life, as she gazed at the men with barrows and donkey carts who collected the refuse from the houses and street corners where other workmen had brushed the dirt into neat piles. As they walked down each street, she could not stop herself peering sideways into shops where hams and ropes of sausages hung from the ceilings. Once a dark little door opened and a little man in black came running out, carrying a book. Further on, a red-faced housewife, with a scarf tied over her head, was angrily pointing with her finger at some dirt sticking to the side of her front step, and called to her maid to bring soapy water. Sefchen couldn't take her eyes off the smart carriages which rolled by, and the carts arriving from the country, laden with vegetables. She shook her head and was excited by the bustle and movement.

'Now, remember the way, dear,' said her aunt. 'You turn right here, then first left after the church,' and she showed Sefchen a neat building with pillars at the front and a tall pointed top. They turned down an unpaved street which was not so clean as the rest of the town. At the bottom her aunt stopped and went up two steps to open a door where she started sniffing. 'No, there's been no one here. Sometimes folk forge keys, but they don't dare to come in here, for I spread it around the Plague will catch them if they do,' and she pointed to certain letters carved over the door. She led Sefchen upstairs and into a cluttered room where she could vaguely see a long table with a high chair on one side and a low bench on the other. These were the only pieces of furniture, except for a large cupboard against the inner wall.

'Now, Sefchen dear, I will take you into my parlour,' and she led her across the top of the stairs to another light little room which overhung the street and showed her a small trapdoor which lifted up so she could study any visitor on the doorstep. Pointing to a brown pile of books in a corner, she said: 'Now, my dear, read for an hour or two. I only have one visitor for certain, and she's as punctual as a clock. Stay in here, and don't on any account wander.'

She looked as if she was about to add something fierce, but instead gave Sefchen one of her crafty smiles. When she had gone, Sefchen looked at the books, but since they were written in Latin, she neither understood them nor liked their musty smell of rotting paper. When she put them down again, she found her hands covered with dust, so clapped them together and took off her mantle and dusted the dirt off her green dress with a handkerchief. As she sat in the window, looking along the street, she heard movements from the next room and the opening and shutting of the cupboard. A few minutes later, she saw a long way away a pale young girl come walking hurriedly towards the house. She stopped outside the front door, and stood shifting from foot to foot as if trying to make up her mind. Suddenly, without warning, she jumped up the steps and banged twice on the knocker. Her aunt hurried downstairs and brought her quickly up again. A long silence was broken by a cry and the sound of soothing murmurs. Later, there was a clinking of glasses, and a few moments afterwards the sound of the two women going downstairs. Sefchen could not resist peeping through the little trapdoor, and saw her aunt go down the steps and look up the street before beckoning to the girl, who came slowly out of the house, extended her hand to the Meistereen and walked unsteadily away, keeping close to the houses for support. Her aunt watched until the girl had turned the corner, when she opened her hand and looked at a coin, and shook her head as if at her stupidity. Then she reclimbed the steps, closed the door, mounted the stairs and once again began to open and shut doors and cupboards. Eventually she came in smiling, a satisfied look on her face, and said: 'I'll sit with you an hour, although I'm expecting no one else today. Yet visitors do come unexpectedly, and I shouldn't want to miss them. I hope you'll do the same,' and she cocked her eyebrows.

Sefchen made herself nod and watched as her aunt sat in the window and looked out, keenly studying the occasional pedestrian. She seemed to know everybody and commented on their appearances freely, remarking a woman's dog must have died, as she had never seen her without it before, and that a young girl who emerged from a house opposite was two months expectant from the way she walked.

'I can always tell, sometimes before the girls themselves.'

At eleven o'clock, she told Sefchen to sit where she was and went into the other room. Afterwards, they closed the parlour shutters together and walked back up the street. Again Sefchen noticed that, although the townsfolk turned their backs on them, they would always look at them out of the corners of their eyes and whisper once they had passed. There was one notable exception: a young man wearing a high hat curled at the brim and smart dark blue coat. He stood at a corner, lackadaisically twirling a gold-topped stick, scanning the passers-by with bored scorn. She thought that she had never seen anyone as proud, with such assurance and confidence.

To Sefchen's surprise, as they drew close, he came to life and turned to stare at her openly, unlike Harry making no attempt to conceal his admiration. She felt herself flushing scarlet. To her annoyance, the moment before they came level with him, her aunt caught her leg in her dress and fell. The young man simply continued to stare blatantly at Sefchen as she struggled to lift her aunt, who eventually creaked herself upright, groaned and, walking very slowly on, whispered: 'Look straight ahead, dear, and lift up your chin.'

Without knowing why, she did as she was told, and as she passed felt rather than saw the young man's eyes trying to make her look at him. Within minutes, her aunt's leg was mended again, and by a quarter to twelve they were back at the Abbey.

For the rest of the day, Sefchen could not think of anything except the town, the glimpses of shops through doors, the discreet displays in bow windows, and the brazen man swinging his cane and staring. Her mind raced from one subject to another, and she thought and rethought each of the morning's encounters. In the evening, the boy brought from Harry the letter telling of his father's illness and recovery, which brought her heart into her mouth and made her fear she would not see Harry until the next day.

But in the morning she woke up excited and certain she would see him. As she ate her simple breakfast in the kitchen, Sefchen looked her aunt straight in the face and said: 'Mr Heine will be coming to see me today. He's anxious to be shown my grandfather's sword.'

Her aunt remained perfectly still, a slice of pumpernickel half-way to her mouth, her eyes wide open with surprise so that Sefchen noticed what small pupils she had.

'You told him about that?' she asked, leaning forward, the piece of bread and cheese still gripped in her hand. 'Ah, so you've become close friends, then? Well, let me offer one word of warning. The family business doesn't prosper and they say that young Heine's to be sent away to learn the trade, for his father's ailing and given to fits.'

The news he might be going to leave came like a slap in the face to Sefchen, and she sat back in dismay. Could this be true? With her aunt, she never knew what to believe, but her doubts increased as the old woman went on: 'You know, you'd be wiser, far wiser, to turn your attention to that young baron who looked at you in the street where I hurt my knee yesterday. There's real money there, and breeding – true, aristocratic breeding. Of course, there's no marriage,' she leered, 'but then you're not looking for marriage, are you, dear? Young Baron Muchien will, I know, make inquiries about you in the town, and they say that he pays well for his pleasures, even if he is proud and a young fool. But he'll need to lay his money on the table, and much of it, for those grand folk can't have everything their way as they used to.'

Sefchen stood up, hating the way her aunt talked about her as if she were a horse for sale or one of her horrible little packages. She walked out into the open air, but she thought she had better go back and ask her aunt nicely to show Harry the sword, as she knew how upset and disappointed he'd be if it was locked away again when he came. Swallowing her repulsion, she went back into the room and made her request, looking down on her aunt in a way which made the Meistereen wince and mutter under her breath, 'No offence, no offence. You're such a sensitive creature.'

'I said,' Sefchen repeated, 'when Harry comes today he'd like to see the sword.'

'Yes, dear, of course. But be sure to take great care, for as I've told you, you must not tamper with it or dangerous things, very dangerous things, will follow. You know how careful I was cleaning it.'

Sefchen assured her she would take every care, but the old woman continued to worry. 'Take no liberties with it. There are those who say it's an old folks' tale that such swords have a thirst for blood. I don't know. I've heard strange tales, and your cousin Maximilian nearly cut off his own leg playing the fool before a cutting, and he's as skilled a swordsman as there is to be found.'

Sefchen always found herself trying to like her aunt, but it went against the grain, and now, following her glimpse of the town, she had a longing to leave the Abbey. If Harry was to leave, perhaps he would take her with him. She would not mind what happened so long as they could be together, and she knew she would follow him to the end of the world.

The Meistereen, rapidly recovering her spirits, went on to say: 'Anyhow, I think you're a sensible girl who won't grant Heine any liberties, especially now that his father's business is in trouble. What a strange boy he is, always mooning on about romances and battles and songs. I can't see him making a tradesman himself. How he'll live, I'm sure I don't know. You don't make gold out of songs. You'll go along to my shop tomorrow, won't you?'

Sefchen nodded and thanked her aunt politely and went to sit in the sun and study pictures of dresses as she had decided she should dress more like other girls. Perhaps, if only she dared, she would go into a shop and study the latest fashion. She knew she could copy anything after a glance. Or perhaps she could get some new pictures. Maybe Harry would bring her some. She felt excited by the idea and found the dresses she had worn for years distasteful. The thought cheered her up, and she looked forward, with excitement, to Harry's arrival, and recited, so she could please, verses from his ballad which she had learned by heart. She flushed with pleasure that she, who only a year before had been little better than an animal in the forest, could inspire such a young man to write such clever words.

It was not until late into the afternoon that he arrived. She heard his approach as she sat in the kitchen, a momentary shower having driven her indoors, singing verses of his ballad as he came through the Abbey. First it was just a sound, and then, as he walked up the old nave, she heard snatches of words interrupted by the wind. Not until he was close to the house did she catch a whole verse:

> 'Blow fell on blow; between each stroke
> She sang her song of axe and oak
> "O iron of mine, O bright iron shine
> And neatly cut the coffin fine!" '

He walked into the kitchen, flung himself down at her knees and, seizing her hand, kissed it and sang:

> 'Then slowly to her side I drew
> And said, "I pray you tell me true,
> Young maiden strange and wondrous fair
> For whom is made the coffin here?" '

He shouted out the last line at the top of his voice, making her smile, at which he laughed with pleasure and, jumping to his feet, shouted again: 'Is the sword here, is the sword here? I have been thinking of it all night. Did you know that all common criminals were hanged and the sword was only used for officers and gentlemen and the cursed nobility? I have decided that when I make a great fortune . . .' he had been about to say 'in Frankfurt', but drew himself up in time, '. . . I shall buy it from your aunt and hang it up over our fireplace and gaze at it every day as an instrument as noble as the guillotine which cut off the vilest heads in France.'

When he talked in this angry way, Sefchen would sit and wait quietly for him to finish. She did not criticize his animosities, but thought of them as a part of him which, because of her stupidity, she could not understand. But, seeing that he was only thinking of the sword, she stood up and said: 'Come, I'll show it you. Though why you should be so interested in such a great ugly thing, I don't know.'

She unlocked the door to her father's old study, which was now used by her aunt for her strange trades. On one side of the room was a counter, and above it rows of shelves stacked with glass jars of bottled herbs and powders labelled with such names as 'Wolfsbane', 'Mandrake' and 'Rhino Horn', while the fullest jar of all was labelled 'Oris Powder'. Higher up stood toads and snakes in bottles of clear spirit, viper's venom in a phial and several bottles marked only with a single capital letter. When Harry saw the collection, he nearly danced with pleasure.

'Ah, but she is a witch, she is a witch!' he cried, throwing back his head and laughing. 'As I told you, she rubbed spittle on my head as a child and saved me from going mad when someone said I was good-looking. My goodness, what objects! But where is the sword? Ah, magnificent,' he said, looking across the room where the huge weapon, over five feet long and still rusty, hung by a piece of leather to a metal rod in the wall. 'Ah, what a blade. And to think that the hundred heads it cut off all belonged to tyrants!'

Suddenly he leapt forward and, seizing the weapon, said: 'Why does she think it would turn on me? Let's take it outside. There's no room to swing it in here, and I should like to feel the power of this hero who's cut off the heads of the oppressors of the poor.'

Directly they left the house, he at once lifted the sword above his head, but remained motionless and quickly laid it down.

'It's true,' he said. 'It's quite extraordinary, but I'm sure this sword possesses some power of its own, a special strength. Feel it for yourself.'

Sefchen eyed it doubtfully. Perhaps it had served good purposes, but lately she had begun to feel a hatred for her family's profession. Now that she knew Harry, the cousins who had asked for her hand seemed utterly repulsive and to be avoided at any price. She would rather have died than marry any of them, and although, in the forest, animals killed each other to live, she realized now that her family killed for profit, which was different. At the same time, she felt a surprising interest and desire to hold it, and as she took the handle in her hands, she felt with a start it was a sharp living magical weapon and, what was more, was asking her to use it, saying: 'Show him, show him you have the power and that I'm to be trusted with you but not with him!'

Also to her surprise, there was nothing malevolent in the sword's message. She felt rather that it was only expressing gratitude to her as one of the family who had used it so skilfully, and telling her to excite her young friend, who so admired success and passion. Not certain she was her own mistress, she found herself raising the sword and swinging it around Harry's head as he stood transfixed, his eyes full of a fearful love she had never seen before. At the same moment, there came into her head the words of the old song. She altered them to fit the moment, and sang with a certainty and a strength she did not know she possessed as she whirled the huge weapon about his ears:

> 'Dear Harry, dear Harry,
> Thou, sure shalt not the last one be –
> Say, wish you to hang on the lofty tree?
> Or wish you to swim in the dark blue sea?
> Or would you kiss the naked sword,
> Given to us by our Lord?'

And then she heard herself perfectly imitating his voice:

> 'I wish not to hang on the lofty tree;
> I wish not to swim in the dark blue sea;
> I wish to kiss the naked sword,
> Given to us by our Lord.'

The spirit went out of her. She rested the sword's point on the ground and, putting one hand on the handle, leaned against it, resting. Harry seemed to awaken and shake himself out of the trance into which they had been lured by the weapon, and as she stood still, he suddenly moved quickly forward, put one arm round her back and jerked her hand up, causing the sword to fall to the ground, where it lay rattling in protest but admitting its impotence to do more for its new mistress. Then he began to fondle her, kissing her on the forehead, cheeks and hair, and lastly the mouth, which closed as his lips touched hers. She felt sure that possession of her had passed from the sword to the young man. He kissed her on the mouth again and, despite herself, her lips opened to him and she felt she was falling into a pit from which she was only saved by his arm around her back. Gently he stroked her forehead and led her to the seat outside the door, saying quietly: 'I love you, and will always love you, now that I associate you with the emblem of freedom. Ah, you should have seen yourself, waving that mighty blade! You were the very picture of liberty carrying the sword of justice.'

She was silent, but leant back against the wall, trying to recover from the experience, which had shaken her out of herself, and made her capable of anything, even cruelty. She realized that if Harry ever left her, there would be no alternative to death. He brought her back to life by saying, in an urgent voice she had never heard before: 'I have not been honest with you. I have not told you that next month I have to leave for Frankfurt for three months to learn the business of banking and to gain commercial experience. I think next year my uncle will set me up in business. My father's fit has made me realize it's my duty to support my family and make a fortune. When I have – which I will do quickly, for I cannot bear to wait long – I shall elope with you to America, the country of freedom.'

'I will go where you go,' she said simply.

He did not appear to hear and went on: 'While I am in Frankfurt, I promise you to come back twice. I shall say it is to visit my father, but it will be to see you. I pledge myself to you, now and for ever.'

He looked at the sword and she saw that he was about to swear by it. Instead, he gave a little shiver and, changing his mind, kissed her hand and turned to walk away, this time singing a plaintive love song. Once she saw him look upwards and wave condescendingly at the trees moving in the wind. She was sure that he thought they were bowing to him. As he turned out of sight, she suddenly remembered a question she had bravely decided to ask him. Determination conquering shyness, she ran swiftly and caught him up at a bend on the path.

He turned at the sound of her rustling dress and saw a vision of beauty, with red locks flying, green eyes flashing, running towards him. Opening his arms, he caught her and held her to him, crying out: 'You are Daphne, I Apollo! The position is reversed, and you are chasing me, and I am going to turn us both into trees. You will bear blood-red berries each year, and we shall live as one for eternity!'

Again he kissed her and she lay weak in his arms. She had not understood what he had said about turning her into a tree, but she knew he had declared passionate love. It was several moments before, blushing, she had the chance to ask the question which had urged her to pursue him.

'Oh, Harry, will you be kind and go to a milliner and fetch me pictures of new dresses? I want to copy one for myself.'

Tears came into his eyes, and he could only nod his head. Kissing her quickly on the forehead, he said goodbye again and almost ran to the gate.

12

That night the sword disturbed her dreams. To begin with, it said it was going to cut off Harry's head, and for a long time she argued tearfully he was her friend. At last it stood on end, and the handle leaned forward and made what she eventually realized were three bows. Then it stated that it accepted him in that role, but if he proved false, he would pay with his blood. She was so relieved that she stopped dreaming, woke up and could not sleep again because of her fears of going into town by herself in the morning.

She set out at seven, when the mist was still hanging about the old walls, making the motionless branches of the widespreading oak trees look ghostly not animated and alive as on windy days when they still, as in her childhood, brushed against the chimneys with a rasping note that suggested clawing hands. Looking upwards as she left the Gothic ruins, she imagined the trees as grasping the fog and holding it as a prisoner who would otherwise disappear. She thought she was right when she reached the old wooden gate, and could faintly see through the mist over the far fields the colourless rising sun.

A townsman on his way to Düsseldorf later told how he had seen, near the Abbey, a green spirit materializing out of the mist. She had been above average height, with a slender waist and surprisingly large bosoms which he had glimpsed beneath an open thick black cloak which half-hid a curious costume which clung closely to the shape of the body, except for a square of bare skin that ran in a straight line above the breasts. He had shut his eyes and crossed himself, which made the lamia, he swore, vanish again into the mist; which was true, for Sefchen, self-conscious in her costume, had walked as fast as she could to try to arrive unseen at the shop. Trying to improve her appearance, she had wound a piece of lace about her forehead, but her long red ringlets fell as before over her shoulders, the ends pulled as usual forward round her neck, creating a startling impression which she would have avoided had she been conscious of its effect.

As she neared the outskirts of the town, she looked about her with a nervousness which increased as she neared the outlying houses. When two young men came out on their way to work, she faltered and stopped, wondering if she should turn and run back to the safety of the Abbey. But a contrary thought changed her mind, and she hurried on with lengthening strides, head erect, heart beating, eyes staring straight ahead and forced herself to re-enter her childhood dream world as, with a mixture of pride and horror, she recited aloud Harry's ballad, which, by now, she knew by heart.

'A fearful dream I had last night
Of chilling joy and fearful fright.
I still see clear its ghostly shape
I fear I never may escape.

'I stood within a garden fair
And I was glad to wander there
And look upon pleasant flowers
That gave me hope of golden hours.

'Black birds were singing in the grove
Full many a charming song of love;
The sun shone with a golden light
On the flowers so gay and bright.

'Sweet perfumes stole among the trees,
While light and loving blew the breeze,
And all was gleaming, all was glad,
And all for me in splendour clad.

'And in this lovely flowery land
I saw a marble fountain stand;
And washing linen in the stream,
I saw a maiden in my dream.

'Pale cheeks, mild eyes, and glances faint,
She was the image of a saint;
But as I looked she quickly grew
A stranger, yet the girl I knew.

'As she washed her linen white,
The maiden sung to my delight:
"O water, water, run and shine!
And clean my linen neat and fine!"

'Then slowly to her side I drew,
And said, "O maiden, tell me true,
Fair as the lilies, tall and white,
For whom wash you this garment bright?"

' "Be ready soon!" she said aloud,
"It is for you I wash the shroud";
And scarcely had she said her say

When quick she parted from the day.

'And yet enchanted still I stood,
Deep in the dark and gloomy wood;
The trees to heaven branches raised
And I stood thinking all amazed.

'And hark! a distant echo rose,
As though some axe struck heavy blows,
In haste through brake and bush I run
And then into a clearing come.

'And central in the verdant space
A mighty oak stood in the place;
And see! the maiden strange and fair
Was hewing with a hatchet there!

'Blow fell on blow; between each stroke,
She sang her song to axe and oak:
"Iron of mine, bright iron shine
And neatly slice the coffin fine!"

'Then slowly to her side I drew,
And said, "I pray you tell me true,
Young maiden strange, and wondrous fair,
For whom make you the coffin there?"

' "Short time is left," she harshly spoke,
"I cut your coffin from this oak";
And scarcely had she said her say
When quick she parted from the day.

'Around me spread all dead and still
A barren heath without a hill;
I could not tell how came I there,
I could not understand my fear.

'And as I struggled on my way
A brighter place before me lay;
I hastened on, I hastened more,
And found the girl I sought before.

'The deathly white but fierce young maid
Now dug the earth with burial spade;
I hardly dared to look, for she

Was fair, yet fearful, still to me.

'And as she urged her task along,
She gently sang an elvish song:
"Spade, my spade, so sharp and tried,
Dig out the grave both deep and wide!"

'Then slowly to her side I drew,
And said: "I pray you, tell me true,
Young maiden strange and fair, and sweet,
What means this grave before our feet?"

'And quick she spoke, "Be still! it's true
This cool, deep grave I've dug for you!"
And when the lovely maid replied,
The grave before me opened wide.

'And as the opening pit I view
A freezing horror thrills me through
And plunging in its funeral night
I fall – but wake again to light.'

Even now, she did not understand some of the verses, and would have to ask
Harry to explain them, but what most enchanted and delighted her was at the
top he had written: 'Dedicated in admiration to the beautiful Sefchen'. She
would be forever grateful this handsome young man had written words which
enabled her, at will, to retreat into the secret world of romanticism which she
had created in the forest and to pass, unseeing, boys, and be ignorant of their
comic attitudes of fear when she drew near, and the affected way they ran, as if
for safety, across the road to cling on to each other in pretended alarm.

Her self-containment lasted until she was in the centre of the narrow
overhung streets of the old town, and was only interrupted by fear she might
go in the wrong direction. But, waking out of her dream, she saw with relief
she had not gone beyond the turning into the by-street at the end of which
stood her aunt's little house.

When she went to bed the night before, the Meistereen had said: 'Sefchen,
even though you're vague, you're a good girl, and since you're nearly grown, I
can trust you to go in my place, for a brewer's agent will be arriving at eight
o'clock. You'll have nothing to do but open the door with this key, climb the
stairs, and go into the back room I showed you, which looks out, as you know,
on to a blank stone wall, so you cannot be seen. You know you'll see there an
old black cupboard in the far corner, with various secret markings on its door.
Pay no attention. They are harmless. But woe betide you or any other who
opens those doors without my permission, for their future will be dogged by
ill-fortune. When you have unlocked the cupboard, open, with *this* key, the

second drawer on the extreme right of the second shelf. Inside you will find six little parcels. Each is done up in brown paper and tied with twine with knots set in red sealing wax.'

Sefchen took the left turn and walked down the street in a happier mood, thinking that, having passed safely through the main streets, she would now remain unnoticed until she reached the shop, but instead the front door of the biggest house in the street opened and a youngish woman with a wide round face, pushing a child before her, stepped down two steps on to the paving. Her large protruding bonnet was adorned with a profusion of lace which hid most of her face, and her free hand was pushed into a muff. All this Sefchen took in before the woman saw her. Instantly her fat, placid face froze into rigid lines. Galvanized into activity, she turned quickly about, almost tripping over the hem of her long skirt and, dragging the protesting child back into the house, slamming the door. Sefchen trembled with dismay at yet another scene of rejection which bitterly hurt her feelings. However, holding her head higher and, she hoped, more proudly, she walked on and opened the door to her aunt's house, went upstairs and carefully followed her aunt's instructions. Distastefully and quickly, she took the small, narrow parcels and dropped them on the table and, looking at her watch, saw she had only a few minutes to wait before the arrival of the brewer's agent.

'What's he like?' Sefchen had asked her aunt in the cold voice which she put on to hide her fears.

'Ah,' came the croaking reply. 'He's a merry man and a friend. Much business has he brought me, and he is to be trusted, as not all are, as you'll learn in life. He always deals with me himself, which is a golden rule. He's a stout, bluff hearty fellow, always with a jest on his lips. If he pinches your cheeks, that'll only be his playful way, for he's a kindly man or I wouldn't send you. To hear the way he talks, fast and loose about anything that comes into his head, you'd think he was gabby, but look at his eyes and you'll see how small they are and how he never laughs with them. That's a good sign. Always watch for it. It means a man is close and thoughtful.'

Sefchen sat down on one side of the table in her aunt's old oak chair and unsuccessfully practised smiling at the lower bench opposite. When her aunt had pointed out the differing heights she had added in a whining voice: 'When you grow older, my dear, you'll find there's always a difference of opinion between those who buy and those who sell, and to sit higher gives you the advantage. Remember that, dear. I only tell you things which will be useful to you later.'

Her thoughts were interrupted by a knocking downstairs. Again she did as she'd been told and went into the front room and opened the little trap to examine the visitor beneath. Since Sefchen did not know what a brewer's agent looked like, she thought this would be a waste of time, but was reassured by the sight of a stout figure resembling the man her aunt had described. Trembling, she ran downstairs, swallowing again and again with nervousness, and opened the door so sharply that she was flung back with it against the wall, and found, standing before her, a stout, red-faced man holding a round hat and wearing a French army coat and large boots. They gazed at each other silently a moment before he bowed and said, if he was not mistaken, she must be the Meistereen's neice, of whom he had heard so much.

She could only nod before turning to run upstairs as quickly as she could and sit on the far side of the table, her bosoms rising and falling as she gasped for breath. Steps followed behind her, and the man came into the room, glanced at the cupboard, sat on the bench, smiled, laid his hat on the table, leaned forward and said with a hearty laugh: 'There's no need to take fright, little one. I'll not eat you. You're much too pretty for that,' and he reached across the table to pinch her cheeks as her aunt had said he would.

Quickly, she sat back in her chair, which made him laugh.

'Oho, a shy one, are you? There'll be plenty to pinch those cheeks later, I'll warrant. But if it's business you want, then business you'll get,' and he banged his fist on the table and laughed again.

Sefchen looked up and saw how his little eyes remained cold and observant even as his face creased up with laughter. She put her hands nervously on the table by the parcels, ready, at any moment, to take them back if he tried to cover them. He did not move, but said: 'Ah yes, your shyness will pass. There'll be many asking for your hand, I don't doubt. Oh, but I'd forgotten . . .' and he stopped as if embarrassed.

Looking up again, Sefchen saw that he was laughing this time in a different way, and that his eyes held a look of apology, almost of regret. Puzzled, she looked down at her hands, wishing, with all her heart, the business was over and done with.

'It's six little parcels you have for me?'

She nodded.

'Each done up fine with wax and string, I see. She does things in style, does the woman of Goch.'

He picked up the parcels, gently tossing each one in the air before clenching his fist on them as if feeling their contents.

'Ah, but I'm satisfied without seeing them. She's an honest, trustworthy woman, your aunt, and reliable. There's many an innkeeper swears by her, but, I don't know . . . except it's not for me to question profitable goods,' and he chuckled again.

Sefchen did not look up, for she knew that all the sympathy would by now have gone out of his eyes.

'Well, I buy six parcels, for which I pay three pieces of gold. Is that what she told you? I have them, here in this purse. Do you want to see them?'

Terrified that he would seize her hand, Sefchen shook her head, and the man placed the parcels one by one in his side-pocket before getting to his feet.

'Oh, don't be afraid, child,' he said. 'I'm no ogre. But what white skin you have,' and his eyes stared intently. 'Here, take the gold,' and he tossed over a little bag. 'I'm as trustworthy as your aunt. You needn't open it. Well, lass, I hope to see you again some day. You're a sight for sore eyes, though you are fearful shy and cold as yet.'

He clamped his hat on his head and turned, and she heard him walk down the stairs and slam the door. Immediately, she ran into the front room and, peering into the street again, saw his back disappearing up the street. Relieved, she scurried downstairs to bolt the door before going to the window seat, for she could not abide the horrible little back room with its black cupboard covered in strange signs. She looked at her watch and saw it was half past ten. Not for anything would she go out until the midday hour, when the streets emptied of the dreaded figures who malevolently bustled about, only waiting to stare at her. No one else called, and by leaving at noon, Sefchen arrived back at the Abbey without being insulted.

From then on, and until his schooldays finished, Harry called daily, and even implored to be allowed to drop in and see her when she was working in her aunt's shop. She refused with an anger that silenced even his enthusiasm. There was something about her aunt's business room which made her bitterly ashamed and determined he should never see the little house. He understood, and from that moment his conversation was about his absence, how he could not live without her, and the continuation of her education while he was away. He said it was essential she should learn French, the most civilized language in the world, and he brought her his old grammars. She took them without enthusiasm. The task daunted her. How could she learn a foreign language? She had seldom heard a word of French spoken, and often misunderstood sentences in German and was sometimes puzzled by Harry's conversation. One day, she wrote down a list of words whose meaning she wished to have explained, and, to emphasize her ignorance, asked him four questions. The first concerned how long it took for children to be born, at which he blushed. The second inquired what sinful meant, at which his mouth fell open. The third asked why men and women married, and the fourth who was God? This last question drove him into a frenzy, and he walked about, shouting, 'It's very much a matter of opinion, but, in my eyes, God is the deity responsible for the wars that have ravaged Europe for the last eighteen hundred years, who has allowed the burning of towns and villages with children and old women inside them and ensured that every crossroads is marked with a dead body to frighten the poor into believing implicitly in his goodness.'

He ranted on and left her, when he had finished, with no idea what he had been talking about. She began to despair of herself, without understanding the fault lay in her beloved's confused teaching. It never entered her head he had no idea how to teach or make love to her, or indeed to control his imagination, which made truth to him as changeable as a tide. But meanwhile his desires persuaded him he loved Sefchen with his whole heart, and to show it bought her a five-year-old French history of fashion. She was filled with excitement and, within a fortnight, had made a new costume copied from the already outdated Empire style. When she first proudly wore it, the high waist hiding the shape of her body, Harry turned pale and indignantly declared he dreamed nightly of her in the old green dress, and whenever he came to see her, he hoped she would go on wearing it. Let her keep the Empire dress to wear when he was away. She was hurt and pleased.

They spent nearly all their time together outside the house, and the voices spoke more and more to Sefchen, warning her against Harry. She hoped it was not herself talking, and told him of the increasing dislike for him, which filled him with frightened pleasure.

'Look,' he said one day, suddenly shuddering as they walked out of the house, 'I felt that cold wind pass by again and I'm sure I saw a woman in the corner dissolve before my eyes! Ah, you may talk of classicism,' he said – and she never said she had – 'but this is wonderful. Ghosts hating me in an Abbey! If I was rich, do you know what I would do? I would send for Casper Friedrich. I know he's a Gothic painter, but he and his friends are, at the same time, part of the revival of German art and civilization. There's a renaissance in Germany now. I can smell it from underneath the coats of the princelings. The talents of the people are at last emerging, and I shall be this movement's leader!'

She listened sympathetically to his dreams and was sure he would be a great man, and when he described his egalitarian theories and the meaning of Hegelism, she would listen happily but uncomprehendingly. But, to her relief, as they came to know each other better, he talked less about politics and philosophy and more about himself and their future plans. Frequently, he'd begin to talk about her education, but she soon noticed that the conversation always ended up in his talking with shining eyes about his own beliefs and ambitions as she sat staring in admiring ignorance at the shape of his mouth and the waves of his hair. However, sometimes her ignorance shocked him. Once, when he told her that he was planning to write a section of a long ballad for her Christmas present, and had, in his mind, a picture of a bridegroom giving his bride a glass of wine which turned into his blood, she said distinctly (for if she spoke quietly he never heard), 'Which day is Christmas?'

'But surely you know.'

She shook her head. He questioned her at once and discovered how, in the forest, no day had ever been marked by celebrations of any kind. He jumped up and down with excitement.

'Really. No birthday presents?'

'No. All I know is that I was born in 1799. I don't even know when.'

'You have never had a Christmas present?'

'No, why?'

'Well, I thought everybody in Germany knew about Christmas or the birth of Christ's day. It's a national holiday, although, belonging to a Jewish family, we hold another feast day. But, for German children, Christmas is the most wonderful day of the year. A month before it, every child receives a picture with many little windows and door tabs sticking out of it. Each day they pull one of these and the door or window opens to show a different picture, twenty, nineteen, eighteen days to Christmas, and so on. Then, the night before Christmas Day, they hang stockings at the end of their beds for St Nicholas to fill with presents. Why he was chosen as the generous national godfather by the German forefathers I can't imagine, as he lived in Asia Minor and never gave anybody anything, except three golden balls to a man to stop his daughters becoming prostitutes, but that's never mentioned. At any rate, they now call him Santa Claus and say he sets off every Christmas Eve in a sledge piled with gifts and drawn by reindeers from somewhere up in the Arctic, which he must find very cold compared to Asia Minor, then he climbs down all the chimneys and fills up all the stockings. On Christmas Day, all men and women make up their quarrels and eat without stopping – pasties, roast geese, beef, turkeys. Even the poor are given feasts in workhouses and hospitals. Mother prepared a big lunch on that day, so we would not feel left out. Everyone gets drunk and merry, the children are naughty and nobody minds, and then, you know, the idea of a Christmas tree . . . but, of course, you won't. Anyhow, the German tree has gone all over the world and presents are hung on it in both America and Russia.'

The next time he came, he brought her a lexicon, which he said was a present from his father, which delighted her, and history books for children, which she enjoyed reading. After that, when she presented him with any example of her astounding ignorance, he seemed pleased to explain the meaning. And so she came to learn many things he, and her aunt had taken it for granted she understood.

He told her of certain words which she should not use and explained grammar, and when she told him how, as a child, she had dreaded lessons, as Cousin Anna would often hit her on the back of her fingers with a hard ruler, he indignantly demanded every detail. When she told him about the pain of the blows, he looked shocked, then laughed and ran into the wood, coming back with a willow switch, and told her that he would beat her if she made mistakes. Afterwards, he would sometimes say he was her cousin, ask her a question and, when she did not know the answer, raise her fist and pretend to switch it. Often he examined her beautiful hands and told her he loved her transparent white skin and how he could see through it the blood throbbing in her veins, which 'run like rivers to your heart'. Then he would kiss a vein in her hand and say he loved her, look at his watch, wait half a minute and decide the message had reached her heart, when he would kiss her again.

13

The next few weeks were the happiest of Sefchen's life, except for once, when Harry arrived at the Abbey early one morning and told her, in broken phrases, how the previous day his father had sent for him, and he had found him sitting looking 'fat, pale and very ill himself'. At once his father said in an embarrassed voice: 'I can understand a young man having a dalliance with a girl. In fact, I have done the same myself. I must warn you, however, that the aunt's a vicious woman, and you should take care not to be inveigled into any close association with her niece.'

When he had delivered this message, which, Harry felt sure, came from his mother, his father lifted his eyes from the floor and, raising a plump hand, added: ' "But don't be put off, my boy. Your mother told me I must warn you, and I've done so. The flirtations of youth are the sweetest part of life. The one thing is to be careful so that they – I mean the old aunt – doesn't trick you into a false position. That could cause all kinds of . . ." he waved his hand, ". . . trouble." I don't know what he meant, but I'm sure my mother must be planning something which I don't like.'

Sefchen, when Harry told her of his father's warnings, said indignantly: 'I don't want to trick you into anything. I want to live with you and love you, but I don't want to marry you. The things you've told me about God have made me realize he's bad, and since he's never done anything good to me, why should I wish to have his permission to stay with you? I think it would be very unlucky.'

As she spoke these words, Harry's mouth fell open with amazement. Although he considered himself a rebel, he came from a conventional background and marriage seemed to him to be the basis of every home, even if you despised God. Now here was this wild creature teaching him liberalism. At the same time, her frankness frightened him. He was happy to kiss her, to tell her he loved her and talk of a vague future together, but what audacity of the girl he was half-planning to seduce, calmly to suggest with innocence and purity he should live with her without being married. He told himself it was ridiculous to have such old-fashioned feelings, and tried to dismiss them from his mind. He avoided the truth, he was not shocked but frightened, for he had never made love to a woman. He had thought of it in Düsseldorf, and once, a few months before, he had with friends gone to the street which housed the low women of the town. They had looked such horrible painted harridans, with strident voices and coarse faces, that the boys turned and fled and he remained an innocent. He thought how stupid he would look if this extraordinary girl suggested he made love to her, for wasn't that what her words suggested she meant. Where, in any case, could they go to make love? The idea of taking her up to the bedroom made him blush, and though he knew that some of his contemporaries took girls into the woods, he somehow could not imagine undressing under the trees. Where would you put your clothes? But then, wasn't it ridiculous to be timid and frightened and confused by inexperience? All he needed was to be courageous, for after she had told him her wishes, he could not help looking at her in a different light and felt sure she was only waiting for him to show he was a man. He must therefore be brave and commanding, but the next day she looked so innocent he thought he must have misunderstood her. But that evening he admitted he was lying to himself. He had heard her clearly and had to admit he was a coward. This, in turn, made him furious, and each day he determined to behave bravely and each day his courage failed. Could it be that cursed sword? Had it placed him under a spell when she had waved it about? Each evening his confidence returned, and each morning, when he woke up in bed, he swore because she was not with him.

One morning he decided, as he drew near the Abbey, to seize the sword and hold it over her head. But as he entered the old nave, the idea dissolved with his courage. What if the fearful weapon should cut her head off? He came to believe that she was looking at him with scorn, when she was only looking at him with love, unaware of the tortured turmoil which arose from his innocence making him incapable of manly action. Once he admitted this, he saw that the only way for him to retain her respect and love was by charming her with conversation. And so, after rehearsing all day, he told her the story of Cupid and Psyche, adorning it with his own elaborations, with which he was exceedingly pleased. As soon as he had finished, he waited for Sefchen's applause, and was disappointed and annoyed when she only said: 'Why, if Cupid had beautiful eyes, which made Psyche fall in love with him despite his size and fat body, was he afraid of letting her see him asleep?'

Harry could think of no convincing answer, and thought Sefchen was laughing at him, which made him feel more stupid than ever. Angrily, he decided that he could no longer take her for granted and that, perhaps, she had been more natural and delightful before he had taught her to be critical. His failure to impress only added to his impotent rage and his sense of insecurity, which left him feeling inadequate and, at the same time, more slavishly loving. Once, as her red hair fell forward, he was so moved by her beauty that he felt a spiritual passion which for an instant persuaded him it was his own intention to rise above all physical things. But later, when they sat talking on a leafy mossy bank, his desire for her returned, and he tried again in a serious voice, for he did not wish to look stupid this time. He told her of Danaë, the only daughter of a king who, when it was foretold he would be killed by his grandchild, shut her in a bronze tower with a flat roof, on which she sat sighing. Excited by his memories, his voice rose and his face flushed as he went on: 'One day Jupiter, flying through the air, saw a flash of brilliant colour, and when he flew down saw Danaë, sighing, sitting in the sun and drying her long red hair as she leaned over the side of the tower. Immediately he felt for her such deep love he thought it would be sacrilege for him to appear to her in human form, as she was more beautiful than the goddesses. And so he climbed high into the sky and transformed himself into a golden shower, some of which as it fell upon her, entered her and, as a result, Perseus was born, who later killed his grandfather.'

She asked him how Danaë's father made the tower of bronze, for she had read that metal needed to be melted by fire in a foundry and poured out of the bowl red hot. What an enormous bowl it must have taken, unless the tower was very low, in which case Danaë could have jumped out. And how hadn't the gold hurt her, falling all the way down from the sky? Harry was once more disconcerted by her practical reception of his story, but, excited by the challenge, he made up some original explanations. The two of them then sat looking into each other's eyes until the sun set, when they wandered back to the Abbey, where voices welcomed them with relief. As Harry walked homeward, he thought how she had stimulated him, while Sefchen remembered the handkerchief he had left behind. At once she put it with the pencils and little presents and ribbons he had given her, in her secret store in the back of a drawer. She held the handkerchief in her hand and shut her eyes, when she saw him as clearly as if he was in the room.

After her questioning his account of Danaë's tower, he told her no more legends, but, the day before he was due to leave for Frankfurt, he brought her a beautifully written copy of a poem which he had translated, 'by an Englishman of whom you'll never have heard . . . but wait! I'll say it to you. The words are engraved in my mind, both in English and in my translation, which I think excels the original.'

He began to recite:

'*Menaphon:* To Thessaly I came; and living private,
Without acquaintance of more sweet companions
Than the old inmates to my love, my thoughts,
I day by day frequented silent groves
And solitary walks. One morning early
This accident encountered me: I heard
The sweetest and most ravishing contention
That art and nature ever were at strife in.
'*Amethus:* I cannot yet conceive what you infer
By art and nature.
'*Menaphon:* I shall soon revolve ye.
A sound of music touched mine ears, or rather
Indeed entranced my soul. As I stole nearer,
Invited by the melody, I saw

This youth, this fair-faced youth, upon his lute,
With strains of strange variety and harmony,
Proclaiming, as it seemed, so bold a challenge
To the clear choristers of the woods, the birds,
That, as they flocked about him, all stood silent,
Wondering at what they heard. I wondered too.
'*Amethus:* And so do I; good, on!
'*Menaphon:* A nightingale,
Nature's best skilled musician, undertakes
The challenge, and for every several strain
The well-shaped youth could touch, she sung her own;
He could not run division with more art
Upon his quaking instrument than she,
That nightingale, did with her various notes
Reply to: for a voice and for a sound,
Amethus, 'tis much easier to believe
That such they were than hope to hear again.
'*Amethus:* How did the rivals part?
'*Menaphon:* You term them rightly;
For they were rivals, and their mistress, harmony.
Some time thus spent, the young man grew at last
Into a pretty anger, that a bird,
Whom art had never taught cliffs, moods, or notes,
Should vie with him for mastery, whose study
Had busied many hours to perfect practice:
To end the controversy, in a rapture,
Upon his instrument he plays so swiftly,
So many voluntaries and so quick,
That there was curiosity and cunning,
Concord in discord, lines of differing method
Meeting in one full centre of delight.
'*Amethus:* Now for the bird.
'*Menaphon:* The bird, ordained to be
Music's first martyr, strove to imitate
These several sounds; which when her warbling throat
Failed in, for grief down dropped she on his lute,
And brake her heart. It was the quaintest sadness,
To see the conqueror upon her hearse
To weep a funeral elegy of tears;
That, trust me, my Amethus, I could chide
Mine own unmanly weakness, that made me
A fellow-mourner with him.'

As soon as Harry had spoken the last words of the poem, he felt so moved
by their beauty that he burst into tears. At once she flung her arms about his

neck, kissed him and held him to her bosom. As he lay there sobbing, the rise and fall of her breasts seemed to soothe him into a dream. Shutting his eyes, he imagined that he was floating on the sea, that all would be well and he would make love to her. But, just at that moment, he felt an agonizing pain on the back of his neck. He had been stung by a wasp and the pain killed his new confidence. He was furious, but Sefchen was not at all upset and calmly walked away to collect herbs, which she put on the sting to soothe the pain. She looked so beautiful and chaste that, he told himself, he was glad their relationship remained spiritual. Then she asked, a serious look on her face, whether next year, when the nightingales sang in May and June, he would not come and recite the poem in the wood, to see if a nightingale answered, although he was not to challenge any bird to death, only to make it sing.

'I used to talk to birds in the forest,' she added musingly, 'and they understood.'

It was their last meeting before he left for Frankfurt. Hand in hand, they wandered to the gate, where he kissed her goodbye on the forehead before walking away, his head in the air. She was not downcast since she remembered he had told her about a girl who waited two years for her lover and spent the time making her trousseau. When she asked what a 'trousseau' was, she learned that every good young German girl spent years with her mother, preparing not only her clothes but also the sheets and linen to make up her dowry. She also remembered having heard that young girls still had painted chests which they would fill and ultimately present to their husbands. Sefchen decided to do the same, and that evening, instead of sitting crying, as she would otherwise have done, she sat up by candlelight and wrote down all the silks and cottons that she needed to make everything her aunt had told her was essential so that she would be able to delight Harry on his return with a present he hadn't dreamed she could make.

Two days later, Sefchen went into Düsseldorf as usual to her aunt's shop, but on the way steeled herself and went into a milliner's to buy needles, thread, and wool and silk materials. Her purchases were so expensive that, by the time she had finished, she found she had spent almost all her grandfather's gold coins which she had kept for herself. It did not worry her, and she looked forward with intense excitement to starting on her trousseau. As she was walking out of the shop, she stopped and, blushing but determined, asked the smart woman behind the counter if she knew of an old painted wedding chest for sale. The woman looked steadily at Sefchen with an expressionless face and cold eyes, as if summing her up, and after a moment said slowly: 'Large or small?'

'Large,' said Sefchen bravely, and received another calculating look.

'By chance,' said the woman, 'my brother has such a chest, but it will be expensive, for my grandmother brought it all the way with her from Bavaria . . .' She stopped, appeared to check herself, and then added hurriedly, 'My grandfather was a soldier, you see, so it will cost you twenty gold Napoleons.'

Sefchen was relieved: 'That will be all right. Can you deliver it to the Abbey?'

The woman, looking equally relieved, nodded her head. 'Yes, my brother will deliver it himself.'

That evening, Sefchen said to her aunt: 'Do you remember how, when I returned here, you took all but ten of the five hundred pieces of gold which my grandfather left me and said you'd put them in the bank, and I could have money whenever I wished?'

'Why, yes, dear,' said her aunt, looking at her with her eyes almost invisible. 'But we must take into account that you haven't lived here for nothing. There's been the expense of your eating. You've no idea the difference it makes to feed two. And then the roof had to be done up before you came and . . .'

Sefchen felt angry, knowing the Meistereen to be lying. The money was hers, and she knew where it was kept, for one day, as she was standing quietly by the door about to scrape the mud from her shoes, she had seen the old woman use an iron hook to lift a small stone in the corner of the kitchen and drop into the aperture something that tinkled. Quickly she had put the stone back and hidden the hook in her pocket. It had taken only a few seconds, and her aunt had started and looked about nervously when she made a noise. Sefchen could see she was wondering if she had been seen and if her niece had noticed. Neither spoke, but the knowledge the gold was in the house, and her aunt was lying and trying to keep it, made her angry, now she needed money and was determined to buy the chest, she only said quietly, 'I know, aunt, you have the money, and while I was only going to ask for twenty gold pieces, now I'll take it all. You only have yourself to blame.'

'Ungrateful child! How dare you! I've looked after you and spoiled you, and now you demand my gold! That's bald ingratitude. I'll have to think about it.'

Sefchen stared and then her instinct, learned in the forest, told her it was necessary to be violent. She knew exactly what she must do, and without hesitation went to the hiding place where her aunt kept the key to the storeroom, slid her hand into a crevice and, taking the key, walked over and opened the door.

She heard a screech: 'You cheating girl! Give me back the key. You dare to steal my savings and I'll whip you and send you to the magistrate.'

Sefchen closed her eyes as she gathered together all her contempt for this miserly, dishonest old woman who dealt in revolting fingers, sold quack potions and skimped her meals, and who, she knew, would sell her, if she could, to any rich old man. As she opened them again, she found her aunt creeping towards her, a long-handled brush raised above her shoulder.

Sefchen tried to make her eyes reflect contemptuous disdain, and the effect on the Meistereen was extraordinary. She stood still, the brush fell to the floor, she gasped as if she had been hit and whimpered: 'I wasn't, I wasn't, I wasn't . . .' before bursting into tears.

But Sefchen paid no attention, again certain of what she had to do and knowing that, if she failed to go through with it, she would never have the courage again. Walking across the storeroom to where the sword hung on its grubby piece of leather, she firmly gripped the handle. As she pulled it down, she heard a whining.

'You ungrateful child. What impertinence! I've fed you and petted you, and now you take my savings. It's wicked to be so thankless!'

A red mist of rage covered Sefchen's eyes and, through the blood, she saw her aunt standing before her with a stoat's head in place of her own. For a few moments, she relived an incident from her life in the forest and saw, as clearly as if it was yesterday, herself standing beside the hangman's clearing and watching, amazed, a circle of stoats dancing on their little hind legs as they waved their front paws in the air. Then, on all fours, they ran round in a large circle before standing up and dancing again. The performance was repeated three times, and each time they passed Sefchen, the animals looked at her, but paid no attention. Then, with squeaking noises, they put their noses to the ground and scattered in various directions. She had been charmed by the scene and delighted by the grace of the creatures.

A week later, she was wandering under the beech trees when a rabbit ran towards her. She was quite friendly with these animals, but they were too stupid to have ever really appealed to her, except when they were very young and it was nice to stroke them. She had never felt sad, either, when she saw the fox cubs eating dead ones. But this rabbit was quite different from any she had ever seen before as it staggered along squealing with glazed eyes, its legs stiff and jointless. About six feet to its right ran a stoat with eyes fixed on its prey. There was something so pathetic about the pursued animal running squealing stiff with terror Sefchen at once felt a hatred for the torturer playing such a cruel game. Trembling, she watched the rabbit take a turn to the left as the stoat began to draw closer. A red mist covered her eyes. She felt the terror of the helpless for its vicious pursuer. The screaming grew louder, the two drew closer, the rabbit's legs stiffer, the hunter happier in its mercilessness, never taking its eyes off the victim. It was choosing the moment to kill. The sight was unbearable and, picking up a broken branch, she ran and hit the stoat as hard as she could. The animal kicked for a few seconds before lying still.

This memory now came back with complete clarity and she knew what she had to do. She raised the sword and, pointing it at her aunt's stomach, moved towards her. The Meistereen edged away and almost fell backwards through the door in to the kitchen, where the two stood face to face, one calm, the other crumpling her apron into her mouth as she shivered with terror. Sefchen calmly placed the sword's point on the ground, lifted it, moved it sideways, made an inverted 'U' over the old woman's head and pointed it towards her stomach again.

Calmly she heard herself say: 'I wish to have my five hundred gold coins back. You may keep ten for the little I've cost you. Fetch the money.'

'Oh, but I don't know where the hook's got to,' sobbed the old woman.

'Well find it,' ordered Sefchen, and started to raise the sword again. Her aunt shrieked, put her hand under her skirts, fumbled among her clothes and, walking backwards and never taking her eyes off the weapon, bent down and slipped the hook under the iron bar and pulled up a stone.

'Take out all the money.'

The Meistereen grunted, lifted up a heavy wooden bowl full of gold coins and staggered to the table.

'Which of these are mine?'

'All are here.'

'Are you sure?' asked Sefchen, moving the sword.

'I promise, I promise,' said the old woman. 'Yours are one hundred of the French and four hundred of the Prussian kings.'

'Count them out,' said Sefchen and, seeing her aunt cast a worried look at the floor, demanded: 'What else have you got hidden in that hole? Go and bring out everything.'

'No, no.'

But, after another movement of the sword, the old woman brought out a rusted metal tin filled with rings, diamond bracelets and clasps. Disgusted, Sefchen told her to put them back and go and fetch a sack and fill it with the four hundred and ninety pieces, and keep the other ten for herself. While her aunt stood laboriously counting the money, Sefchen laid the sword longways on the floor and went and sat on the bench until the piles of gold stood in order. When she asked the Meistereen if she was finished, the woman looked up and let out a blood-curdling shriek and stood, her little eyes protruding, making the most awful noise as she stared at the sword. Sefchen looked down and followed her eyes, and saw the weapon rocking, although she was never sure whether it had moved on its own towards her aunt or if she, stepping forward, had trodden on its handle and caused the blade to rock. Whatever the reason, the effect was dramatic as the Meistereen became hysterical and yelled: 'I'm done for, done for! God save me, God save me!' She went down on her knees crying, 'I admit my sins, I admit thieving, but never will I do so again. Take the curse off me, please, please! I'll be your servant for life, I'll give back what I stole. I'll do anything, I'll work for you. Only spare me, spare me. Call off the cursed sword.'

Sefchen tried to calm her by saying: 'I've never put a curse on you,' but as the deafening screaming continued, she simply said: 'Very well,' and, picking up the sword, walked with it towards the old woman's room.

At this her aunt screamed even louder: 'No, no! Take it away. You saw how it crept at me! Take it away to your room and lock the door.'

Not until Sefchen had gone upstairs and leant the sword in the corner, loudly shutting the door before coming down again, did the old woman stop her noise and sit shivering on a chair. As Sefchen went up to her, she stood and bowed and said: 'I'll help you with your trousseau. I have a fine handloom upstairs. I put it away, but I'll get it out, and there's no better hand on a loom than mine. I shall embroider your linen with your initials and help you with my heart from this day on, if you never again put the curse on me.'

The change in the old woman seemed so complete Sefchen began to wonder whether there might not be some truth behind the old woman's belief in magic, for the sword had certainly produced a strange effect, both on herself and Harry, and now had changed, in a moment, a disagreeable woman who grudged her everything into an abject figure whose only motive was to please.

In the following days the Meistereen taught Sefchen how to spin, weave and embroider 'S' and 'H' on all the work. She threw away her niece's materials, calling them rubb.sh, and produced in their place finer silks and cottons and, from upstairs, a roll of old green Genoese velvet, which she promised to make into a dress in the style that pleased Harry. As Sefchen watched her, she saw that she was terri.ied and really believed that the sword wished to kill her.

14

A week later, a letter arrived from Harry in Frankfurt, declaring hatred of banking and love for Sefchen. He ended it with an elaborate flourish: 'I am, la Grande Mademoiselle, Your obedient servant, The deposed King of your woods, Harry.' During the next month, while Sefchen worked ceaselessly away at her trousseau, she received two more letters in the same style. The second and shorter of them mentioned a slight consolation: 'I have made friends with a young English "buck" who is touring Germany . . .'

Happy and encouraged, she returned to her weaving. Her aunt remained helpful, if less obsequious, but Sefchen knew her character could never change and she still hated her. Her knowledge was reinforced one day when, as they were about to start their simple midday meal, the old woman asked a question. Lost in thoughts of Harry, Sefchen ignored her, only to be suddenly brought out of her daydream by noticing her aunt was gripping the bread knife as she smiled and repeated the question a second time. The smile, Sefchen saw, did not belong to her face, and looking into the bitter little eyes, she saw them boiling with hatred and menace and read in them the thought, 'If you don't answer, I'll cut your throat.' Knowing eyes cannot lie like mouths, she said: 'Do you know, aunt, the sword took itself off my wall last night, and this morning I found it outside my bedroom door?'

She was not disappointed. Within an instant, her aunt was clawing at her arm and begging: 'Chain it to the wall! Chain it to the wall! I've got the chains, and a lock. I'll go and fetch them now.'

Sefchen shook her head, knowing she remained safe from injury as long as the sword was loose. She wondered whether she had a good fairy who told her how to treat the Meistereen and, if so, whether she was also the owner of the voice which she had heard less frequently since Harry went away. It occurred to her that, since her aunt was in a frightened mood, she might for once tell the truth, and so asked her whether she ever heard voices.

'Oh, yes,' the old woman replied. 'When I lived her alone, they were on at me all the time to join them, so they could leave, and, they told me, whatever happened I must stay here till I die, which depressed me. I couldn't get rid of them until, one day, I went to Alberfald, where I have a cousin – yours, too, one who's wise about such things, who said: "All of those that live alone hear voices. Often it is only themselves talking to themselves, and also, if you live among the dead, they don't want you to depart either, which is natural. All you have to fear is your imagination and the past trying to hold you."

'She told me to listen carefully to the voices to see if they were my own, but if that did no good, to bring her the right knee-cap of a pastor or priest. A priest would be the stronger, she said. A rabbi the strongest of all. They must have killed themselves or been murdered or hung. I found one easily enough, although he was only a pastor who had died by his own hand. She had a crucifix carved with Jesus nailed on the cross, and ever since I've worn it about my neck, and the voices have troubled me no more. Our cousin told me an ordinary crucifix would be as good, but where an object has a past, it makes one have more faith in it, even though one knows the tricks we all play. I think this is true, and anyhow, it's worked with me. If you wish, you can have a spare knee-cap which is in my room. It should be a lucky one. It came from a Polish rabbi who murdered his mistress with an iron stake. I'll give it to you as a present, but you'll have to pay for the carving of Christ on it. I'd give you that too, but can't afford to be generous now you've taken all the money. Shall I look it out?'

'No, no,' said Sefchen, 'but I'll listen carefully and see if it is myself talking. The strange thing is that they whisper the same things to me as they did to you.'

'Well, my dear, all I can say is that if I were you I'd try the rabbi's knee-cap.'

'I've said no. I couldn't bear to have such a hateful thing. It must surely be unlucky.'

But the conversation helped her, for afterwards, whenever a voice whispered as she was weaving or embroidering, she decided it was herself speaking and the voice would be silent. This made her wonder whether her sitting alone so much – for she avoided her aunt whenever she could – was not making her queer. And then she wondered whether the belief that the dead had some power might not be true, but as it was a question she could not answer, she soon gave up thinking about it.

After Sefchen had used the threat of the sword against her aunt a second time, the old woman became cloyingly helpful and told her niece that she did not see how they could possibly complete her trousseau in time, for all German girls' mothers started working the moment their baby daughters were born. They had, at most, two and a half years to finish hers, Harry having declared he would make his fortune in two years. The limited time spurred Sefchen on in silent desperation. To her aunt's annoyance, she only went once a week to the shop, and only then because she had noticed that, after joining the bustling life of the town and meeting the odd clients in her aunt's shop, the voices would be silent for a day or two.

Three weeks later, a fourth letter arrived from Harry, consisting of a long and furious complaint that his uncle had arranged for him to work in a greengrocer's. Sefchen could not help smiling at the letter's anger, and thought he was silly to consider it menial to move vegetables and wondered why he had dropped his romantic ending.

The reason for this momentary lack of affection was that Harry's life had changed and he now considered himself an experienced lover, untroubled by ignorance and doubts. This had come about through his fortuitous meeting with a young English 'buck', William, the son of a tradesman called Higgs, who had made a fortune in the war in the Peninsula. His son William was a large fat young man, unwisely proud of his enormous calves and red face, bulbous and marred with pimples, who lived with his valet in the most expensive inn in the town, out of which he swaggered every day, exciting the numerous maid servants who were not averse to earning unexpectedly large sums of money. Harry met him by chance one day in the tap room of his inn, where he was having an argument with a waiter who had, he claimed, made his punch incorrectly. Since William's German was incomprehensible, and the waiter understood no English, Harry saw his help was needed, and the two young men struck up a friendship which resulted in their dining together. Harry was astonished at the amount his host drank, but they ended the evening boon companions, and he was asked to dine regularly every night.

During their second evening together, William asked Harry about his amorous exploits, and, receiving the bashful reply, 'I have had none,' cried out in affected amazement: 'Be damned! You're surely not a virgin? We'll have to put that right,' and told him he would see to it the following evening this incomprehensible abstinence was ended. Harry, worried by his inability to make love, at first welcomed the idea, but was later prostrated by nerves and arrived trembling with fear. But, as soon as he saw the pretty young girl his host had provided, he thought here was the opportunity for which he had been waiting, and easily persuaded himself he was playing the lover only out of love for Sefchen.

The girl to whom William introduced him was both young and knowledgeable, and he found the experience by no means disagreeable. As he walked home that night, he dreamed of returning to Düsseldorf and conquering his red-haired beauty, who was, he realized, superior in every respect to the pleasant but bucolic girl who had obliged him.

During the next two weeks, his host introduced him to a couple more of his mistresses, and each experience added to his opinion of himself and left him wondering why Sefchen had frightened him. Then came his transfer to the greengrocer's, and three weeks later Sefchen received a note, brought by a boy from Düsseldorf, announcing Harry had arrived at midday, after a journey down the Rhine, and would be at the Abbey early in the afternoon. When she received the note, her instinct told her there would be a change in their relationship, and he was coming to her, as she had been willing to come to him. She wondered what she would wear, and thought briefly of white, which, in the books Harry had given her, represented virginity. But that seemed unimportant, and she did not want to have anything to do with the brides who were blessed by God, so decided to wear his favourite old green dress which she had on when he first saw her. She spent the morning cleaning the house – for her aunt was away on business, and would not be back until the next day – making her bedroom spotless, cleaning everything in the kitchen and plucking and throwing a chicken into the pot in case Harry was hungry when he arrived. Then she threw a shawl over her shoulders and sat outside the door and began to read about the ancient Greeks. At first her attention wandered continually, but at last she reached with delight the story of Ulysses, when Harry said: 'Good morning, beloved.'

He was standing before her in a red velveteen suit and a smart cravat, and she, seeing at a glance he had become a man, welcomed him without bothering to question how it had occurred. He felt pleased to have found her sitting dressed exactly as he always pictured him. Seeing her reading, he had crept up the path, taking care not to tread on a twig, until he was able to stand over her and she had to look up at him. He was delighted at the effect he had on her. Her bosoms heaved up and down and blood rushed to her face, giving it the delicate pink shade he had never seen in any other woman. Her welcome filled him with confidence, and he sat calmly next to her on the wooden bench and took her hands to kiss them. She did not speak, but looked at him, her eyes shining brightly beneath her almost black eyelashes. He had forgotten her startling beauty and, fearful the witch in her might steal away his confidence, stood up, raising her with him, and kissed her on the mouth in a way which left her in no doubt that he was her master. Then, for a moment, he gave her a frightened look as the confidence began to seep out of him. Where could he take her? Although the sun was shining, it was a cold afternoon and the undergrowth in the woods was wet. Noticing and understanding his nervousness, she said, 'Let's go inside,' before walking quietly towards the staircase and waiting at the bottom step until he led her up to her bedroom.

After he made love to her, she knew she had committed a perfectly natural act which bound them together far more closely than any promise in a church. She felt a deeper love than she had imagined she could feel, and a passionate hope that she might have a child. Delighted by the idea, she clasped him to her, wishing never to let him go so they would stay together for ever. The future held no dangers for her now, and she was united to her lover. But her happiness was shattered as he pulled away. Opening her eyes, she was startled to see him looking white and ill. Fearfully, she asked, 'Harry, are you ill?'

Opening his eyes, he said dramatically: '*Post coitum omne animal triste est.*'

When she asked him what he meant, he explained and she remarked: 'Yes, I've noticed that's the case with dogs and deer. It is not so with me.'

He looked at her – she said such surprising things – and realized with a stab of excitement her new beauty. As he continued to stare at her relaxed face and the gentle, natural and contented way in which she smiled at him, he wondered why he should have known, only a few moments before and after intense excitement, a feeling of bitter disappointment, as if the spell she had cast over him was broken, freeing him from the magic circle which she had woven around their future. He had seen clearly their future together was a dream excited by his physical longing. Satisfied, he knew their roads lay apart. She was a beautiful nereid of the forest, he a man who must take the open road and lead, by his pen, the countless repressed thousands of Europe to liberty.

These grim thoughts had passed through his mind as she held him in her arms, and had made him move away without looking at her, but as soon as she had spoken, he had looked at her again. He found his despair turning again to love. How could he have momentarily wished to avoid so beautiful a girl? He stared at the blue vein on her forehead as it gently beat below her hair, and knew he had been wrong. She was still an enchantress, he was still spellbound. While, later, his career might lead him away, at that moment he was the most fortunate of men. Taking her in his arms, he kissed her again and his passion revived.

Afterwards, he slept deeply, but she lay awake, staring at his face, sometimes softly touching his lips or hair, wondering whether she deserved such happiness. Later, she quietly got out of bed, dressed, went downstairs, swung the iron pot over the fire and opened a bottle of her aunt's rarest wine. As soon as the chicken and vegetables were cooked, she cut off the choicest portions and placed them in a wooden bowl, then, carrying in her other hand a horn mug of wine, she went upstairs and gently stroked Harry's face. When he awoke, he looked startled, then pleased, which made her happy, and she fed him as if he was a sick child, which made him look even happier.

Sefchen wondered aloud what might have become of her if she had never known him. Would she have been forced into marriage with one of her brutal family, whose hands were soaked in blood? Reaching out, he held her hand and said how lucky she was to have met him, and she nodded. He thought to himself that he, too, was lucky to have met her, for she had taught him the meaning of ecstatic love, which would be useful to his poetic muse, and which he had not even glimpsed during his experiences in the inn at Frankfurt.

The next day, when her aunt returned from the Rhine, she stared at Sefchen and a look of intense interest immediately showed on her face. At last she said, speaking in satisfied tones: 'Well, my dear, you're so touchy that I'm always careful what I say but,' and she screwed up her eyes, 'you can't deceive an old woman.'

Sefchen said nothing.

'You know, my dear, there may be consequences, but consequences which could be turned to advantage if we're careful. Now, would it be . . .' and her voice was sugary with ingratiation, '. . . would it be asking too much of you – and think this over carefully, like a good child – if, the next time your gentleman calls, I should find you together and go and swear on my heart to a magistrate you'd been violated? Of course, he'll pay no attention to me, but if later consequences follow, as they may, he will recall the complaint.'

Whenever her aunt talked in this way, Sefchen felt a horror rising from her feet to her head and became frightened that one day she might do the old woman some harm. Instead, she clenched her fists, said nothing and walked away.

The month which followed was another idyll. Each day Harry came and, if the aunt was away at the shop, they would make love together. Alternatively, they would walk in the woods and talk as before, except that now they were bound together. Sefchen thought the pattern of her future life with Harry was established, and he thought her enchanting and beautiful, and now he would be able to write about love with absolute understanding. It was now arranged that, after Christmas, he was to go to Hamburg, establish the new branch of his father's Düsseldorf business. His mother told Harry that he was a man now, and while he was only going to be put nominally in charge, he had as chief assistant one of his uncle's clerks, who would obviously be a spy. His mother said: 'Your Uncle Salomon says that, while he's not a man who could have ever made his own fortune, he's honest and reliable, will never be disloyal to you, as his master, and will ensure that the business is well run. Whether or not it succeeds, depends on you, and how hard you're prepared to work. Uncle Salomon says always remember to have a quick turnover, and that this won't be achieved by selling velveteen. You'll have the means at your disposal to buy a wide variety of goods. Such opportunities are given to few. You are fortunate. Work hard and, above all, impress your uncle by your seriousness. Your future and the future of your brothers and sister depends on what he thinks of you. He is merciless but fair. If you please him, he will advance you. If not, he will dismiss you. The choice is yours.'

'And I shall take it,' Harry told Sefchen. 'I've decided to make my fortune, within two years, and that then we will go to America together. I will do it, because I cannot bear my uncle's patronizing words and his unkindness to my father. I will do it to spite him. When I was staying with him last year, he either ignored me or patronized me, and laughed at my ambitions.' Harry began to rant feverishly: 'Yes, he lives in splendour, dines with princes, values everything by its cost, despises poets and is determined I shall not write poetry but, instead, wear out my genius by buying goods for fat Philistines and their wives. But I will show him. I will go to London and Paris, find the rarest materials, the newest machines, and amaze him. I will revolutionize the production of every saleable article and become his right-hand arbiter of taste, and when I am indispensable, I will retire with enough money to leave this horrible and accursed continent and become a great poet. You will see,' and he burst into tears.

She cradled his head in her arms and told him of her faith in him. At last he stopped sobbing and immediately began to laugh, and, in high spirits, told her jokes about his uncle before striking his forehead and saying: 'I've forgotten to pay you the compliments I thought of last night. Well, you know, in books, heroines are always difficult and complicated, especially when beautiful, but you, who I'm sure are far more beautiful than they, are never difficult. You do whatever I ask, believe in me, never sulk or complain, and are natural, talking openly about things my mother could never discuss. You are free of rotten conventions. I'm sure the new America is the place for us, and we shall be married and have children.'

She replied sharply: 'I don't want to marry, but I will be happy to have your children. I love you with all my heart, and cannot believe I could live without you.'

He drew her to him and, as they stood close together, persuaded himself that he could feel her heart flooding with love for him. He thought it splendid he could inspire passion in such a beauty, and admitted her loveliness continued to inspire him.

15

The weather stayed comparatively mild until Christmas, and they often walked together hand in hand as he read aloud his ballads and poems. She was so happy she often smiled at her aunt, and once, when the old woman was ill, went three days running to the shop, where all sorts of young men called in to purchase love potions, although one or two of them, as soon as she opened the door, stared at her with open mouths and ran away.

Harry told her how his father had aged and was avoiding work, even the ordering of velveteen, which was a blessing, and how his mother had told him again: 'You must work, not scribble, in Hamburg, otherwise we'll all be at the mercy of your Uncle Salomon.'

One day he realized that he needed some money to buy Sefchen a present for Christmas, as it would be mean if he went away without giving her anything except his verses, although he was sure she would prefer them to anything else. He had seen, in a jeweller's, a cameo of Alexander the Great framed in gold. He admired the face and he thought he would buy it for her, but how? He had no money. Since his mother would give him none, he tried his father. When he asked, the old man looked embarrassed and repeatedly stroked his chin with white plump hands. At length he said: 'Is it for the beautiful young lady in the Abbey?'

'Yes.'

'Ah, I remember when I . . .' But he stopped and sat troubled, thinking. 'Yes, yes, I can get it. One has to please the heart when one is young. Things are difficult now, but I'll manage. Don't worry, you'll have it tomorrow.' The following day, he handed over the few gold coins which Harry needed.

Two weeks before Christmas, he told Sefchen, and she at once decided in return to present him with the trousseau chest, although it would have to remain at the Abbey for the time being. She imagined to herself how amazed he would be to find how, over the past three months, she and her aunt had made, on her loom and with their hands, layers of aprons and towels, pillow cases, tablecloths, petticoats and vests; and had sat up all night to edge the finest linen with a row of old lace purchased from her aunt, who said she had bought it from one of her clients, but in such a shifty way that Sefchen knew she was lying. On top of the pile, she laid an exquisite cambric handkerchief edged with even finer, older lace and embroidered with double 'H's. This was her own gift to him.

On the day before Christmas, she kept lifting the lid to look at the neatly folded and ironed pile, which completely covered the bottom of the chest. How impressed he would be, she thought, at the snow-white linen and shifts, the delicacy of the embroidery and edging. Once again she arranged his handkerchief precisely in the centre. Apart from bunches of flowers, which she had sometimes picked for the old woman in the forest, and which they had usually carelessly left on the table without bothering to put them into water, this was the first present she had ever given anyone. She was restless with excitement and imagined them in thirty years' time, giving their children and themselves presents. She realized what she had missed as a child.

On Christmas morning, Sefchen woke long before the sun and lay thinking how happy she was and how kind it was of Harry to come to her to celebrate Christmas Day. Her heart thudded with excitement and curiosity. She washed her hair and, for the first time in her life, examined her face minutely in the mirror to see if she had faults. Then she slowly dressed herself in the dress of green Genoa velvet which her aunt had made, and which, like her old dress, clung closely to her skin. She went down to the kitchen, and out of doors, and in again, and found the clock had hardly moved. Tedious hours passed until at last she saw Harry's neat figure. She jumped up, unable to stop herself, and ran to meet him, her face flushed with excitement, her eyes unusually bright, which was not at all surprising, as she could think of nothing except his present. He stood still holding, in one hand, a roll of sealed paper and, in the other, a small parcel, wrapped in blue silk and tied with a red ribbon. As his hands were full, she could not run into his arms, but stopped in front of him and, as they faced each other, he wondered which of the verses of his new ballad she would like best, while her eyes, ignoring the ballad, constantly strayed towards the blue box, the first present she had been given since the ill-fated doll.

In the kitchen, the Meistereen curtsied, but in such an obsequious way Harry wondered whether she could be a blood relation to her niece. Taking his time, he placed both gifts on the table and drew up a chair as Sefchen, almost fainting with anticipation, sank on to the bench. Then he lifted up the paper scroll and gave it to her, she broke the wax seal, her hands trembling with disappointment. She did not want another poem. She knew it wasn't a real gift, but merely verses he would have written anyhow.

But he said: 'Read, and afterwards you shall have my other little present.'

She stumbled hesitatingly through his ballad, but not well enough for his taste. So he made her give back the paper, which he read in his musical, ever-changing voice after saying, in a condescending tone, it was dedicated to her.

'Do you like it?' he asked when he had finished.

She hesitated and nodded, longing to open the little silk parcel.

'Which verse do you like the best?' he asked.

She did not answer for a minute. She had forgotten them all, but thinking desperately said: 'The last.'

He looked pleased and said again: 'Are you pleased with it?'

'I love it,' she said. 'Love it. I always love whatever you write,' she added, her eyes straying to the silk parcel as she dreaded another question.

Mercifully, he seemed satisfied and, at last, offered it with a bow. It took her some time to untie and straighten the ribbon and lay it carefully on the table. She was not going to waste the smallest part of her first present. Then she carefully undid the paper and folded it and put it by the ribbon and stared at a blue painted wooden box. At last she opened it, and her heart beat as she saw, laying inside, the picture of a man set in gold attached to a gold chain. Apart from the watch which her grandfather had left her, she had never had an ornament to wear, and the gun-metal watch was not pretty, while this was made of gold, the most romantic of metals. She gazed at it, breathless with delight, and then he made her lean forward so he could slip the chain over her head and place the cameo between her breasts. She could not keep her hands off it, and every time she touched the head or the gold chain, she could have cried with joy.

As for Harry, he felt complacent. How nice to give to one who had nothing. And how kind and thoughtful of him to search for something she liked, not something he wanted for himself, which was, he knew, his mother's custom when she gave presents to her husband. He wondered vaguely what she had for him, and noticed, when she stood up and beckoned, she was terrified he might be disappinted. She led him upstairs and into her bedroom where, against the wall, was a wooden chest painted with flowers. The date '1774' was on the front. It stood three feet high, and he realized, at once, that he could not take it away, and immediately felt disappointed. But then, he quickly thought, how could she have given him anything? As far as he knew, she had no money. She had never told him about the five hundred gold pieces, thinking it would be a nice surprise to give them to him when they started life together. He only thought how strange she should give him a chest not unlike the coffins her past had often brought to his mind. But when they leaned forward and she pushed up the lid, he saw at the bottom a vague whiteness and thought for a moment of a corpse and, without thinking, heard himself say:

'And as the opening pit I view
A freezing horror thrills me through
And plunging in its funeral night
I fall – but wake once more to light.'

'No!' she cried. 'Look, look!'

And, staring down into its depths, he saw a pile of neat garments and linen and, on top, a handkerchief which she bent to pick up and give him. He took it with genuine delight. The edging was beautiful, the embroidery fine, and it felt expensive and elegant. He was pleased, then disturbed, as the box became in his mind a symbol not of his future, but of his future denied. Would he, if he went off with this girl, he thought, his mind working at a tremendous pace, be the equivalent of a piece of fine material, forever shut off from the world he wished to conquer?

She started to tell him of all the other things she had made: the aprons, the petticoats, the towels, the trim nightshirts, the vests, shirts and sheets. He only saw them as chains. But when he looked at her face so blindingly lovely, he decided he did not regret his subjection and kissed her. Surely fate intended them to be united? He lowered the lid and shut the door, and turned to find her calmly undressing. For a moment, he was shocked, but, cursing his bourgeois reaction, hurled his own clothes on to the floor.

After he had left for home, Sefchen paid no attention to her aunt's sniffs, but stood by the kitchen table and remembered the terrible moment when he had looked into the chest and she knew he was disappointed. But was he? She tried to recall each of his movements, and her spirits fell, for, after he had shut the chest, he never again mentioned the contents of which she had been so proud, although he was loving. But, however nice he had been (and certainly he had been nice), it was her present, not herself, that she had wished him to like that day, and now he had gone without thanking her. No, he was disappointed. She should have loved whatever he had given her, because he had chosen it. She had put her whole heart into her gift, working late at night until her eyes burned, and all for nothing. Her heart ached with sadness, and despite all her efforts, she burst into tears. Her aunt, who had been watching carefully, turned away to make sure her niece did not spot the smile on her own face and so missed seeing Sefchen put her hand to her throat, feel the gold chain and at once recover her look of happiness.

For his part, Harry slept well, but woke up with an uneasy feeling of having been unkind. His heart told him he loved her. He jumped out of bed and, for the next fortnight, gave up all discretion and saw her every day. She knew he must have realized his tactlessness, for when the next day, he asked to see the chest, he took out each item and congratulated her on her skill, and asked her to excuse his lapses.

As they went downstairs, he said: 'It's your fault, my love, for when you're with me, my imagination flies into the sky and carries me away from the present into mythical worlds which I could never reach without the encouragement your beauty gives. Please understand that, when I'm so transformed, it's not myself who is rude, but a head emptied by the magic carpet on which your magical personality places me.'

By the time he had finished speaking, she was looking at him doubtfully. He wondered if his words had sounded false. To prove his sincerity, he disregarded manners and conventions, and although the old woman was in the kitchen preparing luncheon and the warm plates were already on the table, he took her upstairs by the hand to enter into their own worlds. He thought of marching kings and of knights participating in heroic epics, while she conceived them as undivided lovers and visualized the little child for which she had always longed.

In the following days, he behaved with the same bravado, although he often had periods of sadness which, she decided, were part of his character and nothing to do with her. When these moods fell on him, she would at once move out of his arms and lie with her eyes shut, only occasionally glancing from under lowered lids to see if he had returned from his dreams. Sometimes his fits lasted only a few minutes; at other times, an hour afterwards he would look at her with surprise while she, with her natural intuition, would smile and very slowly draw herself further away as if she was about to get out of bed. At once he would clasp her in his arms, and she would again feel that they were indivisible and her happiness complete, as he looked at her in amazement, whispering words of love and praise of her beauty, telling her of his fears she might leave him and of his dreams of 'sad stories of the death of kings'.

Three times Sefchen dreamt she was back in the forest, taking him to see the mysteries and wonders of the magical wood which she was never able to convey in words. In each dream, they set out from the old house in the wood and, hand in hand, walked through the trees. Then she introduced him to her young foxes as the birds followed singing. The three dreams all ended with her leading him to the edge of the wood to meet the two young lovers. As they four walked away together, she would wake up at Harry's side. At other times, he would wake her up by muttering snatches of verse, his face sometimes showing intense interest, sometimes fear, but his expression telling her she played no part in his dreams.

On their last day, he wept long and bitterly in her arms and told her, swearing on his heart, that he was in love with her – which he was at that moment, out of gratitude to her for introducing him to a physical passion which he had never thought was in his nature. Innocent, she believed him, and felt sure he would always come back to her. In the meantime, she had ceaselessly thought of their parting, and to make it less bitter had planned how she would overcome her sorrow when he went away. During the next two years, she would think of nothing but filling her chest. If necessary, she would use the sword to make her aunt work at the loom, and herself would work from first light till darkness. Once the chest was full, then, she knew, Harry would return and they would go away to America. By then she would have the boy she had dreamed of, to fill the little clothes she had made, who would look the image of his father.

Her plans for the future made her impatient for him to go, for, as the sorrow had to come, let it come quickly and be over, so she could start her task and put him out of her mind. When the time came for him to say goodbye for the last time, it was not as painful as she had feared. They clung together by the kitchen door before he moved abruptly away. She did not look after him, but at once ran upstairs and started to work the loom.

When Harry had come back, he had lifted up one of her white hands disdainfully and stared, a look of horror on his face, at the number of needle pricks on her finger ends. The next day, he brought her ten wooden thimbles and told her firmly that she must wear them, for it was an offence to beauty to treat beautiful objects as pin cushions. And he had added: 'Do you think Rembrandt stuck needles into his paintings, or Goethe threw ink over his manuscripts? You should realize,' and he looked at her seriously, 'you are a thing of beauty and must protect every inch of yourself, so promise to wear the thimbles.'

She smiled. 'I promise.'

But now she had no time to treat herself like Rembrandt and must either break her word or have a half-filled chest. She sighed and broke her word. Gradually she grew accustomed to her slavery, and almost enjoyed the tedious work which tired her out and scarcely left her time to think of Harry. Her aunt, after Sefchen told her how the sword once rattled in the night and she only with difficulty managed to stop it getting out of the door by tying it to the wall, worked with a will, though she often appeared to have difficulty in concealing her hatred. Sefchen, however, untroubled by guilt or doubt, stayed secure in her belief in a happy future and worked exactly as she had planned. Within two months, they had woven two pairs of sheets, two aprons and an undershirt, all of which she embroidered with the joined initials.

After two months, a letter came from Harry. She hastened through the complaints of the tedium of business, of the meanness of his uncle, of the lack of culture in Hamburg. As usual, she liked best his farewell:

> O Sefchen, you know
> you are the
> most beautiful of
> all women and
> are the
> adored
> of your loving
> Harry

She read the ending again and again and slept with the letter beneath her pillow. Three times in the night she lit a candle over his last words, which filled her with happiness. But, after three days, when she knew every word of his letter by heart, she began to wonder whether it would not be better if Harry complained less and settled down to work. As if to expel her doubts, she worked that night till midnight and only went to bed after she had fallen asleep twice as she sat spinning. Three weeks later, another letter came.

Beloved,

I am still in my position and business goes well. Uncle Salomon is pleased, and I will certainly make a fortune, but if I had you with me, my happiness would be complete. As it is, Uncle Salomon says I may return home for a few days after six months, when a quarter of my sad waiting will be over. I long for a glimpse of your red hair and beautiful face, and, as always, my muse is stimulated by thoughts of you.

Believe me
I am, as ever
Your adoring
Harry

Late one night, a month after this last letter, Sefchen was woken by unceasing knocks at the front door and sat up erect in bed before lighting the candle and creeping softly downstairs. In the kitchen, she saw her aunt already cautiously advancing towards the door.

'Who's there?' she screamed. 'Who disturbs peaceful folk at such a time?'

'Harry!' Sefchen heard a voice cry, above the wind and rain. 'It's Harry, Harry! Let me in. I'm soaked through.'

Sefchen was glad she was at the bottom of the stairs, so could lean against the wall for support, and surprised that her first reaction should be not of pleasure but of worry that he would be angry over her pricked fingers. She looked at them in the candlelight to see if they were badly scarred by needle pricks, and hoped he would not notice the numerous little black holes. As he entered, he shook himself like a dog and water streamed from his cloak on to the floor while she remained standing at the foot of the stairs, her back to the wall, her candle leaning forward, dropping wax on the floor.

At last he looked at her and stopped shaking himself. The candle made her seem the colour of ivory and filled her hair with gold lights. He shook with excitement, unbuttoned the chain of his cloak and let it fall to the ground. Having given a perfunctory kiss to the old woman's hand, he walked towards Sefchen, stopped and looked at her, noticing, with pleasure, that the flame jerked up and down as she stared at him with wide-open eyes. How pleasant to return to this half-fairy figure, who gazed at him with love. At length she slowly raised a hand which felt as heavy as stone. He seized it, lifted it and put his lips to her cold fingers, which lay in his hand as motionless as a broken piece of marble.

Having bustled about, throwing wood on to the fire and lowering the pot, the aunt went to draw Harry some wine, and the couple sat, he on the old chair at the head of the table and she on the bench, still staring at him with surprise Before long, the old woman placed on the table a large wooden bowl, heaped with meat and vegetables swimming in dark brown gravy. He gulped down the food as if he had not eaten for years, and the meal and wine seemed to revive him, but as soon as he had finished, he shook his head as if to rid himself of an evil memory.

Later that night, after he had rubbed himself vigorously with a towel to warm his body, he came into her bed, but made no attempt to make love. Although he drew her towards him, he laid his head to her chest and told her that he had come as quickly as he could from Hamburg, speeding towards her like an arrow, but the roads were so bad that the journey had been difficult. A tragedy had occurred, and there was nobody else he could turn to for comfort. Through his tears, he told her how, when he arrived in Hamburg full of good intentions, his Uncle Salomon had been cold, his daughters friendly, 'but at arm's length'. Undiscouraged, however, he had thrown himself into the business with ardour.

'If anyone worked, I did,' he sobbed on to her shoulder. 'I tried. How I tried! My uncle had given me for a clerk an elderly man with a white wig called Franz Ulman. He was a strong and burly fellow who looked like a farmer but was helpful, very helpful. To begin with, we got along well enough, and I was determined to make velveteen fashionable, and worked hard visiting, oh, I don't know how many tailors and traders. Now I realize why Father is sad. People really don't want the stuff. It's out of *fashion*, which is, apparently, the god worshipped by every fat rich man and woman in that horrible town. Therefore I had to give it up and turn to selling what people demand, for that, Ulman told me, is "the source of success in business" and what he had always done. Yet it made me sad. I had connected velveteen with my father, and selling other stuff did not give me the same pleasure, so I couldn't put my heart into it.

'There was infrequent correspondence between the two firms, and though we were said to be a branch of my father's business, I soon realized this wasn't the case. My clerk ran the Hamburg firm and all my suggestions were ignored. I returned to my books and poetry. What else was there for me to do? Franz was both a loyal friend and pleased to be left free from my interference. At all events, he told Uncle Salomon "the boy is doing well and learns the trade fast". He also told me that the profits of the firm were increasing, and so I thought I could make my fortune, write poems and read Goethe at the same time. I also began to compose a play about Scotland, whose history is written in blood and tragedy.

'Everything was going well, and I was happy, and sometimes dined with Uncle Salomon, who treated me, I thought, with as much disdain as his daughters did with kindness. They are both pretty, you know, and I took to them. Twice a week, the clerk would respectfully say to me: "It would be a good thing, sir, to walk about the business section of the town today. To show oneself is always good policy"; and I'd take his advice and, do you know, rather enjoyed people whispering who I was. Until ten days ago,' sobbed Harry, 'I was content.' Then he gave a little start. 'I mean, of course, as happy as I could be without you, and you must understand, when I write of Scotland and Spain and love, I think of you all the time.'

Sefchen leaned back contented. His behaviour had been like her own. She had sat working all day, trying not to think of him, even though he had been at the back of her mind. At that moment, Harry lifted himself up and banged his head down on the bolster before saying: 'Now I must tell you something. I cannot go back to Hamburg and will never make a fortune. You and I will go away across the sea, away from this cursed country, to whom I owe nothing.'

She was silent as he continued: 'You see, a few weeks ago a promissory note was presented, signed by my father, but referred to our business. When it came in, Franz shook his head and said it was strange, but as it was a small draft and

133

my father a man of honour, it must be a mistake. Would I communicate with him informally, as he would formally, and emphasize that the accounts of the two firms remained separate?

'And then he had looked at me and said: "Was your father well when you left?" I could see he was thinking of asking me another question, but decided not to. Two weeks later, another draft came in for a large sum, and Ulman shook his head and said: "I can't understand it. Unless an explanation arrives tomorrow, I shall have to refer this to your Uncle Salomon. To cash the draft would absorb more than an eighth of our profits." But I wasn't worried, and told him not to bother, as an explanation would certainly be forthcoming, as my father was the most honourable of men. I thought no more of it, but, next day, another and larger draft arrived and Ulman shook his head and, despite my begging and assurances, went to see Uncle Salomon, who sent for me later that afternoon.

'He spoke to me from behind his desk, looking down his hook nose without a smile, and said he had dispatched a special messenger to my father, telling him to send the money to cover the drafts. Then he showed me the hard, cruel letter he had written in which he told my father he was useless and, if the money was not sent immediately, my uncle would close the firm and return me to Düsseldorf. He said unjustly I had not done a day's work, but had sat scribbling senseless words all the time, without making any attempt to learn the business. How he thought he could have known I don't understand, but I suppose he bullied the clerk into telling him. In the last part of his letter, he told my father he would honour his bills on this occasion as he did not wish to disgrace the family, but only on condition that he withdrew from the business and retired to his house, in which case my uncle would make him a small allowance, but only if he agreed never to trade again.

'After that, he was even ruder. The last awful words which he wrote are engraved in my mind: "I consider that I have more than fulfilled the duties of a brother and uncle, since I was not bound to pay debts I had never incurred. I can only hoped that the realization of the shame you have brought to our family will cause you to retire and live quietly and decently, and send your son out into the world to see if he can make his way. That is all I have to say, except that, if you have more debts, kindly inform me and I will honour them, but all must be told to the bearer of this letter, who is to present a copy of it to my sister-in-law, to whom I send my respects and a draft to enable your family to live respectably for two months, after which she will receive another. Will you also ask her to send me, every month, the receipts from the tradesmen."

'Oh, the shame of it, the shame! Uncle Salomon is nothing but a hideous old man who grinds the poor to whom my father gave away his money. Such sad wretches are considered by Uncle Salomon to be despised failures, while, to my father, they were unfortunates to be saved. And now he is to be treated worse than those he helped. I know my mother. She'll be firm and kind, but will show no mercy. I had to come to you, for, as soon as the blow fell, I could not go to them. I, too, will have failed in their eyes. And I dread to see my dear father piteous and broken.'

As he sobbed and held her to him, she moved her arms and held him with one hand, stroking his buried head with the other. 'I would have shot myself, but my passion for you kept me alive.'

She told him she had a little gold, but he apparently didn't hear and went on: 'When I see my parents tomorrow, I shall tell them I am leaving Germany for ever. What has Prussia done for me, or the great Napoleon or his nephew, or, come to that, Murat or the Duke or the Elector? The truth is that all rulers whose subject I have been have done nothing for me or anyone except themselves. Therefore I am leaving for a new world, and you shall be my inspiration. Prepare yourself. I hope to leave as soon as possible by ship from Holland. The Americas call me. I know that the free men there will be appreciative of my genius and honour and help me without making me sit in some dull office. You must, by my readiness to forsake my father for you, realize the depth of my love.' He paused before going on in a sad voice: 'But how could I watch and see one whom I knew as a fount of generosity become a mere pauper at the mercy of a merciless brother?'

At last Harry slept, but Sefchen stayed awake, lying motionless in the darkness. Eventually she moved with infinite care and stretched out a hand to touch his hair, very gently taking it in her fingers to try to convey to the sleeping boy how she loved him with her whole heart and wished him to know in his sleep that she understood the sorrow and shame he felt for his father. Quickly she pulled her hands away, realizing that she was touching him with her pricked fingers. Would he be angry if he woke up? But as soon as she ceased to touch him, she felt lonely and her body longed to lie against his so that the blood might flow through each of them in turn. She had no wish to make love to him, only to feel that they were together, and this was impossible unless she touched him. As lightly as she could, she levered herself with her heels until her thighs touched his and their love separated them off from the rest of the world.

She felt as if she was standing on a hill, looking down on both their empty pasts, which now meant nothing. Gradually she felt a contented drowsiness beginning to blur her thoughts, and realized she was drifting into a peaceful sleep, but the idea made her jump. How stupid to drift into nothingness when she was lying next to Harry and full of happiness. Why waste such time? She moved both her hands gently on to the top of her legs and, selecting soft bits of flesh, pinched them as hard as she could. At once she was wide awake, and knew she had only to touch Harry to become part of him again. She raised herself on her elbow and reached out a hand to hold it above his mouth so she could feel his gentle warm breath, which told her he was loving her in his sleep. Then she touched his lips with the delicacy of a feather and lay against his side, remembering every word he had ever spoken to her, every time she had seen him, and everything they had ever done together. Every now and then, cramp made her shift her position, but if for a moment she lost him, he always came back when she pressed gently against his side. She could not believe that any girl had ever been so happy, and wondered why it was necessary for Harry to be asleep before their minds could finally join together.

At length, the darkness imperceptibly turned to light, and she watched with fascination as his face slowly formed in the morning light and he looked exactly as she had been picturing him, with the same slightly crooked nose, the same delicate skin and, above all, the same beautiful hair, which she softly touched again.

At last Harry woke, and all at once they seemed to snap apart as he jumped out of bed and looked out of the window, saying that, since it was fine, he would stay another day. Then he looked gloomily at her, returned to bed, and fell asleep again. Sefchen went to tell her aunt – who was, she knew, going into Düsseldorf – that on no account was she to mention that Harry was at the Abbey, for if his parents found out, they would be bitterly hurt. As she spoke, she saw a sly look flit into the old woman's eyes and feared that the horrible old creature might deliberately give him away. She thought for a moment, smiled to herself and went to fetch the sword, which she placed on the kitchen table with its pointed end towards the door of the storeroom, in which her aunt was doing up some bundles and making her loathsome potions. The Meistereen came bustling out a moment later, fastening her cloak in a hurry to get into town and spend the gold piece Sefchen had given her to buy delicacies for her downcast lover. She took two steps into the room, saw the sword and shrieked and ran to Sefchen and hid behind her. As she peered round her shoulder, her trembling hand grasped Sefchen's arm.

'Oh, take it away! Take it away!' she shrieked. 'You're a witch yourself. You know my thoughts! I promise I'll not tell a soul.'

'Well, I shall leave the sword there on the table until you return, and if you breathe a word to anybody, it will tremble and I will know.'

The Meistereen's voice suddenly altered and she said, in almost admiring tones: 'It may be that you pretend to be good, but the magic runs in your veins and the power you have over the sword means you have power over many things. A mint of money we could make if only you'd join me in business.' Her voice became almost caressing as she went on, 'Why don't you, dear, now you've a young man to keep? He's not working, and what can he do? Money melts, you know, with a man in the house. They eat worse than pigs, and are always demanding.'

Sefchen said nothing and her aunt turned away after one last nervous look at the sword, but immediately looked around the door again and whined: 'I don't trust you, child. You're too powerful. When I come back, I will tap on the window and you must take the sword up to your room and put it back on the wall. Then come down and tell me all is safe. Otherwise I won't come in. You'll do that for me, won't you? I'm only a frightened old woman, after all.'

Sefchen nodded, and her aunt gave her a conspiratorial smile and was gone. She at once crept back upstairs to see if Harry was asleep, and found him lying on his back, gently snoring. She did not disturb him, but sat happily admiring his beautiful profile and thinking that, although the magical closeness of the night had departed, she was lucky to love such a kind and clever young man. She could not help being pleased, although she knew it was wrong of his father to have made a promissory note – whatever that might be. But for while it had infuriated his uncle, it had meant Harry was sent home to her. Then she looked at the trousseau and gave a little smile, knowing it would never be finished now. She was glad that she still had her four hundred and eighty gold pieces, for although she knew that Harry was clever and would one day be famous, she also realized that he was hopeless with money and it was lucky she would be able to help him when they went away.

The next morning, when Harry looked out of the window, he paused. Sefchen held her breath, expecting him to say he must leave and go to his father's house. Instead he said in a relieved voice: 'It's such a lovely day. I'm in a creative mood. It'll be destroyed if I have to argue with my mother.'

In fact the fine weather did not seem to concern him, for he spent the morning in bed, covering the blankets with sheets of paper. Only after they had eaten their midday meal of young ducklings from Düsseldorf, paid for out of Sefchen's store of gold, would he go for a walk. As soon as they had left the Abbey, he looked about him nervously and said: 'Do you know, I clearly heard voices talking, telling me to be gone? It's most interesting. It's not myself talking to myself, as you suggested. The strange thing is that I've always wanted to be haunted, but these voices upset me.'

He asked if her aunt heard voices, and she told him: 'Yes. She's seen a woman, and a vague man, as I have, but she always frightens them off with a little cross she carries round her neck and which she pulls out and holds towards them, when they vanish.'

That night, Harry questioned the old woman closely. Flattered by his attention, she told him how the voices had asked her to replace them in death, and how the girl and the man had often appeared to her lately. Sefchen knew she was lying, but said nothing, and allowed her to go on interesting Harry.

'But of course,' she said, 'when I see them, I hold out my cross like this . . .' and she plunged her arm down her front and tore out the horrid kneebone crucifix and held it in front of her, '. . . and they fade away,' she ended, nodding and smiling.

Yet her blandishments were wasted on Harry, who leaned forward, looked at her in a puzzled way and at last said slowly: 'Why should the cross on which we nailed Jesus drive anyone away? Is it because evil is stronger than good?'

For the rest of the evening, he asked himself and her, without expecting any reply, countless questions as to why Christians worshipped the cross. 'It's like me worshipping the guillotine, an executioner's axe or a thumbscrew. I find it most interesting.' He would not let the subject drop.

The next day was also fine, and so he stayed on. He was in good spirits, quoted long passages from his plays and took her to a dark, overgrown corner of the wood which, he said, was Scotland, and a bare area beneath beeches, which he called Grenada. In both he recited to her long passages. They went to rest in the afternoon, but during the whole of the next week he only made love to her once, and afterwards was, as she could see, unhappy. He soon fell asleep, and she quietly got up and put on her Genoese velvet dress and then sat waiting for him to wake up. When he did, she saw interest at once return to his face and the darkness of his mood disappear. Each night was a repetition of the first. She had him entirely to herself and would stay awake, happy in her possession of her lover and determined not to miss a moment of the enchanted hours. But, in the mornings, she would be exhausted and as he lay fiercely writing, would go to an empty room, lie down on an old bed and fall sound asleep.

On the tenth morning of his visit, as he awoke he looked out, saw it was raining and said in a gloomy voice: 'I said I'd stay as long as the sun shone and that when the rain came I'd know my father was weeping. Today I must go, but I shall be back in two or three days, once I've confessed my decision and said farewell to all my friends. Please get everything ready. You said you have some gold put aside. That will be useful as I don't know how much my father will give me, if, indeed, he has anything to give.'

She walked with him to the gate as he spoke of their glorious future in America. Passing under the dripping trees, she could not help yawning, for this was the time when she usually slept, and she could not deny to herself that, much as she loved him, she desperately needed to sleep to prepare herself for the long journey beyond the seas. He never stopped talking, and never listened to her replies. And as he kissed her fervently goodbye, she was overcome by an urge to yawn and went back to her bed to sleep all day long.

16

Sefchen anticipated that she would be unhappy and miss Harry sadly on her first night alone, and she lay down, dreading hours of sleeplessness. The next thing she knew, a hand was shaking her, and she found her aunt leaning over her in full daylight, her eyes bright with the hope her niece was dying or ill. But when she found the hoped-for corpse looking back into her eyes, she quickly drew away and, in her whining-worried voice, said it was ten o'clock, and 'since my dear, you're always up with the lark, I was worried'. As she spoke, she looked out of the corners of her eyes at the hanging sword, as if it was about to spring down and attack her.

All day Sefchen washed and ironed her clothes and began to get everything neat and tidy for the long journey. On the next day, she packed her few belongings and then unpacked them and wondered when Harry had ordered the carrier's cart to come to take them down the Rhine valley, and whether he would arrive today, tomorrow or the day after. At the same time, she tried to understand why he should be so anxious about telling his father and mother he was going away. And then she thought how worried she would be when her babies were grown up and said they were leaving, and realized how difficult it was to understand the feelings of parents when you had no children of your own.

As she and her aunt ate their midday meal of bread and cheese – for they had returned to a plain diet once Harry had gone – Sefchen could see that the old woman was giving her little darting glances, which always meant she had something unpleasant to say and was waiting for the opportunity to speak. It came when Sefchen said she was glad Harry had not come today, 'because, it is raining and it would have been wet in the cart'.

'You seem very sure about him,' she said, 'very sure. There is a saying, you know: "You should not count young fowls before they're born." They won't wish him to go, you know. I told you before, they believe we come of a cursed race. The father's pliable, but the mother will fight for her son – fight to her last gasp. From what I hear, she's the authority in that house. The man's weak and willing.'

She spoke almost in triumph, and must have been conscious of having shown her venom, as her next sentence was spoken in her wheedling tone. 'I'm worried for you, dear child, truly worried. Men are born false and women unyielding. Remember that.'

Sefchen smiled and felt sorry for this woman who had never loved or been loved.

On the third day she got up early, locked her chest and lugged it downstairs before unlocking it again to let Harry see how neatly she had packed. Afterwards, she went out for the first time in two days. It was cold and windy, with low grey clouds racing overhead. The trees next to the church brushed their branches along the walls, making a brushing sound she had known since she was a child. It was the kind of day when the voices usually whispered insistently, but, to Sefchen's puzzlement, there was not a sound in the house or a murmur in the Abbey, and not even the glimpse of a shadow half-seen or imagined. Instead, she sensed a contentment in the air. This was peculiar, and she wondered whether the voices had given up their fight as she was going away for ever.

She went back to the house before long, in case Harry should arrive, and, with nothing else to do, began to look through a German–English schoolbook he had given her, in which she was able to compare simple sentences in both languages. She knew a few words of English, but, as usual, found the language difficult and dull. However hard she tried to learn, her mind kept wandering to their future house in the woods in America. She tried to imagine how it would look, but decided a veil lay between her and the future, through which she was not allowed to see. She must have fallen asleep and dreamed she was close to their future American home. All she had to do was to push aside the curtain which hung over the window, and there it would be. Delighted, she ran to the window, lifted the curtain and found herself looking down the nave.

The shock woke her with a start. She stood up, disappointed, and thought how unsatisfactory her dreams had become. Then she heard the front door open, a word or two spoken in the kitchen before Harry's feet ran up the stairs. She went to meet him, but, for some reason, he stopped outside the door. Why didn't he come in? Trying to calm herself and be ready for one of his tantrums, she looked at herself in the mirror, and arranged her red hair forward around her neck before opening the door to find him standing outside, deep in thought. He jumped when he saw her, and pushed her into the room. Then, putting his hand to his head, he said: 'Ah, it's been difficult to get away. My mother thinks you're a devil, you know, and nothing I say can persuade her you're not. But I've told her I have made up my mind to put love and my future before her old-fashioned advice.' He turned, almost barged her over, and kissed her on the lips with his mouth closed before backing away and walking up and down.

To calm him, Sefchen said: 'I can understand your mother not wanting you to go, for I've been thinking how, when we have a son and he wishes to leave our home, I will be sorry since it will be a part of you leaving, and I won't want that to happen. I never understood before last night, but now I see you can only live by looking forward not back.'

While she spoke, Harry continued walking about and she could see that he had not heard a word she said. At last he broke out: 'Ah, but you have no idea

140

what I've been through. When I left here, I couldn't face going home, so I stayed with a friend and only went back yesterday. I saw my father first, to tell him of my decision. He gave me his hand, but his mouth fell open and jumbled, senseless words came tumbling out. Oh, it upset me.'

Harry laid his head on Sefchen's breast, and she told him, as she gently stroked his hair, how she was beginning to understand his sorrows and regretted she must have often been clumsy in the past. Again he did not listen, but started his pacing again, before going on: 'Well, as I said, I was speaking to my father, and was looking sadly at him when the door opened and in came my mother, who said: "Harry, I wish to speak to you alone." That frightened me, for you have no idea how strong she can be. When I was younger, I was terrified of her. If she ever wanted me to do something, I always did it in the end. Things are different now,' he added fiercely, 'but I have to admit my courage drained away as I followed her.

'She took me to the dining room and sat at the head of the table straight as a ramrod – she never rests her back against a support – and said: "Harry, I hear you've been staying at the Abbey for some days, living as man and wife with the executioner's daughter. How could you behave in such a way at such a time?" And instead of adding something severe, as she usually does, for she's hard as a nut and hasn't changed, she lifted her little lace handkerchief and began to wipe tears from her eyes – which made me feel wicked – and said: "I've expected many things from you, yet never this. But, my poor boy, I know why you have behaved in this way. Your father heard from your uncle, you know, and this is why I made inquiries about where you were staying. In future, we are to be pensioners of Salomon. It's harsh, but I understand your uncle's viewpoint. Your father has failed. There can be no softness in business, and weakness is your father's curse. I can forgive him that, but what I cannot excuse is his issuing promissory notes against your business, just when you had started on the road to success, for I know you would have succeeded," and she gripped my hand as she went on: "To deceive his own son is an act of wickedness, not of weakness, and neither I nor God will ever forgive him. Of course, I understand the effect it has had on you, Harry. You could not face the shame and so fled to that woman for comfort. But why not to me, my boy? I would have understood. I would have helped."

'And would you believe it,' Harry continued, 'she got up and held out her hands to me for the first time since I was a little boy, when I used to toddle towards her and she would throw me up into the air? But this time, she laid her head on my shoulder and sobbed. She has never broken down before. I never knew she could. Between the tears, she repeated to me all the old stuff about her hopes, and how, last year, her heart was broken when Napoleon was defeated near Brussels, and how she, not my poor father, wrote to Uncle Salomon and asked him to set me up in a branch of the business, to sustain the honour of his brother's family, as she could see that my father's mind was going. She also asked my uncle to put a man in control of me, and he only agreed after an exchange of three letters.

'She went on: "I can see why you went to the girl in the wood. It was the shame of it, the shame of it, to know you were disgraced by your father. But I know your Uncle Salomon – he's made of iron and will never forgive your running away. Had you stayed, he might have forgiven you. Had you stayed, it's possible he would have let you continue in business. But, because you left, he'll never trust you again, however long you live. Now, Harry," she said, looking straight at me, "you're to go to the girl at the Abbey and explain to her you can't marry her."

'I told her: "I'm not going to, but we shall live together," at which she pursed her lips and said: "Very well, but you must promise not to see her today."

' "I will do that," I said, for I knew you wouldn't mind if I didn't come yesterday. "But I shall go tomorrow, and tell her to get ready."

' "You won't go today?" she said.

'I said: "No – and you know I keep my word."

'She moved away and seemed to think deeply, and I wondered which hand she was going to offer me to kiss. To my delight, it wasn't her left hand but her right, so I think she has accepted the inevitable and we can leave.'

He put both hands to his head and continued to walk up and down, but after a pause he spoke again: 'Oh, how I hate quarrelling with my mother. I can't think why she's so tenacious. She hardly ever interferes, but, when she does, she's so . . . so . . . adamant. It would have been simple if I could just have told my father. But never fear, we are going,' and he came across and kissed Sefchen before resuming his pacing.

But he moved so quickly away from her, she felt a shadow of doubt pass over her and whispered, 'You will come tomorrow?'

He stopped and stared before stating in a loud voice: 'I have told you so. I'll marry you today, if you'll agree. I know a pastor who'll do it, despite my age.'

'No,' she said. 'I don't wish that.'

He stared with intensity and at last, with an effort, looked away and with downcast eyes said in a voice of desperation: 'I will marry you today. It will only cost a few of your gold pieces. Can't you see how our marriage will tie me to you, even if it is said to be irregular?'

She walked happily towards him, because she knew the idea of marriage meant a lot to him, despite his pretences, and said, 'I wish us both to be free. Don't ask me why.'

Her reply made him raise his hands once again to his head, as if in despair. Then he put his arms around her and hugged her harder than he had ever done before and she could see he needed comforting. Why should this be the case when they were about to start a whole new life together? But, to reassure him and stem his tears, she told him she loved him with her whole heart and would, from tomorrow, protect him from the world, ending with the words: 'I know you're clever and brilliant and love me in your own way, but I love you more than life itself, and not most when you're clever, but when you need me, as you do now.'

She had thought that her affection was gradually calming his fears, and was startled when he suddenly laughed and broke away, murmuring: 'You are beautiful . . . I shall be here by eleven,' and clattered away downstairs, shouting goodbye to the old woman.

She ran to the window and watched him walk, almost run, down the nave, his head in the air, declaiming loudly a song of love from his Scottish play.

It seemed a long evening. The minutes dragged on, and for once she was almost pleased to talk to her aunt, from whom she wished to part on good terms, forgiving her her unkindness, spite and dishonesty.

The Meistereen asked: 'Did he offer marriage?'

'Yes,' said Sefchen.

'Ah. So when will the ceremony take place? I should like to be there.'

'I have said I'll not marry him.'

'You little fool!' the old woman screeched before she could check her indignation.

At once she started trying to persuade Sefchen to change her mind, and it was no good not answering or trying to switch the subject. The Meistereen had sensed that she was hiding something and pressed on with her questions until Sefchen turned her back and walked out into the dark ruin and into the wood, her years in the forest having accustomed her to see at night. Usually, she liked to watch the movements of the trees, but tonight they stood motionless, as if watching, and for a moment she doubted whether Harry would come in the morning. But no, she reassured herself, he had promised, and as she had never made an unkept promise, she could not imagine he would break his word. That night she worked until long after midnight, stitching an 'H' and a 'W' on an unmarked sheet. But, despite aching eyes, she could not sleep for excitement. After all, tomorrow she would leave the hateful house and start a new life with her beloved. Twice she lit the candle and found, on each occasion, only a few moments had passed, and it was not until she had counted a thousand sheep that she ceased to fret and worry.

17

The next morning, the ground and trees were covered with a glittering spring frost. She walked into the wood for the last time and felt no sorrow. Her aunt, who was up and bustling, gave her some oat cakes, which she ate vaguely, hardly conscious of their taste, and wondered why she felt sleepy when she should have been excited. She went back upstairs and looked at her English grammar, setting herself a task of two hours' study, but found the book difficult and boring. With determination, she learned two verbs, and repeated them, and thought how dull a language English was compared to German, and how little you had to move your tongue to say the words.

At last it was ten o'clock by her watch, and she looked carefully around the room, to be sure she was leaving nothing behind, and stooped to put on her new leather shoes, which felt painfully tight. A noise in the nave made her run to the window and, looking out, she saw two boys pushing each other forward. One held in his hand a letter. She thought, with terror, something must have happened to Harry, and ran down only to find her aunt was before her and already saying to the boys: 'Who from? From Mr Heine?'

Before they could answer, Sefchen had snatched the letter, seen it was in Harry's hand and run back upstairs. She bolted her door and sat on the window cupboard and stared at the back of the letter a full half-minute before tearing it open.

Beloved Sefchen,

My heart, since I left you, has been torn almost in two by conflicting passions and loyalties. Ah, to think that we should have been, as you receive this, about to float down the Rhine on our journey to freedom! But when I returned last night, my mother summoned me to the dining room, where she sat in front of the little velvet box I had often seen in her bedroom as a child. She looked at me seriously and said: 'Harry, I have thought carefully of all the consequences of what you have told me. I also know that it is your plan to elope tomorrow with this executioner's daughter. Of course, you are a man now, and if you feel you should go, you are free to do so. All that I can do is to explain certain things which I, so you should not worry, kept from you. The surgeon's opinion is your father is failing fast and has not long to live. He has tried everything, even bleeding his neck, to no avail. You must face the fact he is dying and will leave nothing, and I shall have difficulties bringing up the younger children with the small amount my father left me. Had your father not played that terrible trick on you, I would not be so worried, but now must see I'm afraid of being left alone to look after all your brothers and sisters. I do not wish you to think,' she said softly, 'I am forbidding you to go, although, if you do marry her, it will mean that you'll be shunned, your last chance gone. So live with her if you must, but don't marry,' and again she waved down my objections.

What upset me most was her gentle arguments were more difficult to answer than the harsh words I had expected. She continued: 'I wish you calmly to consider whether you have a responsibility to the rest of your family,' and then she asked suddenly, 'Is it true you plan to go to the Americas?'

'Yes,' I replied, though I had not intended to reveal this and had told only two of my closest friends.

'Well, that alarms me,' she went on. 'It's such a long way, and I shall feel lost without you,' and she gave me a little smile which cut me deeper than any angry words could have done. 'Yes,' she said, 'if you feel you must go, then follow your own desires. I do not wish to forbid, as I have the right to, your seeing this girl, who may be good, though I cannot understand her way of life or her agreeing to live with you unmarried. All I ask is that you go for a year to the University of Bonn to make sure this love is worth the destruction of your future. I've written again to your Uncle Salomon, and he declines to help beyond the sum already specified, but I'll not be defeated, I will pay. I shall sell these, my last jewels,' and she opened the red velvet box and took out several clasps and bracelets of diamonds.

'I'm told this girl loves you and that, despite her family profession, she's decent and hard-working. If that is the case, she'll hardly want you to leave your mother alone at such a difficult time, to take care of her fatherless children. Her answer must depend, of course, on her character, and since, in no circumstances, can I see her, that I cannot judge. So all I beg you is to spend a year at Bonn and then, if it still remains your fancy to cut yourself off from your fellow men, civilization, friends and family, go with her to the Americas and leave me in my old age, deprived of the support I had expected from my favourite son. It is up to you. I shall attach no blame to you whatever you do. As a mother, I simply ask that you don't leave tomorrow before explaining my plight to the girl. If she possesses a mite of decency, she will understand that you should remain in Germany during the year of your father's decline and probable death. So, now, if it's your intention to go, please consult her first,' she smiled. 'It will test her true character.'

I thought about her words and knew at once that your goodness would make you say we should wait another year, but I haven't the courage to ask you. I could not bear to see your face, for I know your heart is set on going. As soon as I told my mother, presuming on your goodness, you would not wish me to go, she said she had booked a seat on a coach at nine tomorrow morning. Therefore I shall have set out by the time this reaches you. I need only tell you that I would never have obeyed my mother's wish had I not felt that you, as a mother, would have acted in the same way. It means only a postponement of one year, or, at the most, two. But as I write this, I weep bitter tears at the idea of parting from you. Think not I can forget you now or ever, or that there can be a replacement in my heart, or that we shall not, in due course, go away together. A year is only a brief interlude, and then I shall return. Always remember that if things had turned out otherwise, I would have had to spend a further year and a half in Hamburg, and so, in fact, we shall be leaving six months earlier than should have been the case. When I return, my mother will keep her word, and we shall be free to leave.

I fear that this will be as great a shock to you as it has been to me. Oh, my love, my adored Sefchen, I leave you with my heart breaking, and unless it breaks entirely, will return. I know to ask you to understand is not easy, but I am sure you will see I had to go, for, after you said three days ago how you now understood a woman's concern, I realized you would agree with her point of view and that I could not leave her this year.

She promises to see this letter is delivered after I have left. I will write again, as soon as I reach Bonn, and leave you filled with bitterness and sorrow. Study English, study French, work hard, and I will do the same, and we will be happy in our eventual home. Forgive this confused letter, which, as you can see, is stained with the tears of
Your loving
Harry

After Sefchen had finished, she re-read the letter three times very slowly, each time seeing more clearly she had been living in a dream that could never have been transformed into reality. Harry belonged to one world, she to another, and the claims of birth and position had been stronger than his love. If they were too strong for him now, it could only mean that he did not love her as she loved him. There was nothing she would not have sacrificed for him. He was the culmination of all her dreams in the forest, the only prince with whom she could have lived happily ever afterwards. And now her dreams were shattered. She knew nothing of universities. All she knew was Harry was not coming with her, and never would come. Her hopes were dead. She felt angry at her own foolishness in persuading herself what she had wished to feel instead of following her instincts. Now they ordered her to leave, and she would follow them, for she knew that nothing on earth could make her stay alone with her aunt another year. She had her gold pieces and a few clothes. She would leave at once, avoid Düsseldorf, and travel by the country roads to the Rhine and Holland and go by sea to America where, surely, she would not be despised for something she could not help. She would go, and she would go now.

She took a canvas sack out of the box, threw her gold into the bottom and filled it up with the new warm clothes which she had made for the voyage. She cried a little as she thought how Harry would not be the first person to see her wear them. Then she slung it over her shoulder, and walked downstairs to where her aunt was waiting like a fox by a rabbit hole.

'Ah,' she said. 'Are you going to meet him?'

Sefchen did not reply and saw the old woman looked pleased as she stood between her and the front door.

'Before you go, dear, I must beg for a little of your great store of gold. Fifty of the French Napoleons would cover everything.'

Without a word, Sefchen lowered her sack, moved her clothes, took out the money and threw down two handfuls of coins before walking away. She could not bring herself to say goodbye, but as she went, the corner of her sack caught the edge of the door and twisted her around, and she saw her aunt down on both knees, cackling with delight as she grubbed under the table. Sefchen walked out into a snowstorm.

As she passed quickly through the Abbey, her only thought was to leave Germany and Europe. At the same time, she knew she would love only Harry. Sadness had made her put on her clogs again, and already the snow was getting into them. She looked up and saw the sky hidden by gigantic flakes which, without a breath of wind, fell straight on to the ground, so that even beneath the trees the snow was already an inch deep. She remembered how these violent spring storms had often excited her, but that had been when she was happy. Now her heart ached. As she reached the gate, she said goodbye to the trees, remembering how Harry had imagined them bowing to him. They did not bow now, but stood weighed down, motionless. She closed the gate and turned to her left, plodding down the road from Düsseldorf. Her feet were already frozen, but, having noticed the numbness, she forgot them. Her one wish was to escape. It became difficult to walk, for the snow was falling faster and thicker, and her clogs slipped at every step. She wished she knew where the road led, but it was enough that it should lead away from misery. As she went, her tears began to fall.

She had gone scarcely a mile when she became aware of a faint rumbling sound which gradually grew louder and louder. Turning, she saw a misty, creaking half-obscured apparition gradually transform into a grand coach drawn by four horses, with two men sitting at the front. Despite her unhappiness, she wished she could shelter in the white vehicle, which was driving straight at her. As she drew aside to let it pass, the window was let down and a head emerged to shout unintelligible instructions to the driver, who cracked his whip and urged the horses on.

Their sudden fright made the carriage lurch towards Sefchen, who jumped out of the way and, at the same moment, looked up to see the man who had shouted with his eyes on her. She recognized his face at once. It was the young baron she had seen with her aunt in Düsseldorf, and she remembered with shame how the Meistereen had pretended to hurt her knee so that they had to linger and be stared at. He stared at her now in the same way, and, after the coach had passed, looked back. The vehicle rolled on and was almost swallowed up in the blizzard when, to her surprise, it pulled up.

She at once made up her mind not to travel with the young baron. When she saw him the first time, she had thought he was evil, and now stood still, hoping the coach would start again. Instead, she saw him step down, and immediately afterwards a man at the front landed on the road behind him. The baron, whose name she could not remember, walked towards her and, lifting his high hat, asked politely, but with the look in his eyes which repelled her, 'Please, on such an evening, travel with us. I could never be so ungallant as to allow a beautiful young lady to travel alone on such a night. It would be the height of bad manners. I should never forgive myself.'

She hated the sneering tone of his voice, and again tried to step past him, but the manservant moved to bar her way.

'No, really, I cannot allow it. You must be frozen and will die of exposure if you stay out in such a storm. I shall not allow the world to be made poorer by the loss of such a beauty. God, how it snows.'

He lifted his hat and huge snowflakes stuck to his eyelashes. He wiped his eyes with his right hand and turned to say something to his man. Sefchen knew she must escape and turned to walk back the way she had come. Anything would be better than travelling in such company. She hadn't gone twenty steps before there was a noise behind her and the next instant the baron's man drew level with her and, with a quick movement, linked an arm through hers and locked it to his side while, with his other hand, he gripped her waist. She struggled in terror, but he merely said in a countrified voice: 'Steady, lass. You'll be warmer inside the coach than out of it,' and with a coarse laugh added: 'But how warm, don't ask me – maybe warmer than you warrant.'

She struggled again, but helplessly, with her clogs slipping and the sack weighing her down. She found herself half-dragged towards the coach, where the baron, standing by the open door, once again took off his hat and bowed as the man suddenly changed his grip, lifted her by the waist above the step and roughly shoved her inside, where she found herself lying at the feet of a young man sitting before a small table covered with counters, cards and pieces of white wood with holes in them. She noticed these details as she pulled herself upright, indignant and frightened, and saw the baron climb in, shut the door and lower the blinds as the coach began to move on.

She had never been in such a vehicle before, and was amazed by its size and luxuriousness and how smoothly it rolled along the rough road. The baron said something to his friend, who at once gave a laugh, asked her to move aside and did something to the table which made it disappear into the floor. Then the baron asked politely if she would like a drink, and pulled out a drawer from underneath the seats to show her a variety of bottles. She shook her head, and as he sat down, he made a gesture she should do the same. What could she do but lean back on the soft cushions?

'Well,' he said, 'I was right. You are the enchantress in green, the niece of the old hag at the Abbey. It's a long time since I last saw you. But wait, your teeth are chattering with cold. Have a glass of cognac.'

She shook her head.

'But I insist.'

He poured a glass and held it towards her. She shook her head again, at which he turned to his friend and said, in his sneering voice: 'My dear Hans, I fear our beautiful patient is determined to die of cold. I think you'll agree it's our duty to ensure she lives. I fear that if we put the glass to her mouth, she will break it, but the bottle has two advantages. It holds more cognac, and not even such a determined young lady as this one could bit the top off. At any rate, let's find out.'

He moved over to her side of the coach, placed his left arm round her neck and, seizing her chin, with his right hand forced the silver top of his whip into her mouth and forced it open. She gave a scream and struggled, but he only laughed and held her tighter. The next moment, the other man sat on her lap so that she was at their mercy, unable to move. A bottle was thrust into her mouth and a liquid tasting of fire poured down her throat. Most of it must have gone into her stomach, but some was caught in her lungs, for she choked and gasped to such a degree that she thought she was dying, and still the fiery liquid continued to suffocate her. At last she must have fainted, and only recovered consciousness when one of the young men hit her hard on the back as she gasped for breath. A further blow knocked her forward, and her head almost struck her knees, but, to her relief, she could breathe again. At the same time, she could not think where she was as the coach swam before her eyes and she felt as though she was spinning round and round. She stood up and, from a distance, heard the other man said: 'My God, she's a beauty! Just look at her skin and hair! You didn't exaggerate, did you?'

'No,' the baron laughed, 'but be careful. Remember, I told you she's a witch.'

After a moment she felt the coach pitching and lurching in such an extraordinary manner that she was thrown into a state of total confusion. When she looked at the two men she saw that they were also rolling from side to side in the same way.

'Well, pretty one, since we've so kindly given you a lift, I think it only right that you acknowledge your debt and pay, and we, your hosts, have the right to state in what form the payment shall be made.'

They whispered together, and the other young man moved swiftly across and pinned her back against the seat as one of them wrenched up her skirt. Although she fought back, she could not match their strength, and as she felt a stabbing pain, thought only of Harry and broke into a wail of despair at the terrible intrusion. It seemed no more than an instant before there was a pause and she heard the baron say: 'Your turn. We've not time for niceties, I'm afraid.'

A second intrusion followed, but this time it did not hurt, and while she tried desperately to reject both of them from her mind, the moment the second young man had finished with her, she was all at once aware of a new life flowing into her and felt sure her lifelong wish had been fulfilled and she was to have a baby. She looked up, ignored the baron, and stared in amazement at this stranger, who had given her what she so passionately desired from Harry. As he sat opposite her now, disconsolately fastening his breeches, an intense gratitude and the wish to thank him overcame her. Even though she fought against it, an incomprehensible instinct made her lean forward and kiss the man, who was surely her own Harry, on the lips.

He at once jumped back and said: 'Ugh, away with you. You're an insatiable bitch, aren't you!' and pushed her back on the cushions.

She tried to understand why he should be angry, and then suddenly she knew that he was not Harry and she had been possessed by two men whom she hated. She gave a cry of despair and knew she had to get out of the coach. She reached the door and tugged at a strap which let down the window. The friend leaned forward to shut it again, and pulled her by the hair on to the floor, so that she lay half over his boots. As they talked about her, it seemed that their voices came from a long way off. At last, the baron opened the window and called up to the driver to turn round and drive back to the place where they had picked the girl up. Within minutes, there was a turning, a backing and a cracking of a whip and the coach turned upside down and the right way up again while her mind denied everything that had happened to her. At the same time, she felt pleased to be having Harry's child, and she heard the two of them, as they drank and laughed, call each other Harry. So who was Harry? She tried to keep her eyes on them, but they kept swaying backwards and forwards and in and out of her vision. Clapping her hands to her eyes, she thought she must be having a nightmare which would soon be over.

Then she must have slept, for when she woke up the coach had stopped and the baron was bowing and thanking her and pressing two gold coins into her hand as he declared in his mocking voice: 'I hope we shall have the honour of seeing you before long.'

Then the door was opened and she could see nothing but snow as she was gripped by the waist and bundled down to the man, who stood her on her feet by the roadside. The next moment the coach was moving away and the baron was smiling and taking his hat off to her as he leaned out of the window. As she tried to remember where she was and what had happened, she saw him re-open the door and toss out her sack on to the road, before bowing again politely as he disappeared into the storm.

Slowly the cold brought back her memories. How could she have allowed herself to be raped? But she had not allowed it. She had fought! And then she remembered her delight when the young man had given her a child and how she had kissed him. She cried out in agony. In all the world, there was only one man's child she could carry. Harry's! How, now, could she sail away as all faces would be set against her? She knew the end was near as a voice whispered, 'Come back, come back. You will never leave the Abbey again.' Perhaps it had never been intended she should, and maybe her dream of living with Harry never had any substance, although she would have lived for and loved him. She longed with her whole heart to pluck the alien seed out of her body, although she knew she would never live to bear the child.

Picking up her sack, she stumbled along through the ever-deepening snow, and at last came to the wooden gates, looked up at the trees she had hoped never to see again, and ran, still carrying her sack, towards the Abbey, taking the path which led round the back of the apse where the voices called, clamorous with excitement and triumph. At last she stopped and, looking up, made out the outline of the central arch of the Gothic window. Knowing what lay ahead, she climbed the rungs of the iron bars, height and danger meaning nothing, and quickly reached the gap at the top and stood, looking down on to the ground beneath and on to the house with smoke rising out of one of the chimneys.

She knew she was about to end her life and the pain of living, and never again would she think of a future without a chance of happiness. She breathed freely for the first time since her violation. All was nearly over, and the suffering which had pierced her heart since Harry abandoned her was about to end. She looked up and saw the snowflakes falling straight past her towards the ground. Happily she leapt forward to join them, and from her body, not her soul, came an echoing cry which ended abruptly as she hit a fragment of a broken arch.

Her aunt inside the house heard a noise and wondered whether it could be Sefchen returning and hoped the stupid girl had not allowed her gold to be stolen. The storm had killed the day, and while it was early evening, it could have been midnight. She lit a lantern and, holding it on a stick, opened the front door and called: 'Sefchen, Sefchen, Sefchen!' into the white darkness. Her words echoed round the Abbey walls. No answer came. She lifted the lantern as high as she could hold it. The flickering gleams lit up a grey break in the whiteness of the ground with two shadows bending over it. Whining with fear, she shoved her trembling hand down her neck and, with her crucifix of human bone, walked forwards. The shadows vanished into the air and, drawing closer, the Meistereen saw Sefchen's body lying broken among fallen stones, the head lying sideways, with blood oozing under the untouched face, reddening the snow. Realizing at once she was dead, the Meistereen lifted her lantern again and, ignoring the body, searched for the sack. Soon she saw and seized it and, running back to the house, ripped open the canvas and found to her delight the store. After an hour of careful counting, she was still unsure whether she had 420 or 421 gold coins.

Epilogue

Harry or Heinrich Heine lived on until 17 February 1856, although he never rose from his bed after the spring of 1848, lying for eight years on what he called 'my mattress grave'. His disease was never diagnosed, although it was generally assumed to be syphilis. Sometimes, in that terrible endless period of suffering, it appears his mind returned to the past and his poor disturbed brain dwelt on the beautiful red-haired girl he had abandoned to a terrible death. Propping up a paralysed eyelid with a shaking finger, he had put pen to paper and written, in huge shaking letters, memories of his first great love and the inspiration of his early Gothic poetry. On 12 February, when his last attachment, Camille Selden, visited him, he whispered to her from the bed where he lay with closed eyes that Sefchen had come to him the night before, looking more beautiful than ever.

His broken voice continued: 'I believe she's waiting for me. Last night I woke up to find myself back in the Abbey, and there she was again, singing the old song, holding the executioner's sword in her hand. When I looked into her eyes, I saw no reproach but only hope, and my whole body leapt towards her, only to find I was chained to this death bed.'

He shivered as he held Camille's hand and said he felt waves of grief he had never known before because he had treated Sefchen so badly.

His voice quavered as he feebly went on: 'And then I looked up and she dropped the sword and came to me, wearing the green skin-tight dress I had loved, and threw her arms around my neck and kissed me on the lips and said, "I have waited long long years, but now at last you are coming, and we will be free to go away as you once promised we could."

'As she stood looking at me, to my horror the flesh slowly vanished from her face and body and a skeleton in the green dress stood clasping me. I screamed, and my wife came in and gave me laudanum, but I am terrified Sefchen will come back.'

'Why,' said Camille in her sensible voice, 'why are you frightened? Remember, it is what she thinks, not what she looks like which matters now.'

She felt the frail fingers tighten on her hand, expressing gratitude, and when she gazed at his face for the last time before leaving him, he looked at peace and was smiling. She never saw him again, and until the end of her life felt jealous that the great poet's last happiness had been bound up with an unknown executioner's red-haired daughter whom she had believed was a figment of his diseased imagination.